DR. ROB BRYANT

FRAUD
PRESIDENT

DEFIANCE PRESS
& PUBLISHING

Fraud President

First Edition: 2022

Printed in the United States of America

10 9 8 7 6 5 4 3 2 1

ISBN-13: 978-1-955937-64-1 (Paperback)
ISBN-13: 978-1-955937-67-2 (Hardcover)
ISBN-13: 978-1-955937-63-4 (eBook)

Published by Defiance Press and Publishing, LLC

Bulk orders of this book may be obtained by contacting Defiance Press and Publishing, LLC. www.defiancepress.com.

Public Relations Dept. – Defiance Press & Publishing, LLC
281-581-9300
pr@defiancepress.com

Defiance Press & Publishing, LLC
281-581-9300
info@defiancepress.com

Dedication

My active US Marine sons, Jason and Jonathan, motivate me to be my best. Their names merge to create the main character, John Jacobson. They are the real heroes in my life. Jason is a US Marine Corps Master Sergeant (E8) and married to Joie, a wonderful wife and mother. Jonathan is a graduate of the US Naval Academy, a US Marine Corps Lieutenant Colonel (05), and helicopter pilot. He's married to April, a dedicated homeschooling mother. I'm beyond proud and honored to be their dad.

Thanks to the professional editing done by Defiance, PaperTrue, Pam Taylor, Glen Hammond, and Jonathan Bryant.

Table of Contents

Part V – Losing Ground

Part VI – Imminent Clashes

Foreword

ALL MAJOR CHARACTERS IN THIS novel are fictional. However, the events accurately describe voting weaknesses in recent US elections. Information concerning battleground states originate from the official state election websites. Therefore, could apply to any future US election—unless states improve voting controls. The reader may find the policies of their state interesting and visit the official state voting websites for more information.

This book is the result of over one thousand hours of research, incorporating information found on government websites, articles, descriptions, demonstrations, litigations, videos, and media reports. Compelling evidence of voter fraud cases found by the Associated Press during the 2020 election and others include:

1. Lack of voter ID
2. Non-paper-based voting-machines
3. Computer viruses
4. Mail-in
5. Provisional
6. Absentee
7. Early
8. Proxy
9. Ballot box stuffing

10. Ballot harvesting
11. Voting for inactive voters
12. Voting in more than one state
13. Voter impersonation
14. Unregistered voters
15. Destruction or invalidation of legitimate ballots
16. Organized attacks on polling places
17. Vote buying
18. Misleading and/or confusing information
19. Vote manipulation of protected groups
20. Voter suppression
21. Politicians moving precinct boundaries to their benefit

The table in appendix B lists the top twenty-five states by number of electors. There are ten blue, five red, and ten battleground (purple) states. The states that allow no ID voting or mail-in voting contain 179 of 270 electors needed to win the presidency. Even more surprising are the states allowing no-excuse mail-in votes contain 336 of 270 electors needed to win the presidency! Therefore, how can we say the election process is valid? We have no idea who really voted or how often. This is, of course, by design.

Currently, the US is a politically divided country. The characters and events within this book are not strictly liberal or conservative. Both sides will enjoy reading this book and supporting or defending their political views. I hope this book informs voters of the election weaknesses in their state. I also hope voting reform sweeps the country. I believe all states should require *free* government-provided photo IDs and voting machines with a paper trail. Without them, voter fraud will continue in ever-growing quantities. We currently face a voter fraud crisis leading to illegitimate politicians and potentially a *Fraud President!*

PART I ★ THE PLAN

Chapter 1 ★ Fight or Flight

"THE CANDIDATE IS A REAL son of a bitch," an FBI agent said behind closed doors.

Another agent responded, "The candidate can't be worse than many previous presidents. Dishonest Ulysses S. Grant gave offices to unqualified friends, drank heavily, and guilty of graft and corruption. Herbert Hoover's policies contributed to the onset of the Great Depression. John Tyler was a known racist and defended slavery. Andrew Johnson was almost impeached and fought the emancipation of slaves. Warren G. Harding and his administration stole from the Treasury. Richard Nixon resigned after Watergate, and Bill Clinton lied to the country and Congress, then impeached. Finally, a previous president gave billions to terrorist countries and doubled the US debt."

"Were any of them murderers? Did any of them give US secrets to enemies for money?"

"Many argue presidents are murderers by virtue of declaring war."

"Maybe, but I'm talking about hiring thugs to kill enemies in cold blood! Have any done that?"

"Not as far as I know. And I don't know of any who sold secrets for personal gain."

"Well, this one did both!"

"How do you know for sure?"

"Our investigations reveal a shortlist of the felonies perpetrated by the candidate. We just can't prove it. Witnesses keep dying."

The agents read them silently:

- Record-Gate
- Death of a Secretary of Defense
- Cyber-Hider
- Asia-Gate
- Tour-Gate
- Illegal Profits
- Suspicious Death Investigations
- Illegal Fundraising
- Ambassador's Death

"Holy crap. Those are all open investigations?"

"Yes, and they grow monthly," the other responded, pointing to several file cabinets.

"What's in those?"

"They hold the over fifty voices from the grave."

"Voices from the grave?"

"Yes. They hold the records of over fifty investigations of the mysterious deaths, murders, and suicides of the candidate's enemies, friends, business associates, and pesky reporters, spanning thirty years."

"My God!"

"God has nothing to do with it. An evil human being is responsible for this. There were indictable charges on almost all the cases. But witnesses died, politicians stepped in, files lost, and authorities dropped charges. In addition…"

***

"Joie's coming!" John whispered to himself excitedly. The dream faded as he woke. His heartbeat faster thinking about her and he could sleep no longer. Wanting to look good for her, he rose early and went to the gym for the third time in a week. Working out burned energy, strengthened muscles, and restrained "the animal." From his time in the Special Forces, the animal within, with restraint, remained at bay. Working out helped keep it there. He couldn't afford to put his budding relationship with Joie and his new job at risk by letting the animal gain control.

When he arrived at the gym, a trainer friend asked, "How are you, John?"

"Great! Ready to work on arms, chest, and stomach today. I worked on legs, back, and neck last time."

"I wish I had clients like you here. Are you sure you don't need a trainer? I could help focus your workouts on weak areas."

John removed his jacket, and his massive muscles showed through his netlike workout top.

"Never mind," said the trainer before he walked off, looking to offer his services to someone who needed them.

John stretched, loosened up, then moved to the bench press. He put 180 pounds on the bar, moved the bar up and down some fifteen times, then added more weight. Soon, he was up to 275 pounds. People in the gym began watching him curiously as they continued their own workouts.

Gary, a local athlete on a semi-pro football team, watched with interest. He outweighed John by fifty pounds, and arms twenty inches around hung from his powerful upper body. Annoyed that others watched John rather than him, he asked a few people about John and learned of his military background. He wasn't impressed.

Gary said loudly to a workout friend, "Who's the asshole on the bench press? Does he think he's tough? Our field goal kicker could beat the shit out of him."

John ignored the big man, but deep within, anger began to burn. The beast within awoke, but John remained in control. His abandonment as a child, the loss of his family, and his experience in the military created this beast, and now it threatened to break free.

Gary continued to taunt John and mistook his silence for cowardice. The trainer walked over to Gary and said, "We're here to work out, not cause trouble. Please be quiet. Besides, you don't want to tangle with John, he's—"

"I don't care what he is, or if he is anything other than a coward, which is obvious." Gary grew bolder and shouted, "Hey, coward, want to tangle with a real man?"

John's anger swelled by the second. He barely controlled himself and decided to walk out when the big mouth said, "Hey, you! I hear you were in the Special Forces. I eat guys like you for dinner!"

The gym grew quiet, and those between the two men quickly moved out of the way. One of the others who knew John warned Gary, "Quiet, he won't take much more. You better stop."

However, Gary continued, determined to instigate a fight by giving John the finger. John, the gentle giant, continued to ignore him.

The trainer said to Gary, "I want you to leave, or I'll call the police."

"It'll all be over before they get here. Right, coward?" he retorted toward John.

The trainer decided the only peaceful option was to ask John to leave. He touched John on the shoulder, which was rock hard with tension. John fixed him with a cold stare, making him withdraw his hand and step back quickly. The trainer tried to calm him with a smile. John turned away from them both until Gary approached. John balled his fist, ready for whatever the big man wanted to do. As he began to lose his composure, his muscles started to flex uncontrollably, but Gary interpreted the flinching anger as fear. It was all he needed to continue badgering him.

"So, what are you going to do?" Gary asked, looking down at John with a twisted smile.

His six-foot taller frame made onlookers wonder if John had a chance. Gary turned and looked back at one of his friends, laughing. Confident that John wasn't going to do a thing, he stepped closer.

Wanting the big mouth to just go away, John said, his voice shaking with anger, "Look, I don't want any trouble. I just came in to work out in peace. I'll even work out with you. You look like you could keep up with me."

"You damn chicken! You couldn't lift the weights I clean and jerk, you little frickin' coward. You're nothing but a—"

Suddenly, the animal erupted deep within John. The trainer saw it coming and backed away. Everyone did knowing better than to interfere at this point. Gary already sealed his fate by not walking away sooner.

Everything moved into slow motion for John, although for those watching, his actions were a blur. John whirled around and performed a perfect roundhouse kick to the man's chest. Something in his chest area cracked with a sickening sound, causing spectators to flinch. The man's arms, legs, and head lurched forward as his abdomen flew backward.

Gary, probably unconscious already, fell limply as John continued his spin and brought his fist up, hitting the man squarely in the face. The man's jaw collapsed under his fist. The man flew backward and fell hard, hitting the floor with a crash in a near-comatose state. The fight was over in just two lightning-fast blows. Gasps and murmurs filled the gym, and no one looked directly at John.

John paused, looking at the big man's friend to see if he wanted to join the fight. John wanted him to come—the animal within was now in charge, and the only way to subdue it was to tire it out. "Come on!" John yelled. "I got more. You want any of it?"

The friend looked at his large unconscious friend and quietly gathered their belongings. Without a word, he and the trainer carried Gary out. Everyone kept their distance, afraid they might be next.

John slowly relaxed, lay down on the bench, and gradually regained control of the beast. The others watched him change back to a mild demeanor. In moments, he was lifting weights as if nothing happened. The anger left him as it came, quietly and quickly.

John added more weight and calmly said, "Can I get a spot here?"

Two people rushed over, ready and willing to assist. One of them whispered to the other, "Better with him than against."

The other man nodded in agreement, and bystanders returned to their workouts. The trainer re-entered a tranquil gym. No one called the police, knowing Gary deserved what he received. John worked out for another hour, showered, and drove to the airport.

At the DFW baggage claim E-34, John waited for the love of his life. It was strange to wait for a passenger rather than to be traveling himself. John Jacobson retired from the military as a decorated Special Operations US Marine officer. With an aerospace engineering degree from the US Naval Academy, his intelligence set him apart from most. His tall solid frame and short hair betrayed his military background. A few US Marine tattoos from former units remained hidden under his shorts and shirt. His tanned skin revealed his love of outdoor sports. His large girder-like arms and powerful stride turned women's heads. His hazel eyes bore through his foes yet expressed fond acceptance for friends and acquaintances. John rarely dropped his guard and trusted people slowly, with good reason. After heroic and dangerous military operations all over the world, John was ready to settle down.

Joie August flew back to the DFW Airport for the second time in a month. She couldn't wait to see John again. They'd been through so much together, and their relationship only grew stronger She wondered why he insisted on seeing her this weekend. Was it for personal or professional issues? She hoped it was the former.

After landing, Joie checked her phone and found several emails and texts waiting. She was only interested in one text, though—John's. It read "Waiting for you. Can't wait!"

Joie typed, "Me too. Are you at baggage claim or passenger pickup?"

Within a second, there was a response. "Yep."

Joie smiled. She loved his playful nature. She'd have to wait to find him and counted the seconds. She wore tight blue sweats—a departure from the business suit she wore during the week. The outfit revealed her athletic twenty-seven-year-old body. The monthly physical fitness tests at her job with the FBI required her to remain fit. Her long dark blonde hair swayed freely as she walked into the terminal. Men literally stopped and watched her walk by. Joie paid them no mind and rounded the corner, passing through the revolving security door. Her trained eyes scanned the area but did not find John. Her disappointment was apparent through a slight frown, as per FBI schooling, since hiding true emotions was part of bringing down "bad guys."

She grabbed her bags and headed for the exit to the passenger pickup, scanning her surroundings one more time. When she was almost at the exit, she felt someone grab her bag. She whirled around, ready to take down any idiot trying to steal her belongings, when suddenly she felt solid arms lifting her off her feet. John continued walking, carrying her and her bag as if they were feathers. Joie hit him on the shoulder and tried to scowl at him, but he wasn't buying it and kissed her. She fell limp in his arms. He won the first round, but many more skirmishes were coming. Even though John wouldn't admit it, she was far ahead in victories in the almost yearlong set of bouts.

"So, how is saving the world in the FBI?" John asked, smirking.

"I just save the US. The world belongs to the CIA," Joie responded, liking the mode of transport.

"All I know is you saved me last year," John said seriously.

"The pleasure is mine, you big lug."

"No, it was mine. I owe you my life."

"You saved me right back," Joie returned.

"Enough reminiscing." John set her back down.

"Too tired to finish the journey?"

"I'll never tire of the journey with you by my side," he said without hesitation. He wasn't trying to be corny or mushy; that was just how his loving nature found expression.

"God, I love you and missed you," Joie sighed as they continued to his car.

"Love you too, babe." He looked into her eyes as he pressed the car security button. His Mercedes beeped as he opened the door for her. After tossing her luggage in the trunk, he jumped in and began the drive back to Fort Worth.

"So, John, how is the new job, running engineering for Pseudomics?"

"I love it. We're designing new avionics for some of America's newest aircraft."

"And how's the staff?"

"They're handpicked and awesome. We cleaned house after you brought the guilty to justice last year," John returned.

"That's old news. I only did what any FBI agent *would* do."

"Bringing down some bad guys and saving my butt at the same time was not something just any old agent *could* do. I'll never grow tired of thanking you," John said, remembering the events vividly.

Joie responded, "No charge. I'm glad your job is well. You deserved the promotion."

"You got any exciting cases, babe?" John asked, changing the subject.

"Not anything like the one where we met. But my days are exciting."

They talked about their jobs as he stroked her hand. John tuned in to Sirius Radio for the news. It was background noise as Joie talked.

The commentator said, "Despite allegedly giving favors to foreign governments in exchange for donations to Dreams International, Jeffrey Adams continues to lead in the polls. Senator Adams continues to deny any ties to Dreams International, and there is no proof of that association—"

"John, please turn that off. I'm so sick of politics. The media is so one-sided, it makes me sick."

"You got it, babe. Sorry." He turned it off with a button on the steering wheel.

"So, what did you want to talk about?" Joie asked, almost in a whisper.

"I just need to see you. I want a shot of Joie. Living three hours away by air is tough," John replied honestly.

"I agree it's hard, but my job is in DC, and yours is here in Fort Worth. What can we do? Neither of us wants to quit our job to join the other, right?"

"Not necessarily," John replied, pulling the car over on the shoulder.

"How's that?" Joie asked, reaching for both of John's hands.

John pulled her closer and said, "Pseudomics's headquarters is in DC, as you know."

"Yes," Joie replied quickly, holding her breath.

"Joie, I need to be closer to you. You work as many hours as I do, so being in the same town just makes sense."

"Agreed. Go on."

"I've asked corporate for a transfer!"

"You're kidding? Is it approved?"

"Provisionally."

"What does that mean?"

"One of the VPs offered me a job to work directly for him," John said proudly.

"When does it begin?" Joie asked, still holding her breath.

"That's the provisional part."

"I don't understand."

"My VP asked me to finish my current project. It'll take about six months."

"Six months? That's no time at all. Oh my God! I'm stunned. We need to find a place to live. My one-bedroom place just won't do. We need to—"

John cut her off. "What we need to do is solidify our relationship."

"What the heck does that mean? If it's a proposal, it's pitiful," Joie scoffed, disappointed that he was maybe proposing to her on a highway.

"No, just a preparatory strike."

"You're such a guy. Such a military guy!"

"Yes, I'm all man, seeking the most beautiful and exciting woman in the world."

"Good comeback. You're forgiven."

"Good, let's go. We have things to do."

"You better believe it," she said as she reached over and touched him provocatively. He started touching her back… and thirty steamy minutes later, they resumed the drive.

"Wow! I missed that," John said, catching his breath.

"Me too. So, where are we going?" Joie began composing herself after the intense physical session.

"I'm an old-fashioned kind of guy, as you know."

"Yes, it's part of the reason I love you."

"I need to ask your only living parent for her blessing."

"John, I've told you how she feels about us. She wants me to quit my job, live with her, and take care of her as long as she lives. She wants me to be the recluse she is. She will never approve."

"I hear you, but I need to do this."

"It's a waste of time… but whatever."

"Thanks for agreeing. I have a way with moms. Trust me."

"I always have and always will. My God, that sounds so cliché! But it's true."

"I've trusted you ever since we met," John responded gently.

"Nice to know. OK, let's go."

"Your chariot and driver are ready, my lady."

Joie rolled her eyes and kissed him on the cheek. His rough exterior concealed a mushy interior. She loved both sides of the big man.

John didn't tell her about the fight that morning. Besides, she knew about his temper, what he called the "inner beast." There was no point in discussing it now.

On the drive to Waco, they spoke about work, family, and the future. However, Joie knew disaster awaited them in ways she couldn't explain. John had to experience it firsthand to understand. Joie felt sorry for him, thinking of the pain waiting ahead.

Chapter 2 ★ Voter Fraud 101

IN EARLY JANUARY, TWO MEN met in a conference room in a hotel in Alexandria, Virginia. The warm surroundings felt good in contrast to the freezing winds outside. The dark and expensive meeting room contained lavish mahogany frames encircling the pictures adorning the wall. A beautiful sailboat skimmed across the sea. Another showed a Scottish castle, while another featured a collection of flowers and fruit. The large conference table, built of cherrywood from the Orient, sat in the middle of the room. The twenty dark wood chairs arranged in perfect order, ready for the momentous meeting just weeks away. They had to be ready.

Fred Reider, a short and stocky political advisor with blond hair and freckles, sat at the head of the table. "I'm the cyber expert, and I disagree with your premise. We need a strategy utilizing a single technology or method. Let's not complicate things with several methods, making it more difficult to control."

Todd Shamer was tall, thin, dark-haired, and a highly respected party leader. Obviously displeased, he responded, "No, that's too easily detected. The optimum approach utilizes small and myriad methodologies based upon each state's weaknesses. Being small methods, they'll stay below the radar and remain undetected."

Fred retorted, "Look, think about the entire party. If we involve many operatives in this, they need to understand our approach. Word will get out about our plans. We need one strategy, not several. That's too complex."

"That's where you're wrong, just like with the Manhattan Project. There were many pieces, players, and steps, yet very few people understood the entire mission," Todd said respectfully.

"OK, that makes sense. I'm still not convinced, but what do you have in mind?"

"There are hundreds of cases of voter fraud in every state of the union."

"Is that a fact? How do you know?"

"Google 'voter fraud cases.' You'll find many of them in every state. We'll learn what doesn't work through the failures of others. An example of what does work is the current lack of voter ID requirements in many states."

"What do you mean?"

"It's so frickin' easy. Here's an example—check it out by googling it if you want. The watchdog Department of Investigations sent undercover agents to sixty-three different polling places last fall. They pretended to be voters not eligible."

"Why's that?"

"These agents assumed the names of individuals who died or moved out of town, or sat in jail. In sixty-one instances, or ninety-seven percent of the time, the pollsters allowed them to vote."

"How do we know they actually voted?"

"Are you ready for this? All sixty-one agents cast a write-in vote for 'John Test.'"

"You're kidding?"

"Nope, they wanted to prove it could be done without affecting the election."

"Yes, but we *do* want to affect the outcome."

"Right. So, in our case, they vote for Senator Adams in large numbers."

"It can't be that easy."

"It's that easy in New York, for instance. Blue states claim voter ID checks are racist— a silly argument, since government voter ID is free. Listen to this: Young undercover agents voted using the names of people three times their age and voters who died years before. In one case, a twenty-four-year female agent gave a male's name, and someone who died in 2012 at age eighty-seven!"

"Are you kidding?"

"Nope! We'll train our supporters to vote more than once in weak voter-ID-law states. That's one-third of US States! Prosecution for ballot box stuffing, voter impersonation, ballot harvesting, and voting for inactive voters is virtually unheard of."

"What's the difference between them?"

"Multiple voting comes in many forms. Ballot box stuffing is casting more than one ballot per voter. Placing multiple ballots into a ballot box is easily caught, so our voters will cast votes at multiple voting locations."

"That one makes sense and easily conducted. I think I understand voter impersonation. In states with weak voter ID laws, our voters simply cast votes for others. Is that easy to get away with?"

"Yes, but only in states with weak audit practices. I'll make a list of them."

"Great! Now what about ballot harvesting? What is that?"

"Ballot harvesting is a common campaign tactic in areas with weak police protection, primarily in the inner cities. We'll intimidate early and mail-in voters to give us their blank ballots. Lastly, almost all states have versions of early and mail-in voting laws. With the thugs working for us, this will be easy."

"Seems like a risky proposition."

"It is, so we won't use those methods as much as the other forms of multiple voting."

"Good, agreed. I think I understand voting for inactive voters. But is it simple?"

"Yep, all we must know is neighbors, friends, and relatives that are nonvoters. Then, in the states with weak voter ID laws, they must know the name and address."

"You're kidding! It's that easy?"

"Yes! I love states like North Carolina, Nevada, and Pennsylvania where voters do not have to show any form of ID at all. The polling workers can't ask voters for their ID!"

"That's the law there? I can't believe it! However, let's suppose we get thousands of people to do that in New York. That's just one state. Besides, we're in good shape in New York; it almost always votes our way. That won't change the overall outcome. We need to focus on battleground states."

"Finally, we agree. I've done my research. I've found voter fraud and critical cyber weaknesses in voting methods in each individual swing state."

"Like which ones? We can't win this thing with just a few of them."

"Uh, you mean states like Arizona, Colorado, Florida, Pennsylvania, New Hampshire, Ohio, Iowa, Virginia, Michigan, Minnesota, Nevada, and Wisconsin?"

"You can't be serious. It's impossible to find weaknesses in all of them."

"There's documented cases of effective voter fraud in them all."

"No way!"

"Way!"

"OK, you told me about New York. What about, let's say, Virginia? I live there just outside the DC beltway."

"That one is even easier. Bonnie Nicholson of Virginia pleaded guilty to forgery and election fraud. Despite being a felon and ineligible to vote, Nicholson registered and then voted in the last election. She received five years in prison on each charge, but all suspended, and she only got one year of probation on each charge."

"Yes, but that's been corrected, right?"

"That's the beauty of it. We told the other party it's fixed, but it's not!"

"You're kidding."

"Nope, Virginia liberals favor letting felons vote. There are thousands of felons voting there with the governor's approval. He's writing individual letters allowing them to vote legally."

"I'm not aware of that."

"It's true. Look it up! I'll explain more about that later. How about a famous example from another state?"

"OK, shoot."

"How about the three hundred twelve-vote victory in 2008 in Minnesota that allowed them to pass Obamacare? Months after the Obamacare vote, a conservative group called Minnesota Majority finished comparing criminal records with voting rolls and identified one thousand ninety-nine felons—ineligible to vote—who voted in the Franken-Coleman race. Fox News's random interviews with ten of those felons found that nine voted for Franken, backing up national academic studies that show felons tend to vote strongly for liberal candidates. Minnesota Majority took its findings to prosecutors across the state, but very few showed any interest in pursuing the issue. Only a few were prosecuted."

"OK, so we get felons to vote for Senator Adams. I'm sure they will. The people who want handouts typically vote our way. That still won't get us there."

"Again, we agree. There's a much bigger issue we can use to our advantage."

"OK, I'll bite. Like what?"

"Did you know there are over nine thousand jurisdictions in the United States that conduct the balloting, collecting, tallying, and reporting of votes manually? There are tens of thousands of cases of overseas voters, like our military serving internationally, where ballots aren't counted when they favor the other side. Many states have weaknesses in that category."

"Do many of the swing states use hard-copy ballots?"

"Are you kidding? You don't remember Florida and the 'hanging chad' controversy and the lawsuits on both sides?"

"Yes, but didn't they fix that?"

"Some Florida precincts use digital voting now. But surely, you've heard the FBI is investigating the hack of the Democratic National Committee. Private investigators have identified the suspects, and United States intelligence agencies have told the White House that they have 'high confidence' that the Russian government was responsible."

"What about it?"

"It wasn't the Russians. It was the other party behind it. If they can do it, so can we."

"You have proof it was the other party?"

"Yep. I have it right here in my satchel."

"OK, let's say they did. How do you propose we do it? With all the investigations, it'll be tough."

"There are two recurring voter fraud categories involving voting machines. One of these is due to a lack of testing by manufacturers before installing the systems in the field. Often these companies are selling 'off-the-shelf hardware,' meaning they're more interested in turning a profit rather than providing a quality product. The second problem comes from local governments not having the resources to certify these machines as properly safeguarded. Without the required funds, these counties and states assume the machines are secure enough to resist cyberattacks."

"Is this theory or fact?"

"We've already evaluated it—it works."

"What works?"

"Cyber hacks of voting machines. Hell, I saw a special on network news that illustrated a virus changing votes on a commonly used voting machine."

"You're kidding."

"Nope, and remember, the press couldn't care less. Leaks of party emails and documents indicate party leaders rigged the primaries for Senator Adams. The only network covering it in detail was Fox News. The liberal press practically ignored it and declared the party national conference as a rousing success, despite the fix."

"That's true."

"Then, just weeks later, Twitter suspended the account of a computer hacker who published a spreadsheet purportedly containing the personal contact information of nearly two hundred members of Congress. The hacker, who goes by the Fraudnym Guccifer 2.0, may connect to the Russian government."

"Yes, I remember that."

"Do you remember when WikiLeaks published nearly twenty thousand documents stolen by hackers? Guccifer 2.0 published some DNC information on a WordPress website. The hacker shared other documents with several news outlets."

"Based on your findings, it sounds like cyber fraud is easier than hard-copy fraud, correct?"

"Correct, and we must move quickly, because many states are going back to hard-copy ballots. In fact, Shyla Nelson, the cofounder of Election

Justice USA, told Al Jazeera that a complete overhaul of the system ensures truly democratic elections in the country, including the end of the use of electronic voting machines. She said that until we systematically address the myriad ways in which our elections manipulate—voter suppression, unauthorized registration purges, district gerrymandering, gross exit poll variances, the privatization of voting machinery, and the lack of transparency in ballot processing—our elections will continue to rank among the lowest in the world in terms of integrity."

"She didn't really say that, did she? How can our country possibly compare to the way dictatorships manipulate elections?"

"You're probably right there, but Nelson criticized current government initiatives to protect voting machines from cyberattacks as a failure to address the well-documented reality of election fraud at their root. She noted that the machines are in many cases running on increasingly obsolete hardware and software."

"Interesting."

"Furthermore, the US Department of Homeland Security Chief said the government would examine if the country's election system should consider it as critical infrastructure. This move would trigger greater digital security measures for electronic voting machines. He's actively thinking about the election and cybersecurity right now. But Caitriona Fitzgerald, the chief technology officer of the civil rights group the Electronic Privacy Information Center, told Al Jazeera that the very reliance on electronic voting machines and online voting threatens public trust in US elections."

"Hmm. You're swaying me."

"Good. This may be one of the last elections for which we can use cyber fraud in many states. State governments are addressing election security, and more states are moving back to paper ballots and ID requirements. Studies show paper ballots are an essential element in election security. Without a paper record of votes, it is impossible to verify if the computer has, indeed, recorded a vote in the system as shown on the screen. Furthermore, the lack of a paper record makes recounts or audits meaningless, because any recount would simply corroborate the same count the computer made the first time and would not catch any errors."

"Again, interesting. But aren't there many types of voting machines we'd have to understand, and subsequently create different voting hacks for each?"

"You would think so, but that's not the case. Let's discuss the major types of voting machines used. I included details in of my report, but I'll summarize them for you."

"OK, what are they?"

"Here goes. First, there's the optical scan paper ballot system in which voters mark paper ballots and tabulate them using scanning devices."

"So, we can use the cyber tool after they scan it, or we intercept the paper ballots in transit and replace the other party candidate ballots with Senator Adams. Correct?"

"Exactly! Now you're getting it."

"OK, what's another voting machine type?"

"The second voting system is the direct recording electronic system, DRE, which uses one of three basic interfaces—pushbutton, touchscreen, or dial. Voters record their votes directly into the computer memory."

"So, what's the weakness there?"

"One version of the DRE is relatively easy to penetrate."

"How so?"

"The new DRE system can be equipped with voter verified paper audit trail, VVPAT, printers that allow the voter to confirm their selections on an independent paper record before recording their votes into computer memory."

"Oh, that's bad."

"Yes, but most states use the outdated version without the VVPAT, so the voter can't verify that the correct selection h was made. Frickin' YouTube shows how easy it is to implant a virus that swaps random votes from one party to the other! It's been in the news as well."

"I missed that. I only watch MSNBC and CNN. I can't stand those right-wing nuts."

"Well, I think it's wise to watch enemy channels. Even though the press is on our side to a ridiculous level, there are still a lot of conservatives out there who believe they ought to keep most of their money rather than give to our Congress-approved and court-enforced entitlement programs."

"They're racists!"

"Calm down, I agree. OK, the third type of voting system is the ballot marking devices and systems that provide an interface to assist voters with disabilities in marking a paper ballot by scan or manual count."

"What's the plan there?"

"I propose we leave that one alone. Over half of the people with disabilities vote for our party because we give them stuff through entitlement programs. Of course, the taxpayer pays for it, but that's the other party's problem since it has most of the wealth. Let them pay for it."

"Amen, brother. OK, we'll leave those machines alone. We just need 50.1 percent of the vote, and if over half the disabled persons vote our way, we need no action there."

"Good. The fourth type of voting system is the old punch card voting system that employs a card and a small clipboard-sized device for recording votes. As far as I know, only two Idaho precincts still use these. Once again, I propose we leave them alone."

"Yes, it'd be too much trouble, and Idaho is not a battleground state."

"Agreed. The fifth voting system is the most vulnerable."

"More than the old DRE or optical scanner systems?"

"Yep. Are you ready for this? The final type of voting system is the hand-counted paper ballot system. A considerable number of jurisdictions manually count paper ballots cast in polling places by hand, and even more count absentees and/or provisional ballots by hand. I suggest we focus on this weakness in precincts heavily supporting Senator Adams. Most voting volunteers will look the other way while we miscount, destroy, and invalidate ballots supporting the other guy."

"Wow! They might as well give Senator Adams the majority vote in those polling places. I love it! It sounds like we have two approaches then. A cyber approach using digital voting, and a myriad of approaches in the paper-based states in their area of weakness. Senator Adams is already in the White House!"

"We'll make sure it happens. Besides, Senator Adams will pick three or four Supreme Court Justices. Then the liberal agenda will be a way of life. We'll open our borders, ensure support through entitlements, run up the deficit, and make the rich pay for it."

"I like the way you think. So, we're agreed. We take advantage of state voting weaknesses using paper-based systems and take a cyber approach in states using digital systems."

"You know what's funny?"

"What's that?"

"The president made the rich richer, and the poor poorer. The beauty is that when our party makes more poor people, most of them still vote for our party. Ironic, huh?"

"Frickin' hilarious. If we're richer, who cares about the poor?"

"Careful, that's what we tell the masses about the other party, and it works!"

"Poor saps. Besides, almost half of the country works for the government or receives handouts—I mean, entitlements. They tend to vote for our party. So, we win again."

"Yes, and that doesn't count the additional illegal aliens, felons, and refugees on welfare, food stamps, social security, Obamacare, etc. And without voter ID, many of them illegally vote. With the additional votes we'll get from our little scheme here, we'll win for sure."

"Don't forget we've opened the border and close to a million illegal aliens cross the border yearly. There are bills in several states to issue ID cards to illegal aliens. With ID cards, they'll be able to vote in many states. Even if they don't vote, we'll harvest their ballots and vote for them."

"Love it! We have a great start to use these methods and technologies to win the election. Let's meet again next week to discuss the various approaches we'll use in the battleground states of Arizona, Colorado, Florida, Pennsylvania, New Hampshire, Ohio, Iowa, Virginia, Michigan, Minnesota, Nevada, and Wisconsin."

"You're right. We must be ready. She's coming."

"She?"

"Scarlett!"

"Shit. We're not prepared for her."

"Are you going to tell her that?"

"Hell no. We'll be ready!"

Chapter 3 ★ Mother August

AS THEY DROVE TOWARD WACO, John said, "I know the general direction, but not the exact location of your house. You'll have to guide me from here."

"Will do. John, I'm sorry you've never met my mom. But you'll probably understand when you meet her."

"You've met my dad many times. I come from a strange family, too," John returned, thoughtfully.

"I love your dad. He's done a lot for us. I miss him. Too bad he's working overseas. How long is he going to be working in the Middle East?"

"He said he's working on a case with US diplomats and be gone at least a year."

"Too bad. He's a great man. I wish I had a chance to meet your mother. I'm sure she was a terrific lady," Joie returned in a loving voice.

John replied, "Yes, she was. I miss her. But I'm sure your mom is great too."

"She's different. You'll see."

"What, you come from someone strange and different? I'm shocked," John joked.

"You'll see."

Thirty minutes later, they turned onto a state road, then spent another twenty on a rural route. Finally, they turned another corner and drove half a mile on a paved road. Beautiful trees and well-maintained bushes lined both sides. It suddenly occurred to John that this wasn't a road—it was a driveway!

The road ended in a circular driveway in front of a three-story mansion. The house was massive, with beautifully sculptured landscape gardens and sidewalks that circled it. Polished granite covered the eighteen thousand square foot manor. Tall, four-foot-wide columns flanked a colossal entrance. The house was as wide as John's entire apartment building, he thought admiringly. Joie looked at the house, too, not with pride but sadness. She looked like a lost little girl.

"You used to live here?" John asked, still amazed by the estate's size.

She nodded, opened the car door, and got out without a word. Like a puppy, John followed her up a beautiful stone path lined with meticulously sculpted hedges through large iron gates to the front door, where she rang the doorbell.

Joie reached over and squeezed his hand. He ran his finger along the side of her hand, but she let go. She withdrew as a soft melody permeated the house, a haunting melody John recognized from a trip to London. Just as he was trying to place it, it stopped.

The front door opened, and there stood a butler in a tux. Recognizing Joie, he stepped forward and gave her a formal hug. She hugged him back in a friendly manner. He stepped back, opened the door, and motioned them to come in with a slight bow at the waist.

"Madam will be so glad to see you. You haven't called in some time," the butler said, forcing a smile as they both walked in.

Closing the door behind them, he motioned for them to wait. He disappeared through large sweeping doors on the other side of the enormous hall, which, although exquisite, was cold and sterile. A minute later, he reappeared and signaled for them to follow.

John thought it was odd that Joie's mother hadn't greeted them; rather, the butler escorted her through her own home like a guest. They walked through several more antiseptic rooms. The mahogany wood furniture reeked of money. A colossal grandfather clock counted the seconds as they walked by. Gold-plated china decorated a grand cabinet. Everything in the house displayed dramatic aesthetic décor yet felt noticeably frigid and impersonal.

The butler led them to a veranda, on which there was a table set for one.

The woman sitting at the table looked pampered but ancient. Her expensive sequined dress hung from her body, which seemed made of only skin and bone. The formal attire seemed so out of place within one's own home. Her gaunt face and wrinkled hands clashed with her recently styled hair and freshly painted pink nails. Her eyes were lifeless, and her lips curled down with years of dissatisfaction. She could not be more than fifty years old yet easily looked seventy. No amount of makeup could cover the premature signs of age.

Joie went to her and gave her a gentle kiss on the cheek. The old woman smiled cordially, but that was all. Joie turned to John and said, "John, I would like to introduce you to my mother, Sandra August. Mother, this is John Jacobson."

Mrs. August held out her hand in a manner to which he was not accustomed. Her palm was down, and her hand half closed. She seemed to want him to kiss the back of her hand, as if she was the Queen of England herself. He complied like a pauper. She nodded formally toward the chairs around the table, and they sat down. Joie gazed at her mother as if she was a stranger. They sat in uncomfortable silence until Joie said, "How are you, Mother?"

Her mother looked at Joie, her face expressionless. "I'm moderately well. I'm surprised to see you. Where have you been?"

It seemed odd that Joie's mother didn't know what was going on in her only daughter's life. John looked from mother to daughter and back again. It was like watching a tennis match. He wondered what kind of "'return" Joie would make. He also wondered why Joie called her "Mother" rather than "Mom." It seemed aloof and formal. However, it seemed appropriate given the mansion was just as stark.

"I've been working, Mother. I have an excellent job! You know where I work."

John wondered why she didn't say she worked for the FBI. Did her mother know?

Mrs. August continued, "I find it totally ridiculous that you work. It is so commonplace of you. You could live here with me and not have to worry about such mundane things."

Mrs. August turned to John. "And do you work at the same place as my daughter?"

"No, ma'am. I work in Fort Worth for a company called Pseudomics."

Mrs. August looked at him as if he was an indigent and retorted, "I see."

This didn't sit well with John, and before thinking he blurted out, "By the way, I don't take offense you think my work is commonplace. My job is at the leading edge of avionics technology and is especially important to our government's defense."

Joie looked at John with a forced smile. She approved of how he conducted himself. Mrs. August, on the other hand, looked unimpressed. She rolled her eyes and turned her attention back to Joie as if he wasn't worth her time.

"When will you move back home?"

"I'm not going to, Mother. I can't! Please don't ask me again. I'll visit you more often, but I can't move back home. I'm an adult with my own life and career. You and Daddy never understood that."

Joie looked at John out of the corner of her eye, slightly embarrassed. He watched the conversation as an outsider.

Mrs. August replied, "I am so sorry your mother is a bother. I can't help being concerned with my only child's well-being. Even after what you did to your father."

A tear rolled down Joie's face at the mention of her father. She fought back emotions, wiping the tear from her face. "Mother, you know I didn't mean for anything to happen to Father. It wasn't my fault!"

"You and I both know differently," Mrs. August said as she swiveled her chair toward the gardens, turning her back to them. As far as she was concerned, the conversation was over. She spoke the final word and satisfied with the amount of pain she inflicted on Joie during the first round.

Joie looked defeated but shook her head, gaining control of herself.

"Mother, we're here to talk to you about something. May we stay a while?"

"If you feel you have time to spend with your mother, you may stay. Jeffrey will take you to a room where we can speak. Wait here while I prepare."

Joie stood up and John followed her lead. Mrs. August slowly stood up and walked regally into the house. John wondered why they had to go somewhere else to talk. Joie walked to the elaborate concrete railing and stared without emotion at the beautiful gardens. John held her from behind.

"Are you sure you want to do this, John?"

"Yes, I'm sure."

"OK, but prepare yourself for resistance."

"I can handle it if you can," he replied.

They waited silently until Jeffrey returned. He led them through several more ostentatious, cold, and sterile rooms to a living room with extravagant leather furniture. It seemed too masculine for a woman.

"This is nice, Mother. I see we're in Dad's living room rather than yours," Joie noted, kissing her on the cheek.

Joie's mom feigned a kiss in return. "So, to what do I owe the pleasure?" Mrs. August asked formally.

John started to speak, but Joie cut him off. "John wants to get to know you better."

"That'll take more than two visits a year," she responded, frowning.

"You're right, Mother. We'll do better."

" 'We'? Are you two a couple now?"

John interjected, "Yes, we are. I love your daughter."

Mrs. August glared, disapproving of his interruption, but asked, "You are engaged?"

"I'd like to speak with you about that," John continued.

Mrs. August immediately clamped up and said abruptly, "Go upstairs and freshen up. We'll speak during dinner."

She rang a bell, and the door swung open seconds later. "Yes, madam?" Jeffrey asked, bowing.

"There'll be three for dinner in one hour."

"Yes, Madam," the butler said, bowing and disappeared as quickly as he had arrived.

John thought it strange that the butler and his employer acted so formal and distant toward each other. There was no apparent affection after years of faithful service. John marveled at how this cold woman could have raised such a warm, intelligent daughter.

Mrs. August said, "Joie, you know the way to the bedrooms. You are staying the night, aren't you?"

Joie looked enquiringly at John, wondering if this was part of his plan. John nodded, and Joie simply said, "Yes, Mother."

Joie led John up the enormous winding staircase to the landing above. She turned left and said, "Let's stay in the guest suite."

"OK, whatever makes you comfortable. This is for both of us."

"Thanks for making this bearable, John."

Joie opened double doors into a suite of three large bedrooms and two marble-covered bathrooms. Her countenance waned, and she hung her head in despair.

"Joie, is this a mistake? Do you want to leave? I want this weekend to be special."

"It's OK. I know your heart is in the right place," she responded with quivering lips.

Joie could stand toe to toe with dangerous criminals and could beat almost any man in combat—even him, if she caught him off guard—but her mother reduced her to a trembling little girl.

"John, I need to fix my face and work on my attitude. Can you please go into the other bedroom and change for dinner?"

"Of course, my lady," John said, kissing her gently on the lips.

"Dinner is formal," she replied, returning the kiss helplessly.

She pulled his strong arms around her. He sensed that she needed his protection and squeezed her tight. She felt safe and stood motionless for a moment. When she let go, he released her, walked into the next bedroom, and closed the door. As soon as it closed, he heard her break into tears. He wanted to go back but knew she needed privacy.

John changed quickly into the best clothes he brought and hoped it was formal enough. He heard Joie's muffled moans through the door.

He asked through the closed door, "Joie, do you need more time?"

"Yes, John. I'll need another half an hour. It takes me longer than a Neanderthal like you," she attempted to joke.

John grunted like an ape and heard her chuckle. "Do you mind if I look around a little upstairs?"

"Sure, go ahead. You'll love my dad's study at the other end of the hall."

"Will do, Joie," John said. He walked out of the opposite door into another hallway. At the top of the stairs, he passed the landing and gazed into the living space below. Jeffrey stared at him. John smiled and kept walking. The butler didn't return the smile, instead walking away toward the room where Mrs. August was. John wondered if he was in trouble.

John continued down the hall, looking at family pictures along the hall in lavish large dark wood frames. Joie appeared alone in most. The chronological arrangement of the pictures of her youth told the story of her upbringing. He smiled seeing her as a child; she was beautiful yet appeared so out of place wearing expensive clothes. She appeared to smile less as she matured. He continued to investigate the hall, passing other bedrooms, a library, and a sitting room before he finally reached the office.

The huge dark door contained detailed carvings. He opened it slowly and took in the extravagant desk, pictures, bookcase, and plush carpet. He walked in respectfully, as if entering the Vatican. He knew Joie's father made a fortune from patents in the oil business, but this was overwhelming. What struck John most was the museum-like atmosphere of the room. It remained undisturbed despite his death occurring back when Joie was in high school. The ten-year-old technology still adorned the desk as if it was used yesterday.

John walked behind the desk, swiveled the plush leather chair, and sat down. He surveyed the room, taking in each detail. Mounted on one wall was a diagram and the picture of an electronic component. Since he loved electronics, he rose and approached it with admiration. The device picture, wiring diagram, and notes indicated that it was a digital counter of some sort. It received signals and counted them. The notes indicated that it could reflect the actual number of signals or reduce or increase the count. It included a patent number and picture of a check for three hundred thousand dollars made out to Mr. August. It was dated fifteen years ago.

John continued looking around when the door opened. There stood Joie in a stunning evening dress. She astounded him. He looked down at his semi-formal pants and shirt, obviously underdressed in comparison.

"Joie, you're gorgeous."

"Thank you, kind sir," she said, bowing like a princess.

John laughed. "Do I need to go to town and buy a tux?"

"Not on your life. You're not leaving me here alone with Mother. Besides, I'm the one under the microscope, not you."

"OK, my lady. May I escort you to the ball?"

"Why, yes, my gallant knight."

John offered her an arm. She wrapped hers around his bulging forearm and they turned toward the hall, each closing one of the double doors. They walked back to the landing and down the stairs without a word. He sensed her tension rise as they approached the dining room. Joie opened the door and a twenty-person table, complete with settings, sat in the middle of the room. Mrs. August sat at one end and looked at her watch, indicating her impatience.

John pulled out a chair for Joie on Mrs. August's right. After she sat down, he went over to a chair on the other side of the table. As soon as he was seated, Mrs. August rang a bell. Moments later two doors swung open, and two housemaids placed napkins on their laps, filled their glasses with water, poured a twenty-year-old red wine, and promptly disappeared. Seconds later, they returned with salads for the first course.

Finally, Joie said, "This is lovely, Mother. Thank you."

"You're welcome. Now, tell me why you're here," she replied curtly.

John marveled at her callous cut to the purpose of their visit.

Joie took the lead and responded, equally businesslike, "Our visit has two objectives. First, we wanted to see you. It's been too long."

Mrs. August opened her mouth to respond, but Joie cut her off, saying, "Secondly, John has a question for you."

Joie and Mrs. August turned to John, but he was speechless. This is not how he pictured this moment. It was more like an interview than a loving family gathering. However, he took a deep breath, manned up, and said, "Mrs. August. I've come here to ask you an important question."

She looked at him as if he was an insect and said, "I don't loan money, if that's what you want."

"No, ma'am, of course not. We're doing fine. I've been promoted, and Joie is a field agent with the FBI."

"Yes, I'm aware of your stations. What is your important question?"

"Mrs. August, I'd like to ask your blessings for our marriage."

John knew better than to ask for her permission; her answer was obvious. For the first time, Mrs. August's expression was not condescending or sad. Instead, she appeared surprised. She glanced at Joie and then turned back to John.

She gathered her emotions, opened her mouth, and flatly said, "No."

Chapter 4 ★ Polling 101

IN FEBRUARY, SCARLETT SCHEDULED A summit to discuss the way forward. Fred and Charlie brought a few subordinates to assist them, and Scarlett brought two guests. They gathered in the same conference room in Northern Virginia where they met before. Scarlett Schuller needed no introduction, so she skipped such pleasantries. That wasn't her style anyway. She sat in the vacant seat at the head of the table, leaving no doubt as to who led the meeting.

Scarlett looked forty years old but was much younger. Bitterness and stress took their toll, despite her fortune. Her brown curly hair always looked unkempt, yet her blue eyes missed little.

Fred was the first to speak. "Scarlett, you said we had two weeks to prepare the cyber and voter fraud strategies. We've made progress, but we're not yet ready to present our ideas and potential solutions."

"Relax. I do expect an update, but first I want to introduce two new members to the team." Scarlett pointed to the first stranger, a woman around thirty years old, and said, "This is Lizzy Warden. She's a highly respected and successful polling expert. She owns her own polling agency and assisted Senator Adams from the beginning. Please welcome her."

Most of the attendees nodded in her direction. Two of them, not knowing what to do, clapped. The others looked at them, surprised, and they stopped, embarrassed but hoping they scored points with Scarlett. She smiled at them, and they relaxed—mission accomplished.

Lizzy stood up after the introduction, her attractive figure clad in an expensive brown pantsuit highlighted by her dark-blonde hair. After nodding at everyone, she sat back down.

Scarlett continued, "Our second new member is Gavin Principle. Senator Adams assigned him to this group to ensure our success. He's a, uhm . . . let's just call him a problem solver."

Gavin stood, and the group welcomed him with nods—no clapping this time. Gavin's thirty-year-old frame sported a thousand-dollar suit with a wide starched collar. His short hair betrayed a military background. There was no doubt his solid 190-pound physique poised for action. He smiled and showed perfectly straight and stark white sharklike teeth. He sat back down, and all eyes remained on him until Scarlett cleared her throat.

She continued, "Senator Adams asked me to introduce these two new members. They complement our current strategies. Lizzy, please update us on the line of attack for polling."

Scarlett sat down as Lizzy stood up. She reached into her briefcase and removed ten copies of a forty-page report. She passed them around and began, "As you'll see in the report, our polling approach is complete. In fact, it's already in place and working well."

"How long has it been in place?" Todd Shamer asked curiously.

"Since 1976," she replied.

"1976? What are you talking about?" Todd asked, surprised.

Lizzy replied, "Allow me to explain. In 1976, polling showed Ford ahead of Carter by 1 percent. It was Ford 49 percent and Carter 48 percent. This was the first time in recent presidential election history that there was such a close race. It was also recent enough for high-tech voting apparatus, network coverage, and modern statistical modeling. As you may remember, Carter won with 50.1 percent, compared to 48.1 percent for Ford. This was a full 3 percent swing. The polling worked, though."

"How did it work? It was wrong," Todd said. However, his tone was too challenging. Scarlett and Gavin glared at him, and he shrank down in his chair.

Lizzy continued, agitated now, "You see, Todd, the media and pollsters seemed to favor the liberal candidate and might have rigged the polls. The conservative voters, thinking Ford would win because of the polls and because he was the incumbent president, stayed home; therefore, Carter won. It's a textbook case pollsters study for ideas on how to sway voters."

"Oh, I see. Interesting," Todd noted, hoping to regain Scarlett and Gavin's good graces. It seemed to work; they nodded approval in his direction and turned their attention back to Lizzy.

"Please turn to page one of the handout. Let me summarize our polling stratagem. Here are the ways we'll influence polling. Most voters don't ask the following important questions. One: Who created the poll? We'll hire polling companies favoring liberal agendas this year. Therefore, they will write the questions favoring Senator Adams. Two: Who paid for the poll? Guess what? This time, our candidate's party will. We have super PACs and affluent donors already giving millions for polling purposes. Three: What was the size of the survey? If the sample size was not large enough, it might not be statistically valid. Four: How were participants chosen? Were they in precincts that historically vote for our candidate's party? In this case, they will be.

"Five: Who participated in the poll? The poll will select higher percentages of segments within society and industry supporting our candidate's party. For instance, educators, unions, inner cities, government employees, etc. Six: Did the results include all participants interviewed? It won't! Seven: When was the poll conducted? Was it during the day when more of the other party were working? It will be. Eight: How were the interviews conducted? Was the interview with pollsters influencing participants by emphasizing or understating certain words? Nine: Did the poll use the internet? We'll put up the survey on websites visited by more liberal voters.

"Ten: What was the sampling error? The larger the poll, the less the potential sampling error. Therefore, we'll use smaller polls and stop when we have the result we want. Eleven: Were there phantom results? In other words, did the pollster throw in interview or question results of their own? We're doing that now. Twelve: What was the order of the questions? We'll ask how important previous political experience is to them. This makes voters think of the candidate with the most experience and then favor Senator Adams with the questions that follow. Thirteen: Were rumors spread and lies told about the opponent in the area before taking the poll? They most certainly will be! Fourteen: Were there previous polls favoring Senator Adams conducted in the same area or voter group? There will be! Fifteen: Finally, were the polls conducted in areas containing exit polls and previously satisfactory results for our candidate's party? They will be."

Lizzy paused, giving everyone a moment to catch up. "Any questions?"

Fred spoke up, "What confuses me about the polls is simple. Senator Adams is ahead in the polls. Yet, when Ronald Jackson speaks, tens of thousands attend. When Senator Adams speaks, typically only hundreds show up."

"That's why polling is so important. We must confuse voters with stats."

Todd added, "So the strategy is to influence the polls in our favor, then use technology to rig the election supporting the polls?"

"Precisely," Lizzy answered with a nod of approval.

Scarlett chimed in, "Thank you, Lizzy. Now, let's continue with a status report on our two voting strategies. Todd, you're up first. How is the state weakness approach coming along?"

Todd stood as Scarlett listened intently. He adjusted his necktie nervously while looking at Gavin. Gavin returned his gaze without emotion.

Todd began, "My team feels we need to focus on large cities in the battleground states, focusing on their specific voting problems."

"Why's that?" Scarlett asked.

"First, the larger precincts in the battleground states contain large urban populations with predominately liberal leanings, as shown in recent presidential elections. Pennsylvania, for instance, contains Philadelphia County, which encompasses Philadelphia and the surrounding cities and has a county population of 1,526,006. Since they are liberal leaning, we can easily find those supporting our cause. According to a recent poll, eighty-five percent of Senator Adams's supporters would vote our way no matter what the media reports."

"I like that. Go on," Lizzy said.

"The other PA counties we'll focus on are Montgomery, Bucks, Delaware, and Lancaster. Their populations range from five hundred thousand to eight hundred thousand. These five counties, along with Philadelphia County, contain almost five million voters! We'll focus on other urban precincts in the other swing states. If we focus on too many precincts, it'll be too hard to manage. Therefore, in the ten swing states, we'll focus on the most populated precincts. That's only one hundred precincts. That's doable!"

"Agreed. So, what will you do in those precincts?" Scarlett asked.

"We will use voter ID fraud, felon voting, losing ballots from the other side, and buying officials to falsify counts. These are just a few methods. I'll explain more later," Todd answered.

"Approved," Scarlett said emphatically. "You mentioned focusing on precincts with voting machine issues. Give me an example."

"Let's talk about another swing state—Florida."

Everyone chuckled, and one attendee said, "You mean the state that screws up every election?"

Todd responded, "Yep! Miami-Dade County spent twenty-five million dollars on DRE voting machines, which caused the cost of elections to rise from one to two million dollars to six to seven million. It also negatively affected several elections. Better yet, the machines yield no paper trail. The reason for this is that adding paper verifications of votes would cost another fifteen million dollars. The option of scrapping the DRE machines and switching to optical scanning machines is even more costly. Therefore, Miami-Dade now uses touchscreen iVotronic machines from Omaha-based ES&S installed in 2002 to remedy flaws in the paper-based system."

"Sounds promising," Scarlett said.

"That's not all. The system is so bad that a recent case of voter fraud involved more than two thousand five hundred 'phantom requests' for absentee ballots, for which many were granted. If the voting official was one of ours, most would be granted."

"Nice," Scarlett affirmed, thinking out loud.

Todd continued, "Finally, after a recent special election, a glitch left hundreds of votes uncounted. This led to several resignations of county election supervisors and officials, which means we replaced many of them with officials willing to help us with voter fraud. Of course, there's Broward

County, where we fix elections every year by only counting our provisional and absentee votes, stuffing boxes, suddenly finding thousands of questionable votes after the election, destroying the other sides votes, and more."

"Wow. Wonderful job and informative report," Lizzy replied.

Todd smiled in relief. "Most county voters lost confidence and grew cynical about whether their votes counted. Many will stay home, so our strategies will exacerbate the results in our favor. In addition, coding errors by county personnel caused the iVotronic system to undercount votes in five local elections. The adjacent Broward County, which also relies on iVotronic machines and is one of the most populated counties in the US, had similar voting miscounts. The state mandated a tight deadline for a switch to automated voting systems, leaving county officials scrambling to meet the timetable. However, precincts are resisting and plan to add printers to existing machines. Not only will this cost millions, but each county is doing it differently, causing more confusion and creating openings for our plans."

"Is that it?" Scarlett asked with a smile.

Todd continued after a pause for effect. "We are looking at a voting machine called Dominion. It is manufactured in China and used in Venezuela, Cuba, and other dictator countries. It is designed to flip votes from one candidate to another in predetermined ratios. It is already used in many liberal states. We'll also install them in the swing states."

"Wow! Love it. Excellent. Approved," Scarlett beamed. "I expect a spreadsheet of the fifty target precincts in the ten swing states, with the specific strategy suggested, by our meeting next week."

"But that's not enough time for—" Todd began.

"Excuse me, I don't think I heard you correctly."

Gavin sat forward on cue, staring impassively at Todd.

"I misspoke. We'll be ready," Todd said in acquiescence.

"Great. Thank you, Todd. Awesome job," Scarlett said, and Gavin relaxed. "That brings us to you, Fred, for the cyber approach. You have the floor."

Fred stood uneasily. "As we've previously discussed, many US states use touch-screen computer voting systems without a paper trail. These are susceptible to simple viruses planted in the machines that change the actual results. The beauty is that we just need to infect one machine, as some machines link to others in the precinct. However, many precincts link all machines. That's why we have the results just minutes after precincts close. Therefore, we can infect one machine, and the virus will spread to all the other linked machines."

Lizzy interrupted, saying, "Yes, that's true."

Fred continued, "It gets better than that. Almost all ballots get counted by the computers, whether paper or not. In almost every case, this counting is nontransparent and inaccessible for verification by voting officials. The few states that audit the computer counts by hand only examine a tiny percentage of the ballots, and in most cases do not perform it according to proper statistical procedures."

"You're kidding!" Scarlett exclaimed.

Fred continued, encouraged, "Nope. In other words, the results of our elections, based on computer counts, are largely unverified. We're testing viruses now. The first one works on every voting machine we've tested."

"You said 'viruses.' There's more than one?" asked Scarlett.

"Yes, there are two. The first virus is for voting machines without a paper trail," Fred answered.

"Oh, that ought to be simple. I read a story where an eleven-year-old child hacked a voting machine in minutes," Scarlett retorted.

"That's a true story. However, hacking into one machine is simpler than interjecting a virus on many diverse types of voting machines," he replied respectfully.

Scarlett responded, "Well what about the college students that produced a virus that changes votes on a modern voting machine?"

"I wasn't aware of that one. I'll check it out."

"You do that," Scarlett replied patronizingly. Fred made a note as Scarlett returned, "What's the second virus for?"

"It's the more complicated one. It'll intercept the digital signal of the voting results from entire precincts to the state election boards. It'll slightly change the count in our favor. We're working on it, and *may* have a prototype by next week's meeting," Fred said proudly.

"You mean you *will* have the prototype by next week's meeting. Right?" Scarlett asked.

"No promises, but we'll do our best to…" Gavin sat forward again and stared at Fred with blank lifeless eyes. Fred responded quickly, "Right."

"Magnificent," Scarlett said with a fake smile, gesturing for Gavin to relax. He did begrudgingly.

"Any other business?" Scarlett asked. She looked at Lizzy, Fred, and Todd. They all nodded their heads. A man from the back row, however, raised his hand.

"Yes?" Scarlett asked, markedly disturbed that she was wasting her time with someone so insignificant.

"Ma'am, there are two members of our team missing today. They are not answering texts or calls. Should I be concerned?"

"Why, do you want to join them?" she snapped, looking at Gavin. This time Gavin simply jotted down his name in a small black book he retrieved from his breast pocket.

"No, ma'am. I'm fine."

"Meeting adjourned," Scarlett proclaimed, hitting the desk with her fist like a judge using a gavel. Everyone quickly filed out. Scarlett looked at Gavin, then nodded toward the attendee who asked the last question. Gavin smiled and followed him out of the room. He never asked another question, because he was no longer a member of the group and had a permanent limp.

Chapter 5 ★ The New Job

"NO? YOU WON'T GIVE US your blessing? Why?" Joie asked.

Mrs. August gave her a brief blank stare, then stood to leave.

John spoke up, "Mrs. August, I'll be good to Joie. I care for her deeply. What can I do to change your mind?"

"I don't know you well enough to make that decision. However, I do know my daughter. I doubt you know her as well as I. For instance, do you know she killed her father?" Silence fell thick over the room. "This conversation is over. You may now leave my home."

John looked at Joie, confused by Mrs. August's words.

Mrs. August rang the bell loudly and the butler immediately appeared. She whispered to him, and he gestured for John and Joie to follow him.

"You can't be serious, Mother. What's happened to you that you treat your only child this way? You know I didn't kill Dad. He was sick!" Joie protested.

"I will not tolerate lies in my home. Jeffrey, show them out now," she said, walking to the closest door.

"Mother, we'll get married anyway! John was nice enough to ask you out of respect. That says a lot about him."

Mrs. August left without another word, wearing a look of total disgust.

Jeffrey patted Joie on the back softly and said, "Madam is just having a tough day. Give her time, Miss Joie."

"Jeffrey, you've always made excuses for her. She chooses to be hateful," Joie said, tearing up.

"It'll be OK, Miss Joie," Jeffrey soothed, pointing toward the door.

John joined in, saying, "She'll come around," reassuring her as best he could despite the disappointment.

Jeffrey led them to the front door. Their bags were packed and waiting for them. Joie looked at Jeffrey, betrayed. He simply said, "Sorry, Miss Joie. I'm just following orders."

John and Joie left, disillusioned. Joie was silent for quite some time on their way back to Fort Worth. John gave her time to recover. Finally, he asked, "What did your mom mean when she said you killed your father?"

"It's a long story. I'll tell you about it someday," Joie responded in despair.

He closed the conversation. "OK Joie, it's up to you if we marry without your mom's blessing. I'll follow your lead here."

"Thank you, John. You're so patient."

"No problem. Can I ask another question?"

"Sure, but I may choose not to answer if it's about my mom. I may not know the answer myself."

"Well, it's a family-related question."

"Shoot."

"Do you have any siblings, or were you raised alone?"

Joie thought before saying, "Define 'sibling.'"

"Are you kidding? I mean, do you have any brothers or sisters?"

"You're asking if my parents had any other children?"

"Yes, silly. That's what I'm asking."

"No. Now let's change the subject. I've got a headache thinking about my family."

"Will do, Joie. No more family questions—for now."

Joie forced a smile and put her head on his strong shoulder. The conversation was over, and he'd wait as long as it'd take for her to deal with it.

After a long silence, Joie asked, "What are the first steps in your new job?"

"Funny you should ask. I was just thinking about that myself. I've scheduled my first staff meeting Monday. I'll lay out my plans for the department, then meet with them individually for feedback. How does that sound?"

"Yep, that's probably what I'd do," Joie responded, brightening slightly.

"How about you? How's the new assignment?" John asked, encouraged by Joie's conversation.

"Part of my new duties is working on FBI's unsuccessful cases to strategize better approaches in the future."

"That sounds exciting," John said, faking a yawn.

Joie hit him in the arm. She loved his sense of humor and needed it now more than ever.

The rest of the weekend flew by in a haze of passion. Two days later, John drove Joie back to the airport. When almost there, Joie said, "John, I'm sorry about my mother's reaction."

"No problem, Joie. We're adults and can plan our next steps together."

"You're right. Thanks for putting up with my family issues."

John's smile swelled into a laugh. "Are you frickin' kidding? Your family is a walk in the park compared to mine."

She giggled. "Good point, my love."

John grew serious and said, "Joie, I'm going to wait until the right time to ask you the question I wanted to ask you just weeks after we met. There's no hurry, is there?"

"John, I'd marry you today if you'd ask. But I agree, my mother pretty much killed any wedding discussions this weekend."

John laughed. "You always know how to summarize the situation."

She pretended to swing at his shoulder but leaned in and kissed him on the cheek instead.

John parked and walked her into the airport. They talked for another hour before she entered security and disappeared. Time together always passed much too quickly. Back at home, the night passed slowly for John without Joie by his side.

***

The next morning John arrived at work early, completed notes for his first meeting, and walked the halls. He headed for the conference room ten minutes early.

"Good morning, *Mr. Jacobson*," his new secretary, Debbie Stevenson, said, emphasizing his name and smiling brightly.

"It's so good to see you again, Debbie," John said, extending his hand.

"It's good to be seen, John," she shot back, shaking his hand enthusiastically.

Debbie was a natural beauty, especially when she wore a mid-thigh dress and tight blouse. She was around thirty but looked younger. Her straight hair matched her light-brown eyes. Her full lips and light makeup made her a temptation for John, even though she wasn't beautiful as Joie. He kept his distance, but she became a trusted friend.

"Are you ready to attend your first engineering department meeting?" he asked.

"You bet. Let's get this operation going. I've instructed all group engineer leads to attend your briefing at eight a.m. sharp," Debbie said, taking a seat near the head of the table. John dropped his notes on the chair at the other end.

"Great, thanks. I appreciate you getting the word out for me. I'll expect you to communicate with the entire group."

"Yes, sir," Debbie responded, making a note of it. John sensed that their collaborative effort would lead to success. Tommy Kinnaird, the president of the division, was the one who promoted John to this post, and John was ready to impress him.

Minutes later, engineers entered the conference room. Some were familiar faces, but most were new. At eight o'clock sharp, Debbie closed the door and returned to her seat.

"OK, let's get started," John said as everyone opened their laptops and smartphones to take notes. John liked their eagerness.

"The Aviation Division of Pseudomics is branching out. We have new products and services for midlife aircrafts, as well as the latest aircrafts in the military inventory. As many of you know, we're also retrofitting commercial aircraft in a growing division of its own. Most of us will work in both divisions on demand. It's a pleasure to lead this group. Most of you know I am a fellow engineer. My door is always open to you. I've worked with some of you before and look forward to getting to know the new engineers on the team. My strategy is simple."

Engineers began typing, and John smiled in approval. "First, satisfy the customer. Second, meet or exceed the technical requirements of the product or service. Third, align the form, fit, and function of each component into a holistic system within the aircraft's mission parameters. Fourth, ensure the cost of the delivered product or service is less than the price quoted. Notice I spoke of profit last. If we take care of the customer's needs, they'll take care of our profits. It's a symbiotic relationship enjoyed by the most successful enterprises on the planet."

John stopped speaking momentarily to ensure his team understood the overall strategy. They seemed to agree and appeared eager to comply. Just then, the door opened and in walked a slovenly dressed thirty-five-year-old engineer. He looked for a free chair and sat down with a thud. All eyes moved from him back to John. As a trained US Marine officer and now a commercial company junior executive, John knew exactly what to do. If he didn't set an example, more of this behavior would ensue. It was easier to gradually relax control than to get it back after it's been lost the first day.

"What's your name?" John asked.

"Steve Hamm," the man responded sheepishly.

"Please stand up."

Steve stood nervously.

"Please apologize to everyone for disrespecting them by being late for the very first group meeting. Their time is valuable, and you've disparaged them."

Steve obviously regretted his tardiness and said, "I apologize. My child was sick this morning, and it took me time to drop her off to school."

"Understood. I hope this is an anomaly and not a trend, Steve. I hope your child recovers quickly. Please be seated."

Steve sat, saw everyone taking notes, opened Word on his smartphone, and readied himself. He sat up straight, looked at John respectfully, and mouthed, "Sorry."

John winked at him. Steve, relieved, decided he'd be the most dedicated employee this month.

John passed out the new catalog of products and services, a list of clients, and contracts. "I'd like each of you to circle the products and services you are familiar with. I'll pair you so that your strengths will make up for the weakness of your office mate. Also, circle the clients and contracts you're currently working on. You'll become a subject matter expert in your area, and we'll depend heavily on each other to grow. Collaboration is the key to success. Understood?"

They replied in unison, "Yes, sir."

"I'll be around later to see each of you individually. Any questions?"

They either said no or shook their heads, to which John responded, "Good. Then let's get to work."

Everyone filed out, and most stopped to shake hands with John on the way. Debbie then began scheduling his day, making appointments with individual engineers as well as his new boss, Robert Beyer.

Chapter 6 ★ A Six-Pronged Approach

"WELCOME, EVERYONE, TO OUR MARCH planning meeting," Scarlett began. "As you may know, our little group began with me, Todd Shamer, Fred Reider, Lizzy Warden, Gavin Principle, and a few others. However, to conduct our plan, we've added more members to the team. We now have an electrical engineer, a computer analyst, a software programmer, a hardware expert, a political consultant, an election specialist, and a media expert."

Everyone in the room either shook hands or nodded to each other. Scarlett continued, "Each of us can make suggestions, but I have the final say. I am in charge! If there's any question about that, I can ask Senator Adams to contact dissenters directly. Will that be necessary?"

Everyone in the room shook their heads, trembling in fear. There was no doubt from news stories that Senator Adams would retaliate violently for disobedience.

"Good, let's continue then. Senator Adams has a six-pronged approach to winning the election. Arranged in order of importance, they are: the press, party support, lies, social media, election fraud, and the Hillton Boys."

Most of the attendees looked confused. She read their faces and said, "I'll take you through them one at a time. First is the press. That's the easiest."

"How so?" Fred asked.

Scarlett glared at him for interrupting, and he cowered in his seat. She continued, "Allow me to explain. As you know, the press favors our candidate. In fact, the press favored our party since the mid-fifties. They deny it, but everyone knows it. I mean, face it, our candidate's party gave billions to terrorist nations, freed some of the most dangerous terrorists from Guantanamo. He encouraged sanctuary cities, paid for the release of hostages, protected criminals and illegal aliens while chastising the police, emitted non-vetted refugees, and wrote executive orders even the Supreme Court said were illegal. He lied about healthcare coverage and costs, directed the IRS to audit/tax conservative organizations more than liberal ones, and increased the size of our national debt more than all previous administrations combined! Why did our party and Senator Adams approve these clandestine efforts? Simple—they mean votes! Besides, the press barely touched any of it! Senator Adams lied under oath and destroyed evidence under subpoena. While Ronald Jackson slams the press, which consequently hates him, Senator Adams ingratiates the press, and they love it."

"May I say something?" Todd asked nervously.

"Yes, go ahead. But be quick; we have a lot to cover."

"OK, thanks. The irony is that Senator Adams has not held a press conference in months, and the press doesn't complain about it. Therefore, there's little they can pick apart. However, the opposing candidate holds several press conferences each week, giving the press ample ammunition against him. It's beautiful."

This time, Scarlett smiled in agreement, and Todd smirked at Fred for scoring points with the boss's representative. Fred didn't respond and waited for his turn to shine—it was coming.

"Does prong one—the press—make sense to everyone?" she asked.

They all nodded. She continued, "Prong two is party support. Our party is more unified than the other side. Most of our constituents are uninformed or don't watch political news; many don't have internet access or, for some, even a TV. They vote our way because we give them things. We've convinced our voters the other side is racist, and now they believe that the police shoot more blacks than whites out of racism. Our party members are so upset that they're shooting at the police and organizing violent protests. Hell, a recent poll of our party indicated they don't trust Senator Adams but would still vote for him even if prosecuted of a crime. Now that's party support!"

They all chuckled in agreement. "Prong three is to *lie*. If the press or the authorities accuse Senator Adams of anything, the response is to lie. It's worked over thirty years in Senator Adams's career. Because of prong number one, the press won't challenge him. Senator Adams can lie as much as needed."

Again, everyone agreed. She continued, "Prong four is social media. The largest platforms are Facebook, Google, Twitter, Instagram, and Snapchat. They are liberal leaning and will lock conservative accounts and delete opposing ideas while promoting liberal posts. They do this already and even thumb their nose at congressional investigations. We'll get these social giants to increase these activities just before and during the election. Questions?"

Everyone smiled, knowing this was a well-known political weapon.

"Prong five is election fraud. Senator Adams is aggressively promising things to the inner cities for votes. We're also bringing hundreds of thousands of refugees into the country, giving them welfare and healthcare and swearing them in as quickly as possible. Our party politicians are moving precinct boundaries in favor of Senator Adams. We're removing the other side's voters from registered rolls. We're also creating misleading and/or confusing ballots. Lastly, liberal secretaries of state are amending voting laws to include not validating signatures and increasing mail-in voting where voter ID is virtually impossible to check. Senator Adams is leading these strategies. Now, he needs help from this team. Where are we on the election fraud methodologies?"

Fred Reider was the first to speak up, beating Todd to the punch. "We have two approaches. I'm leading the cyber approach. We'll use technology to digitally increase votes for Senator Adams. As previously discussed, optical scan paper ballot systems use paper ballots, which tabulate by scanning devices. So, we use a cyber tool after scanning happens. It'll change a small number of votes."

"Why a small number of votes?" Scarlett asked.

"Because those machines have a paper trail, and if it's too obvious, simple audits may catch the inequity."

Scarlett nodded in agreement. "OK, I agree with this approach. Go on."

Excited, Fred continued, "The second cyber approach is with DRE systems. Voters record their votes directly into the computer memory. The voter's choices store in the DREs via a memory cartridge, diskette, or smart card. The older version of the DRE that is most widely used doesn't confirm the vote, so the voter can't verify that the vote cast is correct."

"I'm not sure I understand," Scarlett said.

"The latest version of the DRE system includes a voter-verified paper audit trail printers that allow the voter to confirm their selections on an independent paper record before recording their votes in the computer memory. These paper records preserve a record of the vote and, depending on State election codes, made available in the event of an audit or a recount."

"Oh, I see. So, we use cyber fraud with the outdated version."

"Correct," Fred responded.

"OK, approved. Anything else?"

"Yes, we are working with battleground states to use the Dominion voting machine that flips votes in our favor. We've tested them, and they are working as programmed. It will be difficult for the opposing side to prove voter fraud."

"Excellent. Approved. Put a team together to devise and analyze potential scenarios. I expect a report in two weeks. I'll take them to Senator Adams."

"Wait, we need at least a month!" Fred protested.

"OK, how about one week?" Scarlett hissed.

"Two weeks it is," Fred said, yielding.

"Now let's discuss the battleground state weaknesses we broached last time. Are you ready, Todd?"

"Yes!" he answered hastily. "First, we intercept optical scan paper ballots in transit and replace the other party candidate ballots with Senator Adams. Similarly, the hand-counted paper ballot systems used in a substantial number of precincts count paper, absentee, provisional, and early voting ballots by hand."

"You're kidding?" Scarlett asked, now interested.

"No, it's no joke. Thousands of precincts use party officials from both sides to validate votes. So, we use voter ID fraud, felon voting, lose ballots from the other side, and buy a few officials to falsify counts."

"Shit. I can't believe it. I didn't think arcane systems like that still existed."

"There are thousands of them, and what is even more exciting is that most swing states contain hundreds of precincts that fall into this category."

"You're back in my good graces, Todd. I'll expect a list of solutions for each swing state in two weeks," Scarlett said, actually smiling.

"Done," Todd beamed.

"OK, let's meet back here then. I expect you to be ready. Meeting adjourned."

"Wait. You forgot prong six—the Hillton Boys," Fred said.

At first, there was silence; then Scarlett began chuckling. Todd joined her. Several of the other members began laughing too. Soon Scarlett, Todd, and five others laughed so hard that they were out of breath. The laughter slowly died.

Fred said, "Obviously I'm missing something here. Who are the Hillton Boys?"

Scarlett composed herself and said, "I thought all party insiders knew about them."

"Well, I don't," Fred responded, offended that she didn't consider him an insider.

"OK, allow me to fill you in. The Hillton Boys are a small group of Senator Adams's supporters who work on the, let's say, *dark side* of politics."

"Dark side?" Fred asked.

"As dark as it gets. Let me give you a history lesson about Senator Adams's rise to power."

Everyone settled back, ready for the story most of them knew in parts but not in its entirety. Scarlett leaned back in her chair. "As you may know, Senator Adams is only fifty years old, yet he served as a city councilman, mayor, state senator, US house member, and now a US Senator."

"Wow," one attendee stated out loud.

Scarlett raised an eyebrow at the interruption but continued, "Wow is right! Now he is the ranking member of the US Senate Appropriations

Committee. It's a standing committee of the US Senate. It has authority over ALL discretionary spending legislation in the Senate."

"You mean Senator Adams can direct spending where he wants?" Todd asked, wondering if there was a raise in his near future.

Scarlett smiled, knowing she had their attention, and replied, "Yes, pretty much. It is the largest committee and has thirty-one Senate members. The chairman and ranking member are two of the most sought-after committee positions in the Senate. Why, you may ask? Because it wields power due to its control mass monies. Senator Adams hides much of his activities as a part of his duties. It's beautiful!"

"That is powerful," Fred whispered with greed in his eyes.

Scarlett's smile grew brighter as she said, "Yep, but his real rise to power comes from support from the Hillton Boys. The first known use of the Hillton Boys came in 1987. This was down South, where Senator Adams began his career. They became famous with several murders."

"Murders?" Fred asked, shocked.

"Yes, murder. The Hillton Boys pave the way when anyone challenges Senator Adams. Allow me to explain."

"Please do," Fred said curiously with growing fear.

"First, there was the murder of Mr. Barry Smith, who led the investigation of a journalist's death while investigating Senator Adams early career. Mr. Smith was murdered as well, so that's a twofer. Then came Ralph Buck and Bill Black, who both investigated Senator Adams. Mr. Buck died of a crushed skull on railroad tracks. Mr. Black received a shot in the back. Then from 1988 to 1993, several people with information on the Buck and Black deaths died violently. One died in a motorcycle accident at the end of a high-speed car chase. Another stabbed to death. A third died of a gunshot wound to the face. A fourth shot in the head, mutilated, then burned to death and left in a trash dump. The fifth decapitated and ruled dead due to natural causes. The sixth, one of the original Hillton Boys and the prime suspect in the deaths of Buck and Black, was killed in a robbery, subsequently proven to be a setup. The seventh shot to death in the front seat of his pickup. The eighth contained supporting documentation for grand jury proceedings and shot in the head along with his wife and three children."

"Holy shit. All those deaths were the consequence of those people investigating the original deaths of Buck and Black?" one of the attendees asked.

"Yes, but there's more. There were more murders during the follow-up investigations. An employee of the NSA working in the electronic intelligence division found dead in the back seat of a car. An associated attorney shot to death. Finally, a freelance reporter found dead in a hotel bathtub, his wrists cut over ten times, his research stolen from the room and never found. An obvious case of suicide. Finally, one of the creative Hillton Boys murders targeted an attorney with incriminating information, who died of a heart attack despite having no history of heart issues. He was young and in great shape."

The entire room was quiet after hearing the extensive list of murders by the Hillton Boys. The hideous nature of the murders cast a shadow across the room. No one spoke, and Scarlett continued in an excited tone, terrifying the attendees, "In 1992, the Hillton Boys struck again. Two men who worked for Senator Adams disagreed with him in public. They died in a mysterious plane crash. Then a member of Senator Adams's national committee stood in opposition to him and later found dead in his hotel room. No autopsy allowed."

"Damn. That's horrible," one attendee commented quietly before realizing that he said it aloud. Scarlett stared at him and he looked at the floor, sorry he had said anything.

Scarlett glared but continued, "The Hillton Boys took out one of Senator Adams's speechwriters who argued with him over the content of her speeches. She died in a car accident with no known witnesses. Then a prosecutor was killed in a skiing accident. He spoke to Senator Adams only hours before his death. But the Hillton Boys outdid themselves when four bodyguards of Senator Adams all died of identical wounds to the left temple.

"Later in 1993, four military men who escorted Senator Adams to a speaking engagement all died when their helicopter crashed in the woods near Quantico, Virginia. Reporters were barred from the site."

The room was deadly quiet, and a few attendees looked sick as Scarlett continued, "A witness apparently hanged himself after claiming to have negative information on Senator Adams. A lawyer investigating the quantity of drugs running out of Senator Adams's district died of unknown causes. He also exposed the investigations. I'm sure you all recall the White House deputy counsel and longtime friend of Senator Adams who was found dead of a gunshot wound to the mouth and ruled a suicide.

"The Hillton Boys struck again when an investigator 'fell' from the top of the Lincoln Towers building. Then two members of an advisory committee to Senator Adams died in a plane crash in 1993."

Scarlett was now almost frothing at the mouth with excitement. The room was morgue-like. Undaunted, she continued, "The chief of security for Senator Adams's national campaign—shot through the rear window of his car. When the car stopped, he received three shots. The dossier he compiled against Senator Adams. Never found. A fundraiser for Senator Adams died of an apparently self-inflicted gunshot wound. Two attorneys investigating Senator Adams 'committed suicide' within one month of each other. In 1994, a member of Senator Adams's Campaign Finance Committee died in an airplane explosion. The Hillton Boys specialize in airplane crashes despite it being statistically the safest form of travel. Man, they're good!"

Scarlett looked around the room. The team members were dazed. However, to ensure they understood the full power of Senator Adams, she added, "A reporter died of undetermined causes just prior to releasing 'sensitive information' to a London newspaper. Then another witness to the allegations died of a gunshot wound; ruled a suicide as well. A police officer with knowledge of many of the deaths died on the grave of one of the victims. Another apparent suicide. A man who oversaw Senator Adams's Secret Service detail died in a bomb blast in 1995."

Once again, Scarlett surveyed the room. One attendee threw up when she looked at him. She continued with a smile, "One of the most famous deaths related to Senator Adams was the secretary of defense who died in an Air Force jet crash carrying thirty-five passengers. That number included fourteen business executives with criminal ties to Senator Adams. Soon after, an assistant secretary of commerce who missed the flight died in a separate plane crash. Another famous death soon after was that of a retired CIA director. They found him dead after investigating one of the apparent suicides. Then a computer specialist and prominent entrepreneur who received a presidential appointment died of a blow to the head from a weapon never found. Another investigator died in a car crash just before testifying and just days before our party's national convention."

An attendee showing signs of extreme distress stood up to leave the meeting. Scarlett frowned at him, and he sat back down. He bent over, held his head in his hands, and covered his ears. Scarlett continued in her deceptively chipper manner, "A lawyer was trying to help the people swindled out of their life savings by Senator Adams. They found him in a vehicle with a gunshot wound to his head. Another financial advisor, tied to campaign violations against Senator Adams, died of ricin poisoning. A journalist, the son of a famous journalist, apparently committed suicide after bragging that he had information against Senator Adams. A friend, banker, and political ally of Senator Adams went to prison for eighteen felony convictions, then died of an apparent heart attack. Another investigator died in a car crash after discovering a pile of documents in the trunk of an abandoned car on his property and turning them over to the authorities. A programmer received a gunshot wound to the head near his house. He was an executive and member of the board of directors of companies providing software for a suspicious database system. He was behind the administration's plan to develop a secret computer chip to bug every phone and email in America. Finally, a prosecutor died as he crossed a street, just ten days after Senator Adams received notice of potential indictments for fraud. The driver—not charged."

Scarlett finished her account of the trail of death and mayhem following Senator Adams almost in a trance. There was a long silence as she composed herself and attendees tried hiding their fear and disgust.

Scarlett looked around the room as if looking at fresh meat. Gavin joined the stare. She finally said, "Is there anything else to discuss?"

The sickened attendees shook their heads.

"Now the meeting is adjourned."

The group left quickly, deeply shaken. Two attendees resigned and moved that night. Both disappeared. No one considered the matter for obvious reasons. One of the statisticians at the meeting calculated that the chances of that many murders being associated with one person by chance was over two billion to one. He didn't dare show his findings!

Chapter 7 ★ Meeting Bosses

JOIE WALKED BRISKLY TO THE third floor of FBI Headquarters at 935 Pennsylvania Avenue, NW Washington, DC.

"Hello, my name is Joie August," she said to the receptionist.

"Welcome, Agent August. My name is Becky," she brightly returned.

Becky sized up Joie and seemed pleased. Sensing this, Joie replied smiling, "Thanks, Becky. This is my first day working for Sr. Agent Lundberg. What's he like?"

"You'll love him. He's a fair boss as long as you you're successful in putting bad guys away."

"Seems reasonable. I'm so excited about working with career investigators at the bureau."

"We're glad to have you, especially being a woman. The FBI is such a testosterone group."

"I'm used to it. My fiancé is a Neanderthal as well."

Becky laughed and asked, "This is your first home office assignment, right?"

"Yes, it is. Any advice?"

"How could I give advice to you? From what I hear, your first field assignment in Fort Worth was a stellar success. Trust me, your new colleagues here are either jealous of you or respect the hell out of you! Many agents are ready to help their own career by collaborating with you. You're a fast-rising star."

"I'm sure that's not true, but thanks for the ego boost, Becky."

"You're welcome, Agent August. Go get em', girl!"

"Thanks," Joie said, blushing.

Becky winked and said formally. "Agent August, please have a seat. Agent Lundberg will be right with you,"

Joie nodded and sat in the waiting area for Agent Lundberg's meeting to end. Ten minutes later, the receptionist motioned for Joie to go in. Upon entering, ten middle-aged men stood up. Mike was sitting behind his desk but stood up as well. Not sure how to react, Joie walked to an empty chair and waited for directions.

"Gentlemen, this is Joie August. You've undoubtedly heard about her from her first case. Please welcome Joie to the team," Mike said.

The men applauded. Joie, embarrassed by the applause from career investigators, quickly sat down, red-faced. She was just a newbie and over-whelmed with the reception. Joie's modest reaction made them smile in approval.

Mike continued, "Joie, we've read about your first case with great pride. Welcome to the team!"

The men turned toward her, and she realized they expected her to say something. She cleared her throat and said, "I'm honored to work with you. I was lucky to survive my first case and hope to learn from you all so I can live a little longer."

The men chuckled and again nodded in approval of her humility. Each introduced themselves in turn and she tried to memorize names, but nerves caused her to fail miserably. Still, they liked her already. She was intelligent, unpretentious, driven, and gorgeous—all tools an FBI agent must utilize. After introductions, they sat back down and turned their attention back to Mike.

"OK, gentlemen—oh, and lady—let's talk about our assignment. The deputy director tasks us with a specific goal. As you know, the FBI and the DOJ face a severe lack of faith because of dismissed charges against a likely guilty presidential candidate. Our task is to assess the investigation and draw lessons for the entire bureau. I've documented your assignments in this portfolio," Mike said, handing out a stack of papers.

Each took their copy. The table of contents clearly outlined the strategy and gave each of them individual assignments.

"Please read the document and email questions. We'll return after lunch to chalk out a unified approach. Understood?"

Everyone nodded. Mike stood up and said, "See you at one p.m. right here."

As they filed out, Mike invited Joie to sit. "Forgive me for ambushing you, but you're quite famous, and they wanted to measure the person to the myth. I'd say you exceeded expectations."

"Thanks, Agent Lundberg. But I'm a little overwhelmed working with such seasoned agents."

"Call me Mike. Don't let them intimidate you. Keep in mind, most police officers and FBI agents never fire their weapons in the line of duty. You have already done that, and much more. You'll be fine. Just be yourself and share your thoughts. You're a valuable team member."

"Thanks again, Agent Lundberg—I mean, Mike. I need to read this folder so I'm ready for the meeting."

"Yep, dismissed. See you after lunch."

Joie went to her cubicle on the fourth floor and began reading right away. An hour later, she had a visitor. She recognized him from the meeting but could not remember his name.

"Hello, my name is Chester Hammond. Call me Eric."

"Hello, Eric. It's good meeting you."

"You're an outsider, and I want to get your thoughts on an aspect of the case."

"Of course, but I don't know how much help I can be as a newbie."

Eric smiled. "That's what I need—a fresh perspective."

"Shoot, Eric. I'm all ears."

"Here's the issue. I personally know one of the senior investigators on the case Mike mentioned," Eric began.

"Wow, it must be great to have the opportunity to collaborate with a senior agent on such an enormous and history-making case."

"Agreed. He's a great guy with over thirty years of experience. His name is Greg Elgen. He's highly respected and has no political affiliation. Well, at least none that he's ever expressed to his peers. He knows the deputy director personally. That's the kind of career we all want."

"I hope to meet him someday."

"You may get to. Of course, he can't talk about many of his cases. All the career investigators sign confidentiality agreements for reasons of national security."

"Yes, I heard," Joie responded.

"Did you catch the director's press briefing about the charges?"

"Yes, of course."

"Did you agree with the charges?" he asked, studying her expression.

"Yes, the charges were clearly delineated."

"Agreed. What did you think of the findings?"

Joie nervously said, "I was as shocked as the nation. The charges were clear—Senator Adams's actions clearly broke the law, but the director said it wasn't prosecutable."

"Exactly." Joie wondered where he was going with this before he asked, "Do you want to know who else was shocked?"

"Who?" Joie asked, curious.

"Greg Elgen!"

"What do you mean?" Joie asked, confused.

"Greg not only investigated but also helped compose the director's statement to the press."

"Once again, what an honor."

"Yes, and very dangerous."

"Dangerous?"

"Yes. You see the director read the statement exactly as written until the last sentence."

"Last sentence?"

"Yes. Greg's copy says, 'Therefore, the FBI recommends DOJ pursue the criminal indictment of Senator Adams for each charge.' "

"Holy crap!" Joie exclaimed.

***

Two thousand miles away, Debbie, John's new secretary, scheduled his day in accordance with his desire to work long hours. He attended meetings four hours per day. Six hours per day, he immersed himself in tracking hours, projects, corporate requests, sales brochure approvals, and customer meetings. He signed contracts, reviewed bids, P&L reports, and the accounting required by the government. For the remaining two hours, he walked the halls speaking to employees, peers, and other divisions in the ten-story Pseudomics Corporation Office in Fort Worth on West I-20. He didn't mind the long hours since Joie was busy in DC. John's social calendar only included working out, company parties, conferences, and meetings.

One evening, John walked through the office complex speaking to engineering staff. Walking past his old office, he saw his drafting board and CAD computer. He missed the simpler days of generating drawings and kit lists but loved his current job more. Now that he was the boss, he could create a better work environment and generate greater profits.

As he turned the corner by the break room, he saw Steve—the latecomer to the first meeting—and said, "Evening, Steve. How are you?"

"Fine, sir. And you?"

"Please call me John."

"Thank you, sir—I mean John," Steve said nervously.

"I hear remarkable things about your work, Steve."

"Well, after our unfortunate introduction at the first department meeting, I feel I have to immerse myself in work."

"I appreciate the arduous work. How's your daughter? Is she better?"

"Yes, she is. She's back at school. Thanks for asking," Steve replied, smiling for the first time.

"Her name is Rebecca, right?"

"Yes, it is, John," said Steve, moved that his boss took the time to learn his daughter's name.

"Glad to hear she's better. Please give her my best," John said, extending his hand.

"How did you know her name, boss?" Steve asked, intrigued.

"I try to get to know the families of personnel who have a future here," John answered over his shoulder.

Steve beamed and went back to his office, working with renewed enthusiasm.

John texted Debbie, thanking her for sending him Steve's daughter's name. She texted back, "Just part of the job, sir."

John spoke to a few other employees before meeting the entire staff in the conference room. They reviewed several reports, charts, and P&L graphs. At the end of the meeting, John congratulated them for their performance. All was going well.

Finally, John reported to his boss, Robert Beyer, at 5 p.m. The door to the office was open, and John knocked on the frame. His boss, on the phone, waved him in. John walked in and sat down. While he waited, John surveyed the pictures, awards, and trophies around the office. The bookshelf contained top-selling business books, novels, product catalogs, company brochures, and technical manuals.

After a moment Mr. Beyer hung up and said, "Thanks for coming, John."

"No problem, Mr. Beyer. It's good to finally meet you."

"Call me Rob. It's great meeting you as well. I've heard complimentary reports and observed good results from the engineering group already. Congrats!"

"Thanks, but it's easy, since I love my job."

"Glad to hear that as well," Rob said, eying John's size and demeanor. Rob heard John was huge—the rumors were true!

"So, you asked to see me, boss. How can I help you, sir?"

"I just wanted to meet you. Tommy Kinnaird, the president, speaks highly of you."

"That's good to know. He's an outstanding leader."

"Agreed. I also wanted to brief you on other division projects."

"I'd love to hear about them," John replied enthusiastically.

"As you may already know, our division manages aerospace, government, and commercial contracts. You're probably familiar with the aerospace contracts, right?"

"Yes, I believe I'm familiar with all of them."

"Good, then we'll just review the government and commercial ones. We may call upon you to assist on engineering-related requirements from other divisions."

"I've heard that and look forward to it."

Rob pulled a six-page document from a pile on his desk and began leafing through it. John knew about most of the contracts because he read the monthly corporate newsletter and management bulletins meticulously. However, he still listened intently, seeking current information. The commercial division contracts bored John; he preferred the military contracts and high-tech jobs. Pages five and six contained the aerospace, military, and government contracts, and that's when John sat up.

Rob noticed his movement. "You're like me. The government contracts can be exciting, especially the military ones."

"I concur, sir. Being a retired captain in the US Marines, I miss the action."

"Me too. The US Army was my home for twenty years," Mr. Beyer said proudly.

"They have an important mission. Trying to keep the ground the marines take," John joked.

Mr. Beyer's smile disappeared. "The US Army is the largest occupying force in the world, with weapons the marines only dream of having."

John, taken aback, said quickly, "Boss, I meant no disrespect. In the field, the army and the marines are brothers in arms."

John listed the army first, hoping to make up for his blunder. Mr. Beyer's smile returned, and he said, "Just messing with ya. Some of my best friends are grunts. We're both retired now, so once again, call me Rob."

John, somewhat relieved, said, "And some of my most respected acquaintances are US Army officers with twenty years of service."

"Relax, marine. We're OK."

John hoped they were back on good terms. They returned to the government contract list, and John noticed a few "black projects." Each had a name, stipulated the branch of government (DOD, DOS, DOJ, etc.) from which they came, and included a brief description.

"Can you expound on any of these?" John asked, pointing to them.

"What's your security clearance level?" Rob asked.

"I used to have a top secret clearance, but I now have an SCI clearance. As you know, the only one higher is SAP, which is for the president, the cabinet, the joint chiefs, and some congressmen, based on the need to know."

"OK, I have an SCI clearance as well. I've just been briefed on these verbally. I've not seen documentation on any of them," Rob said, looking at the list.

"Well, let me know if I can assist with any of those. They're the most fun." John looked down the list of twelve secret projects. "This one looks weird."

"Which one?"

John pointed and said, "This one. The branch of government is 'Presidential,' the name of the project is 'Fair Game,' and the description says, 'Digital Safeguards.' "

"Yeah, that one is different. I know little about that one."

"Well, like I said, if you need help on any of the government, especially DOD projects, please let me know. I'm your man. Also, there are three other engineers with top secret clearances who can lend a hand."

"Will do, John."

"Thank you, sir—I mean, Rob."

They spoke another few minutes about work before Rob's phone rang and the meeting ended. John still regretted making the army crack and hoped Rob would forgive and forget. Besides, just like Steve, he wanted to impress the boss.

As he left Rob's office, John decided to learn more about the project "Fair Game." Unfortunately for him, certain interested parties noticed his search for information.

PART II ★ THE HILLTON BOYS

Chapter 8 ★ File Cabinets

JOIE RETURNED TO MIKE LUNDBERG'S office and said, "I just spoke with Agent Hammond. He said you know what I'm about to say, so I'm not breaking confidences."

"Yes, I've been briefed. Go ahead," Mike said curiously.

"Let me get this straight. The last sentence of the copy of the FBI career investigator's report, which the FBI director and the US attorney said they'd accept as submitted, was different from what was read to the nation?"

"Yes, the FBI director read the lengthy and incriminatory charges exactly as submitted. The entire nation was therefore prepared for indictment. But instead, he concluded by saying that the investigation findings were not prosecutable. The press core was speechless."

"As was I," Joie said out loud.

Mike replied, "Oh but there's so much more. If you remember, the FBI director admitted two days later in front of a congressional panel that Senator Adams allowed access to classified documents."

"Allowed access?" Joie asked.

"Senator Adams followed all the protocol of storing classified information on government computers. There's no accusations about using personal computers or servers."

"So, what's the alleged charge?" Joie asked, confused.

"There was a breach of security. More than one outside entity broke through security from the outside using passwords. They were Senator Adams's passwords. Each of these breaches occurred just after Senator Adams received favors from various organizations and even foreign governments."

"This is proven?" Joie looked surprised.

"Yes, the sequence of events is proven, but it's purely coincidental. Adams says someone stole his passwords."

"Stolen. That's the best story he can come up with?" Joie scoffed.

"Correct," Mike responded, smiling.

Joie sat back in her chair, amazed at the information. She thought a minute before saying, "May I be candid with you about political issues?"

"Yes, proceed."

"I know we're government employees and therefore supposed to be loyal to our commander in chief…"

"Of course. Speak freely."

"After 9/11, Director Mueller worked with the CIA and Homeland Security to restructure the FBI's areas of responsibility as terrorism, counterintelligence, cybercrime, public corruption, organized crime, white-collar crime, violent crime, civil rights, and now even weapons of mass destruction. Correct?"

"Yes, that's correct," Mike said, impressed she could quote the list from memory.

"If that's the case, mishandling of classified information falls into at least the first three categories. Agreed?"

"Yes, so there's real teeth to the law. However, terrorists can hack unprotected mainframes. Think about it—many of the government's mainframes are over thirty years old. Security is high, but the technology is poor, so hackers can get around it easily," Mike responded.

"Thirty years old? Damn. No wonder so many government employees use servers instead."

"Sad but true. That's one of the reasons the government prosecutes employees storing classified documents or personal or unsecured servers. Jail time can be significant."

Joie responded, "But Senator Adams stored his data on mainframes rather than servers, right?"

"Yes. However, in this case, we believe Senator Adams allowed access secretly. After each alleged access, monies funneled into Dreams International. This is where the investigation breaks down again. It's difficult to track the monies from Dreams International to Senator Adams."

"How so?"

"There is no ironclad proof that Senator Adams is associated with the charity. It's just that with each amount paid to the charity, Senator Adams's personal wealth increased by similar amounts. Of course, this, too, is circumstantial evidence. Therefore, this investigation also falls into counterintelligence and cybercrime."

"I know the evidence is circumstantial, but there's so many charges. How could we possibly not prosecute?"

"You can't be naive enough to believe politicians live by the same standards as the rest of us, surely?" he asked, a little surprised at her shortsightedness.

"I know, but the findings of the case were so clear! I just can't accept illegal actions as the norm. That's too depressing to think about."

"I agree. The US now has almost as low a respect for the FBI, the attorney general, and the DOJ as it does for Congress."

"It's such a shame. I became an agent to make a difference."

"Me too," Mike responded sadly. He thought for a moment and then said, "Come with me."

Joie followed him to an office down the hall. He entered a code on a keypad and placed his right index finger on a biometric scanner, then entered another code. The door swung open. Filing cabinets lined the walls of the room.

"What is this?" Joie asked.

"This is our division's hard copies of the most wanted criminals in the world."

Joie scanned the cabinets and saw categories: Ten Most Wanted, Most Wanted Terrorists, Crimes Against Children, Violent Crimes, Notorious Murders, Kidnappings & Missing Persons, and Seeking Information. The list continued as the cabinets disappeared around a corner.

Some cabinets contained names, such as Amanda Kay Jones, Heather Renee Inks, Carlos Ramos, Tammy Jo Alexander, Ranger Lacy, Tahja T. Williams, Yaser Abdel Said, Abdelkarim Hussein, and Mohamed Al-Nasser. She recognized most of them. Apprehending such criminals and assisting in their prosecution made careers.

"Our task is daunting, isn't it?" Mike asked.

"Yes, imposing for sure," was all Joie could say, still reading categories and names. She also saw countless names from the Taliban, ISIS, and the War on Terror.

"Didn't the president just release many of these from prison and Guantanamo?" Joie asked, pointing to the names on the folders.

"Yes. After millions of dollars and hundreds of thousands of hours of work, he released some of the most wanted criminals in the world with the stroke of a pen. It's enough to make me retire."

"I can see why you'd lose heart. Didn't he release two hundred twelve more prisoners through an executive order recently?"

"Go ahead, depress me even more," Mike answered, trying to joke, but unable to smile.

"Sorry, boss. Is this why you brought me in here? To see what we do?"

"Well, yes. But more specifically, I wanted to show you open Senator Adams's investigations," Mike said, walking over to four file cabinets standing apart from the others.

As they approached, Joie said, "I'm a student of history. Especially of US presidents. Whatever is in these file cabinets can't compete with former presidents."

However, he responded, "Were any of them murderers? Did any of them give US secrets to enemies for money?"

"Not as far as I know," Joie replied cautiously, looking at the file cabinets.

Mike removed a key ring from his pocket and opened the first one. He opened the top three drawers, saying, "Brace yourself."

She looked inside at the thick folders that bore names such as:

- Record-Gate

- Death of Secretary of Defense
- Cyber-Hider
- Asia-Gate
- Tour-Gate
- Illegal Profits
- Suspicious Death Investigations
- Illegal Fundraising
- Ambassador's Death

"My God. These are all open investigations?" Joie asked in amazement.

"Yes, and they grow weekly," Mike responded.

"What's in the other three file cabinets?"

"One full cabinet is for Dreams International. It explains how Senator Adams went from broke to having hundreds of millions in the bank in just fifteen years."

"Damn! Sorry, I'm just shocked," Joie exclaimed.

"Me too. Damn is appropriate."

"I'm afraid to ask, but what are the other two cabinets for?" Joie asked, pointing.

"They hold the over fifty voices from the grave."

"Voices from the grave?"

"Yes, they hold the records of over fifty investigations of the mysterious deaths, murders, and suicides of Senator Adams's enemies, friends, business associates, and pesky reporters, spanning thirty years."

"My God!"

"God has nothing to do with it. An evil human being is responsible for this. We had indictable charges on almost all the cases. But witnesses died, politicians stepped in, files lost, and authorities dropped charges." Mike's phone dinged, and he said, "Let's go back to my office. Someone is waiting for us."

"Do I want to know who?" Joie asked, still scanning the room.

"Yes, you do."

"OK, boss." She still stared at the file cabinets. A chill went down her spine.

Mike locked the file cabinets and closed the door to the room, which clanged as the heavy locks shut tight. They grabbed a cup of coffee on the way back and when they returned to Mike's outer office, Joie noticed the office door was closed. It had been open when they'd left. Mike's secretary said, "He's waiting for you, Mr. Lundberg."

"Thanks. No interruptions, Becky."

"Yes, Mr. Lundberg," she said, opening the door for them.

Upon entering, Joie saw a fifty-year-old man sitting in the corner facing the door. He held a folder close to his chest and watched their every move. He was thin, sporting a receding hairline, a wrinkled face, and a black suit and tie, making Joie think of *Men in Black*.

He continued studying Mike and Joie as if memorizing their every move—in fact, he was.

Mike spoke first. "Mr. Greg Elgen, I'd like to introduce Joie August."

Joie extended her hand, and he looked at it before shaking. He looked tired, stressed, and paranoid. He trembled slightly. Joie couldn't decide if was fear, a nervous tick, or some kind of nerve-affecting degenerative disease.

"Joie, Greg is the career investigator I told you about," Mike said with respect in his voice.

"It's an honor, sir. I hope to measure up to your and Mike's expectations. I respect your accomplishments and your service to the country," Joie said sincerely with deep respect.

"The pleasure is mine. I heard about your first case. I'm impressed," Greg responded, taken with Joie's beauty.

She smiled and sat down along with the others.

Mike began, "Greg, I told Joie about your investigation, findings, and recommendations."

Greg responded, "Good. I want to collaborate with you, Mike, because I trust you with my life. I also want to work with someone new to the bureau who doesn't have ties to the upper levels. What we're discussing is dangerous."

"Believe me, I know. I just showed Joie the files, so she'd know what we're up against," Mike said, looking at Joie and trying to read her. It wasn't difficult; she was shaken. This case was dangerous, and they all knew it.

"Joie, are you sure you want to discuss this? If I assign you to work with Greg, it will get dicey."

"Dicey, I can manage. The files you just showed me are more like *The Twilight Zone.*"

Greg retorted, "Yes, but few aliens rack up a death rate like Senator Adams has."

"Well, maybe the *Alien* series with Sigourney Weaver rivals it," Joie said, trying to lighten the atmosphere.

"The difference is, the alien was on its own. Senator Adams, on the other hand, is protected by the administration, the attorney general, the DOJ, party leaders, the press, and half of the voters in America."

"Good point," Joie conceded.

Mike gestured toward the file Greg still clutched. "Is that the file?"

"It's one of many. This one just contains the FBI director's press statement."

"That's the one we want at this point," Mike said, switching on his desktop computer.

He pulled a CD out of his top desk drawer and inserted it into the drive. It brought up a video of the FBI director. Greg opened the file and handed Joie a transcript.

"Follow along, Agent August," Mike said, looking at the screen.

She still liked the title of "Agent," even after three years of service. It somehow still sounded new and distinguished.

Joie looked at the transcript as the video began to play. She remembered the press statement well; most of America did. The press statement video and hard copy were identical. They walked through the eight charges of "reckless and careless handling of classified information." With each charge came the description of Senator Adams's violation of the law. It built up to a climax with just one possible outcome—an indictment. However, the video departed from the text at the end. The final words in the transcript were: "Therefore, the FBI recommends the DOJ pursue the criminal indictment of Senator Adams for each charge. The lengthy list of charges is now in the hands of the US attorney general."

However, the director's actual words were, "Although there is evidence of potential violations of the statutes regarding the handling of classified information, our judgment is that no reasonable prosecutor would bring such a case. Prosecutors necessarily weigh a number of factors before deciding whether to press charges."

Mike closed the video, Greg closed the file, and Joie closed her eyes.

She whispered, "What am I getting into? Am I going to end up another file in the room down the hall—a dead witness?"

Chapter 9 ★ Two Steps Forward, One Back

IN JUNE, THE NEXT VOTER fraud meeting commenced in Northern Virginia. The attendees once again included Scarlett Schuller, Senator Adams's representative; Fred Reider, the cyber lead; Todd Shamer, the state weakness lead; Lizzy Warden, the polling expert; and Gavin Principle, the *problem solver*.

"Let's get started," Scarlett began authoritatively. "I'm happy to report that I've briefed Senator Adams, and he approved the overall strategy. However, we need to show progress. I hope you're ready."

"I'm ready," Todd said emphatically.

"Great, you have the floor," Scarlett said, ready for good news.

"OK. So, as you know, Senator Adams gave us access to super PAC monies to fund our project. The states we're focusing on are Colorado, Florida, Pennsylvania, New Hampshire, Ohio, Iowa, Virginia, Michigan, Nevada, and Wisconsin."

"Remind me why we're focusing on those states?" Lizzy asked.

"Because they are the swing states."

"You mean battleground states?" she asked.

"Well, that's what the press calls them," Todd responded sheepishly.

"Then that's what we should call them. Remember, the press favors our party, so let's use their terminology," Lizzy responded arrogantly.

"Will do, Lizzy. So out of the one hundred target precinct—"

"One hundred precincts?" Lizzy asked, cutting him off again.

"Yes, ten states times their ten largest precincts equals one hundred precincts," Todd said, a little too impatiently.

Lizzy looked over at Gavin, who sat forward, eyeing Todd as if he was breakfast.

"Sorry for my impertinence, I'm a little tired. Anyway, I'm excited to report we now have a warden in twenty out of the one hundred precincts."

"Warden?" Lizzy asked, gesturing for Gavin to stand down. Gavin's disappointment was obvious.

"I call them wardens because almost every county uses different names for their precinct voting helpers. However, most precincts break it down like this: There's a warden who supervises the other precinct officers before the polls open, during the election, and while the ballots are processed. The warden is responsible for maintaining order and ensures that the required materials are available and posted in the proper places. The wardens also assign other election officers to their stations based on the size of their precinct and anticipated voter turnout. They designate the schedule for breaks, meals, and voting. This also includes responsibility for completion of forms, handling of challenged ballots, and ensures proper help for voters omitted from lists."

"Omitted from lists?" Scarlett asked.

"Yes, this is where voters without IDs, like felons and illegal immigrants or those voting in multiple precincts, will be allowed to vote by the wardens on our payroll. Keep in mind that it won't be too hard, because these precincts heavily favor Senator Adams, and most wardens will look the other way. Hell, sixty percent of our party will vote for Senator Adams even if he's indicted, so breaking the law is not a big thing for them. More importantly, many of these states don't require ID at all."

"Really?" Scarlett asked.

"Yep, the most liberal states don't require them. So almost anyone can vote; and of course, we'll also lose ballots from the other side and falsify counts. Remember, we have PC on our side."

"PC—political correctness?" Lizzy inquired.

"Yes, we're the party of extreme political correctness. Don't forget this PC craze makes it easy to lie," Todd said.

"What do you mean?" Scarlett asked, intrigued.

Todd huffed a little impatiently due to Scarlett and Lizzy's tag-team questions. His almost undetectable attitude did not escape Gavin's attention, who wore an evil grin.

Todd noticed and continued respectfully, "There's documented cases, especially in the liberal precincts, that if the voter can't produce an ID, all they have to say is, 'What? Do I look like an illegal alien to you? Maybe I look like a terrorist? Do I look Islamic to you, you Islamophobic SOB?'"

"That works?" Scarlett asked skeptically.

"Yep. In many cases, they vote without ID because the voting official doesn't want to appear racist."

"Excellent. I like that. OK, will we just have wardens on our payroll per precinct?"

"No, each warden will hire at least one clerk and inspector," Todd responded, looking at Gavin, who no longer focused on him. Todd breathed easier.

"What are their duties?" Scarlett asked impatiently.

Lizzy beat Todd to the punch, saying, "The clerk position keeps a record of all facts relating to the proceedings of the election required by the law. They are also responsible for maintaining the election record and filling out forms. In other words, they help prove election results. Right, Todd?"

Todd, disappointed Lizzy stole his thunder, just nodded.

Scarlett then asked, "What does the inspector do?"

This time, Lizzy was not sure and gestured for Todd to answer. He said dryly, "The inspector monitors the other voting areas. There's at least four of them. They maintain control of the check-in area and ensure peace in the entrance, the queue, the voting area, and the check-out area. The ones supervising the voting area check off the names of voters as they enter."

"So, we only have to hire three hundred voting officials to pull this off?"

"Yep! One warden, one clerk, and one inspector in the one hundred largest precincts."

"How much will this cost?"

Todd pulled out a calculator. "I figure $25K for each warden, $15K for each clerk, and $10K for each inspector. That comes to 100 times $25,000, plus 100 times $15,000, plus 100 times $10,000—that equals $2.5 million for wardens, $1.5 million for clerks, and $1 million for inspectors. So, $5 million in total."

"Why would they risk jail for $25K or less?"

"Because most precinct voting officers are either unemployed or retired. They won't ask for much. Besides, our precincts want Senator Adams to win. Between these three polling positions, they will throw way ballots on the opposing side, count ballots for Adams without signatures or with incomplete addresses, count ballots for dead voters, and mail ballots to liberals only. Lastly, they will make excuses to kick the opposing side out of the room while we count ballots."

"Really? How can they do that?" Scarlett asked, enthralled.

"We can claim they are being disruptive, cheating, or whatever reason they want. The media supports us, so they will not report it. It'll be easy."

Scarlett exclaimed with glee, "Makes sense! Wow, only five million dollars to win the US presidency! That's chump change! That's less than what Senator Adams will spend on advertising each week."

"Don't forget about us! We expect a much greater reward than precinct wardens," Todd said, pointing to everyone in the room.

"You'll get everything you have coming to you," Scarlett responded with a smile.

Todd hoped she referred to money rather than the Gavin type of reward.

"OK, well done. When we meet in two weeks, I expect you'll have wardens on our team in all hundred precincts," Scarlett said to Todd.

"Of course," he said, sitting and sweating as he thought of the difficulty of the assignment.

"That brings us to you, Fred. How are we doing on the cyber approach? I hope you've made progress." There was a threatening undertone to her voice.

"Yes, I have good news," Fred said, standing up. He walked to the corner and removed a cover from a DRE voting machine. He rolled it to the end of the table, and people moved out of the way so that everyone could see.

"If you remember, voters record their votes directly into the computer memory. The voters' choices store in the DREs via a memory cartridge, diskette, or smart card. The older version of the DRE is most widely used, and it doesn't confirm the vote on a paper copy, so the voter can't verify the vote cast is the one they intended."

"Yes, we remember," Scarlett said irritably, gesturing for him to go on.

"OK, I need three volunteers," Fred said, and three people walked over. One of them was Lizzy.

The first tester stepped in front of the machine.

Fred continued, "I have three voter access cards just like the ones voters will receive. First, we insert the voter access card into the slot to the right of the screen. The card should be face up, with the arrow pointing left, and should push firmly into the slot until it clicks. If it's inserted incorrectly, the screen informs the voter. Then the voter reads the instruction screen. Please note before you begin the voting process that you can magnify or change the contrast of the screen to help increase readability. To begin voting, touch the Next button on the screen."

The first tester pressed the Next button.

"After pressing the Next button, we see each ballot page until you have reached the end of the ballot. Please select Senator Adams."

"Wait, what if I want to vote for Ronald Jackson?" Scarlett asked.

"OK, please select Ronald Jackson," Fred instructed.

The tester chose Ronald Jackson so all could see.

"Now choose down-ballot candidates below presidential and state issues. In this case, it's Ohio. Choose any you want."

The tester chose candidates at random by touching the box on the screen next to each choice. An X appeared, designating the selection. Instructions were clear on how to change or cancel a selection. The tester touched the box again and made another selection. The tester chose to write in a few down-ballot candidates. The name appeared on the screen.

"Are you done?" Fred asked.

"Yes," the tester replied.

"OK, now onto the summary page to review your choices. Notice the items in red are races left blank. If you want to vote for a race left blank, or change your vote for any race, just touch that race on the screen and taken back to the proper page to make or change your selection."

The tester filled in one and left two blank.

"Now, we cast our ballot. This version of the voting machine does not have the option to print a verification of the vote. In other words, no paper trail! Remember, every precinct in the one hundred we've chosen has more of these machines than ones that print. Please touch the Cast Ballot icon on the screen.

The tester cast the ballot.

"Now, remove your voter access card and return it to me, your friendly poll worker."

The tester handed the card to Fred.

"OK, let's repeat this with the other two volunteers," Fred said.

Lizzy and the other tester repeated the sequence. One chose Senator Adams, and one chose Ronald Jackson. When completed, they also handed their voting access cards to Fred.

"If you remember, two voted for Ronald Jackson and one for Senator Adams. Now we remove the disk in the back of the machine using the key only the warden has," said Fred.

He unlocked the back of the machine, ensuring everyone in the room could see. He removed the disk.

"Now Lizzy, please insert it into the laptop computer on the table." After Lizzy complied, Fred continued, "Now we read the results in ASCII text form. Please see the results. We have two votes for Adams and one for Jackson, instead of two votes for Jackson and one for Adams. The virus in the machine has done its work."

Lizzy, Scarlett, Todd, and the others looked amazed.

"That's awesome, Fred!" Scarlett cried excitedly.

"Thank you. I'm prepared to send the virus to our precinct wardens. With your approval, of course," Fred said, relieved at Scarlett's reaction.

"Approved. Now tell me how you are doing on the other virus you'll use on the optical scan paper ballot systems. If I remember correctly, we must intercept the results after the ballots are scanned, since we can't change them individually because of the paper trail."

"Well, that's a bit of a problem," Fred said nervously.

"Why?" Lizzy and Scarlett asked simultaneously.

"For two reasons. First, the virus isn't working yet. But more importantly, many large precincts compare the pre-scanned results against the scanned," Fred replied apprehensively.

Scarlett thought about it, whispered something to Lizzy, and then turned back to Fred.

"OK, I'm not pleased. However, since Senator Adams is already leading by ten points in the polls, the first approach we discussed today may be enough. Send Virus A to the Wardens, and keep working on Virus B." Scarlett said, looking at Fred with a disappointed expression.

Fred said under his breath, "The Dominion voting machines may be enough anyway."

"We already have that. I want Virus B to ensure victory. Understood?" Scarlett asked, her tone indicating it was a rhetorical question.

Fred nodded his head and sat down, terrified, eyeballing Gavin. He stared at Fred, just waiting for the moment he disappointed Scarlett too much. Fred gulped and averted his eyes.

Todd, feeling confident with Scarlett's approval of his accomplishments, said, "Can I ask a question?"

"You may," she replied as if talking to a five-year-old.

"What happened to two more of our staff? They haven't been seen since our last meeting."

"They were relieved of their duties," Scarlett replied with a sadistic smile.

She turned to Gavin, who focused his attention on Todd like a hungry man looks at a meal. Todd noticed and immediately regretted having asked. Gavin waited for Scarlett's permission to "relieve Todd and Fred of their duties," but she shook her head. Gavin sat back, disappointed. Everyone in the room stared at Todd, who shriveled in his chair and wanted to disappear—though not in the way Gavin made people "disappear."

Chapter 10 ★ Project Fair Game

JOHN WALKED THROUGH THE HALLS of his division talking to employees and assessing productivity, employee morale, and customer satisfaction. He passed an executive's office as one of them poked his head out. "John, do you have a second?"

"Of course, sir," John responded curiously.

John walked in and stood at ease in front of the exec's desk in military habit.

"Relax, John. Thanks for your time. I just wanted you to know your name came up in the staff meeting this morning."

"Really, sir?"

"For God's sake, relax, John! Call me Calvin."

"Will do, Calvin," John said, sitting down.

"I just wanted you to know that your boss bragged about you during our meeting. Your division's profits are increasing, and customer satisfaction is at an all-time high. He even read an email from a US Army pilot who loves the effect of the new equipment on his aircraft's capability. In addition, in our last employee survey, you have one of the highest ratings in the company! We know you're working twelve-hour days."

"I love my job, Calvin," John beamed with pride.

Calvin stood and shook John's hand. "I'm delighted to inform you that you're invited to the off-site management meeting. This year it's at the luxurious L'Auberge de Sedona in Sedona, Arizona. Congratulations!"

John's shock was obvious as he muttered, "Thanks, Calvin! I'm honored."

"You should be. You're the only non-exec invited."

John's mind wandered through the rest of the conversation and quickly returned to his office to make a call—Joie had to know! She wasn't in, so he left a message and then stepped out of his office to Debbie's cubicle.

"Debbie, can you buy a ticket to Flagstaff for August nineteenth to the twenty-third?"

"You're invited to the company off-site?" she replied, surprised.

"Yep, I just heard."

"Frickin' impressive, boss!" Debbie exclaimed, loving the fact she worked for a rising star.

"Thanks, but it's you and the employees making me successful."

"Yes, but who manages them?" she retorted.

"I think it's you," John said with a smile. Debbie beamed at the ridiculous yet sweet comment.

The next ten days flew by. On Friday the nineteenth, John flew to Flagstaff, drove to Sedona, and checked into L'Auberge de Sedona.

"My God," John marveled to himself as he took in his two-bedroom suite overlooking the golf course and the beautiful Sedona red rocks.

As he unpacked, he heard the door key beep as someone entered the suite. John, not expecting anyone, hid behind the door, waiting to pounce. It opened slowly, and someone simultaneously knocked.

"Room service, Mr. Jacobson?"

A maid poked her head in, likely having heard a beefcake checked in and hoping to get a semi-nude glimpse. John grabbed the door and jerked it open. The maid jumped back, shocked. "So sorry, Mr. Jacobson. Do you need anything? Ice? The bed turned down? Anything at all?" she stuttered, looking at the lean, muscle-bound man before her.

John assessed immediately that she was, in fact, a maid and said, "No thanks. Try knocking next time!"

The maid closed the door and left petrified but disappointed. John went back to unpacking when he heard the door lock beep again. He wasn't buying that it was another maid, so he moved behind the door again. The door slowly opened as someone said, "Maid service."

John swung the door open. The person wore a hat and a jacket with the collar turned up and surveying the hall for witnesses. John grabbed the person so hard, they came off the floor. He put one powerful forearm on the front of his neck and the other on the back of his skull. One jerk and the person would fall to the floor, either a quadriplegic or dead from a broken neck.

However, the person brought an elbow up to John's solar plexus, causing him to bend over in pain, gasping for breath. He straightened, preparing to kill the person with a lethal blow to the abdomen when he heard a familiar voice say, "This is a fantastic way to greet your fiancée."

John looked more carefully through the disguise and recognized the love of his life. Joie stood before him in a ridiculous spy garb.

"My God, you scared the bejeezus out of me!" John groaned, rubbing his stomach and catching his breath.

"You think I'd allow you to come here without me? The FBI doesn't pay as well as Pseudomics." Joie smiled, rubbing her neck.

He grabbed her and literally swept her off her feet. He kissed her passionately and threw her onto the bed. "Now we're talking!" she exclaimed.

They resurfaced three hours later. An exhausted Joie said, "Are you ready for dinner, now that we've had dessert?"

"Lead the way, my lady," John responded, kissing her again and jumping out of bed.

Joie, enjoying the view, begrudgingly rolled out of bed herself. John enjoyed the view as well.

After dinner, they strolled around the lavish grounds and talked about their jobs. Joie told John the unclassified portions of the file cabinets, meeting her boss, and meeting two career investigators.

John's response was twofold. "Joie, I'm so proud of you, but please be careful. From what I hear in the news, you're investigating one of the most dangerous politicians to ever run for president."

"I'll be careful, John. Besides, if I can kick your butt, I can take on anyone," Joie said, smiling.

"Look baby, I'm not kidding," John said gravely.

"Sweetie, I carry protection." She patted her concealed weapon.

"OK, Joie, but if you get into trouble, send for me, and I'll be there."

"I promise to do that," she said, kissing her knight in shining armor.

John returned a kiss so soft it melted Joie's heart.

The rest of the weekend included fine dining, walking the grounds, and ample time in bed. On Sunday night, John drove her back to the airport and Joie sadly said goodbye. John woefully kissed her one more time, knowing their next weekend getaway was probably months away.

John returned to his elegant room alone, but everything he saw reminded him of Joie. He slept briefly, worked out, then went to the conference center early. An hour later, in walked Pseudomics executives, vendors, partners, and customers from all over the world. John, honored to attend this meeting, sat beside his boss, Rob. For the next two days, they listened to presentations from the most profitable and high-tech divisions of the company.

One of the last presentations was called "Confidential and Company Private Projects." The presenter, David Koksma, spoke about classified projects at the nonconfidential level. He concluded by saying, "We even have a project for the president of the United States to ensure fair voting in the next election."

John and Robert looked at each other and back to the speaker. David completed his speech, followed by an award ceremony for the most successful managers. When the conference ended, John and Robert followed David Koksma out of the conference into the hall.

"David, can we have a word with you, please?" Rob asked him.

"Of course," David responded, eyeing John's size and pointing to a couch nearby.

When they took their seats, John cut right to the chase. "David, can you tell us more about that last project you mentioned in your presentation, about fair voting practices?"

"I'm sorry, I can't discuss it. As I said, it's a secret project."

"You're speaking to two men with SCI level clearances."

"Let's see them," David responded.

Rob and John pulled SCI clearance cards out of their wallets. David checked the names and pictures against their name tags and faces.

"OK… I see the clearances, but what's your need to know?"

"We are working on a related project."

He eyed them once again, opened his laptop, and accessed a classified web site. He entered passwords through several levels of security, PINs, and a fingerprint ID. He scanned the list of names in a list and found theirs.

David looked up. "OK, ask me what you want to know, and I'll tell you if I can."

John began, "My fiancée is a federal agent and is investigating a case that may be linked to this one."

"How so?" David asked curiously.

As John explained much of what Joie told him, David listened intently. Finally, David looked around and whispered, "OK, here's what we're going to do…"

* * *

When Joie returned to DC, it was already July. Once again, she met Mike Lundberg, her boss; Chester Hammond, her colleague; and Greg Elgen, the FBI career investigator.

Mike spoke first, "Sadly, there are only two investigations open to us concerning the many charges against Senator Adams. In other cases, politicians protect Senator Adams, or witnesses disappear."

"Which two?" Joie asked.

"Cyber-Hider and Dreams International."

"Makes sense," Greg said, and Chester agreed with a nod.

Mike continued, "Greg, you know the Cyber-Hider case the best. Especially since you investigated the case and even helped write the director's statement. I think the next step is to speak with the deputy director, Clark Hermenez."

"Holy crap, you know Hermenez personally?" Chester asked.

"Yep, we go way back," Greg responded dryly.

"Wow!" Joie exclaimed, proud to know an FBI insider like Greg.

"I'm close to retirement, so my influence will go away soon, but we might as well use it for the time being."

"Hell yes. Greg, you speak to Hermenez, and we'll talk about Cyber-Hider after," Mike said.

"Will do." Greg made a note on his notepad.

"Now, let's talk about Dreams International," Mike continued.

"Yes, let's," Joie said, anxious to learn more.

Mike pulled a file out of his desk and began reading. " 'Today, *New York Times* bestselling author Ed Klein revealed on *The Sean Hannity Show* that sources have confirmed to him that not only is Dreams International under federal investigation, but that at least one insider is also prepared to testify in a court of law against Senator Adams. Reports of legal troubles for Dreams International began last week when *The Daily Caller* reported that a joint FBI-US attorney probe is currently underway. Many documents support the charge recently released by Judicial Watch that alleges that Senator Adams received payments for national secrets in exchange for contributions to a charity called Dreams International. While the charity appeared to be legal and legitimate, there were accusations that it secretly funneled funds to Senator Adams's offshore accounts. Dreams International suddenly appeared while he served as ranking member of the US Senate Appropriations Committee.' "

"Shit, you have to be kidding," Chester said, and Mike looked up.

"Nope. We're a long way from stopping Senator Adams getting into the White House without solid evidence before this election. A US attorney for the Southern District of Virginia is leading the ongoing investigation. He successfully prosecuted dozens of Wall Street executives and powerful politicians. He is reportedly working with the BBI and several district attorneys in and around Washington DC."

"So, there is a current FBI investigation?" Joie asked aloud.

"Yes," Mike and Greg answered together.

Mike continued reading, " 'This investigation includes public corruption, mishandling of classified information, and collusion with Dreams International. Sources confirmed there are several witnesses willing to testify. At least one of those sources used to work for Senator Adams yet now works for Dreams International.' "

"Doesn't that help prove Adams is associated with Dreams International?

Can we see the investigation files?" Chester asked.

"No, it's still circumstantial, but yes, the files are right down the hall in a file cabinet," Mike responded.

"I've seen the file cabinet. It's chock-full," said Joie.

Chester looked at Joie enviously, wondering why Mike hadn't shown him the cabinets as well. Mike noticed his discontent and chose to ignore it.

He went on, " 'Sources are saying that they're willing to testify that this was an alleged *quid pro quo*. In other words, Senator Adams gave favors and secrets in exchange for contributions to Dreams International. One source claims to have overheard Senator Adams speaking directly to a donor to Dreams International. That would help us indict Adams.' "

Chester responded, "Well, that's damning evidence. We also have a list of documented cases in which Dreams International received funds from foreign powers immediately after Senator Adams gave favors to their country."

Mike searched the file and began reading again, " 'According to several sources, Adams was dead broke in 2001 yet now has hundreds of millions from book deals and speaking fees. The only problem is that, according to tax filings, the book deals and speaking fees are worth approximately ten million dollars. Where did the rest of the money come from? As explained by *The New York Times*, a Mexican businessman purchased up to one-fifth of the US plutonium assets. His firm then sold it to Russia's atomic energy agency. This deal appeared in Russia's Pravda with the headline "Russian Nuclear Energy Conquers the World." An acquisition of this size and nature requires approval by the US Defense Department, which would be easily done with Senator Adams's position in the Senate. Coincidentally, at the very same time, the same firm made a 2.35 million dollar donation to Dreams International, and more uranium sold to them. Also, the firm paid Senator Adams five hundred thousand dollars for a speaking engagement. But the contribution went to Dreams International rather than to Senator Adams so that it would nontaxable.' "

"Damn, I can't believe it," Chester said.

"Believe it. It's documented in FBI's investigation files."

"Shit," Joie muttered, not realizing she said it aloud.

"Is there more?" Chester asked.

"That's just the beginning," Mike said. He flipped more pages in the file and scanned through the text. " 'Dreams International reportedly accepted millions of dollars from the head of a Colombian oil company before Senator Adams approved military aid to Columbia. The report centers on donations from the oil company. Finally, according to *The International Business Times*, thirteen corporations together paid millions for speeches from Senator Adams in exchange for favors. The companies are Dell, National Retail Federation, Oracle, SalesForce, Starwood Hotels and Resorts, Goldman Sachs, PhRMA, BHP Billiton, Biotechnology Industry Organization, Microsoft, VeriSign, Project Management Institute, and AFLAC. *The Washington Post*'s analysis found that "53 percent of donors gave one million dollars or more to the charity are corporations or foreign citizens, groups, or governments. Some of the major donors on *The Post*'s list are "the governments of Saudi Arabia, Australia, the British bank Barclays, and major US companies such as Coca-Cola and ExxonMobil." ' That's what we're dealing with."

"So, how illegal is this?" Joie asked.

"That's what we have to prove. We must prove that Senator Adams is associated with Dreams International, and then prove that the funds made their way into his pocket." Mike continued, " 'Vox also said that the size and scope of the symbiotic relationship between Senator Adams and their donors are striking. At least one hundred eighty-one companies, individuals, and foreign governments that have given to Dreams International have also lobbied the US Senate Appropriations Committee, according to a Vox analysis of charity records and federal lobbying disclosures. The charity's acting CEO acknowledged problems with reporting on federal 990 tax forms in a statement issued on Sunday, in which she contended that information about donors was available but not appropriately listed in filings with the government.' "

"That's convenient," Chester commented.

Mike concluded, "If you liked that, get this. A former assistant to Senator Adams now works for Dreams International! Unfortunately, that's circumstantial evidence. We still must prove that Senator Adams connects to Dreams International and that it made payments to him."

"Right," Chester agreed.

"And that leads us to Cyber-Hider," Greg said.

"Why?" Joie asked.

"Because although Senator Adams utilized secure government main-frames, hundreds of documents suddenly disappeared concerning Dreams International and Senator Adams. When the investigation began, Senator Adams deleted thirty-three thousand documents AND wiped another main-frame clean. These documents were on a government mainframe, so this is destruction of government property! However, when the FBI explored the mainframes, we could retrieve many files from the cleaned mainframes and found hundreds of classified files. Many clearly marked classified, according to the FBI director."

"Senator Adams deleted the documents and erased mainframes?" Joie asked.

"That's what we have to prove. It's a felony to destroy classified documents without approval," Mike responded.

"How does he get away with it?" Joie asked, looking at documents in front of her.

"Keep in mind, as the ranking member of the US Senate Appropriations Committee, Senator Adams has great authority over ALL discretionary spending legislation in the Senate. That means he has friends in high places willing to protect him if he funnels money their way."

"So, Senator Adams can spend US tax dollars any way he so desires?" Todd asked, wondering if there was a raise in his near future.

Mike retorted, "All he does is recommend bills with spending he likes, and of course he adds little line items no one really challenges. He can hide his little projects easily. Sad!"

"That is sad." Greg shook his head in disgust.

Mike pulled out a document and began summarizing it. "The chairman and ranking member of the Appropriations Committee have enormous power to bring home special projects—sometimes referred to as 'pork barrel spending'—for his or her state as well as having the final say on other senators' appropriation requests. For example, in fiscal year 2007, per capita federal spending in Hawaii, the home state of then-ranking member Tom Phillips, was fifteen thousand dollars—double the national average. However, now Hawaii has 11,772 special earmarked projects for a combined cost of $14,787,988,500. This represents about 3 percent of the overall spending in the $388 billion Consolidated Appropriations Act of 2005 passed by Congress."

"Damn, no wonder my taxes are so high!" Greg said repugnantly.

"Yes, and if the ranking member can do that in the open, just imagine how much money can be spent illegally on Senator Adams's career and personal wealth," Mike said, nauseated at the thought. "Joie, you and Chester investigate Dreams International, and you, Greg, speak with Deputy Director Hermenez about Cyber-Hider."

They jotted down their assignments and filed out of the office. Down the hall, unbeknownst to them, stood an imposing figure. He watched them leave, pulled his phone out of his pocket, and called a number from memory.

"Scarlett, this is Gavin Principle. Tell Senator Adams they just left the meeting. The attendees were Mike Lundberg, Chester Hammond, Greg Elgen, and a new FBI agent, Joie August. You want me to act?"

Scarlett paused and asked, "Joie August? Are you sure of the name?"

"Yes, why?"

"I know her personally. It's a long story. Wait for now; don't act. Besides, Ms. August complicates things. I need to think."

"OK. I'll wait for now, but I think we ought to send them a message by taking out at least one of them."

"OK, you've convinced me. You have permission to kill one. You can murder…"

Chapter 11 ★ Vital Encounters

THE NEXT CYBER VOTING STRATEGY meeting began in Northern Virginia in late July. The attendees once again included Scarlett Schuller, Fred Reider, Todd Shamer, Lizzy Warden, and Gavin Principle, the *problem solver*.

Scarlett again began the meeting. "Thanks for attending this important progress status meeting."

Fred whispered, "As if we had a choice."

A few attendees heard him and snickered, to which Scarlett responded, "Excuse me, Fred. Do you have something to contribute?"

"No, ma'am," Fred responded sheepishly.

Gavin eyed him, hoping he'd soon get the order to eliminate this impertinent member of the team. Fred cowered, regretting his comment.

"As I was saying, let's get started," Scarlett said, still looking at Fred, willing him to interrupt her again. "You seem eager to speak, Fred. Let's begin with you. We saw the virus in action on the DRE voting machine during the last meeting. Senator Adams approves of the move, so Todd can send the virus to our precinct wardens when they're all in place. Now, let's talk about the cyber approach, Fred."

"OK," Fred began nervously. "As you may remember, optical scan paper ballot systems include a paper trail that verifies votes. Therefore, we must intercept the results after the precincts have scanned the ballots. The larger precincts compare the pre-scanned results against the scanned. That's still a problem, because our in-house versions of the virus didn't work properly. So, I awarded a small contract to a programmer. He's developing a virus capable of accomplishing this. It cost only fifteen thousand dollars. I call the program 'Fair Game'. The programmer is working on it with reasonable results. We're not there yet, but I know this guy—he's brilliant. He'll get it done. Also, he doesn't know the purpose of what he's creating. He just knows we need it to change digital results slightly. Therefore, it's doubtful an audit would ever catch it."

"OK. I'm still not pleased we can't do this in-house. Are you sure this can't be tracked back to us?" Scarlett asked, her tone menacing.

"No, it can't. The programmer doesn't know me personally. So, he'll never know you, or our real agenda."

Scarlett thought for a moment, then said, "Damn, it sounds dangerous outsourcing this, but OK. Lizzy, you work with Fred on this to ensure security and positive results. Gavin, you fix the damage if things get out of control."

Lizzy nodded, and Gavin looked thrilled.

"I'm not happy with your update, Fred, so work to finish your tasks."

"Yes, ma'am." Fred gulped thinking about the size of the assignments.

Scarlett, still staring daggers at Fred, said, "Todd, your turn. What progress do you have to report?" Her frown changed to a smile as she turned to Todd.

"As you know," Todd began, "we're focusing on the ten largest precincts in the ten battleground states. Therefore, there are a hundred target precincts, and one warden in each on our payroll. Last week we had twenty out of a hundred county voting wardens on our team. I'm pleased to say we now have thirty-five!"

"Excellent, Todd. I'm glad you're making progress," Scarlett said, smiling again at Todd. She glanced back at Fred with a frown. Fred averted his eyes.

"These precinct wardens are prepared to supervise the other precinct officers before the polls open, during the election, and while processing ballots. They'll work with their clerks and inspectors, ensuring successful voting for voters without IDs, felons, illegal aliens, refugees, et cetera. They'll also lose ballots from the other side and falsify counts."

Scarlett asked, "The total cost is still five million dollars, right?"

"Well, a few wardens of the largest precincts want more than the offered twenty-five thousand, so this may cost almost six million."

"That's still a deal. Hold the costs under six million dollars and I'll be pleased."

Fred once again whispered, "Sure, my project costs fifteen thousand and she's pissed, yet Todd's costs six million. That seems fair."

"Gavin, I think Fred needs a little pep talk. Would you take care of that for me after the meeting please?"

Fred looked at Scarlett in disbelief. Gavin's evil grin sent a chill down the spine of all the attendees.

"That won't be necessary! I apologize—" Fred began, but Scarlett cut him off.

"Too little, too late," she replied, smiling.

Fred hung his head, wondering if he would be attending the next meeting.

"Anything else?" Scarlett asked.

Attendees shook their heads no.

"Meeting adjourned." She nodded to Gavin.

Three days later Fred showed up at work with an arm in a sling, his jaw covered in bruises, and a black eye.

***

John and Rob, his boss, went up to the seventh floor of the Pseudomics building. They entered their codes to pass through the security doors and walked to a corner office where they entered their codes again to pass through a second set of heavier doors. They had an appointment with the programmer responsible for project Fair Game, Luther East.

They knocked on a heavy closed door. Seconds later, a small man opened the door. He had red hair, pale skin, and a slight build, and his head twitched nervously. He was the poster child of programmer jokes. John towered over him and moved to sit down quickly in a vacant chair so that the programmer wouldn't die of fright, which he almost did.

On the desk was a plethora of diagrams, part catalogs, and notes. Something caught John's eye. One of the diagrams was one John saw before, but after working on hundreds of aerospace and military projects, he couldn't quite place it. On the corner of the diagram appeared a name that made his blood run cold. It read "Patent owned by Mr. Ray August." It was Joie's dad!

Luther noticed John looking at the diagrams and tossed his jacket on top, covering them. John tried hiding his surprise at the origin of the drawing. John looked back at Luther, who was eyeing him suspiciously.

Robert began the conversation, saying, "Mr. East, my name is Robert Beyer, and this is John Jacobson. We'd like to speak with you about a program you're working on called Fair Game."

"And like I told you on the phone, that program is secret," Luther responded, glancing warily at John, who could obviously break him in two. "I know you both have SCI clearances, and they're even higher than my secret clearance. However, unless you have a very compelling need to know, I can't tell you anything."

John smiled pleasantly, trying to calm Luther. It seemed to work, as the programmer relaxed slightly. Robert continued, "We know you can't give us details, but can you describe the program's purpose?"

Luther thought about it and said, "I can tell you it's for the Department of State, it's presidentially approved, the name of the program is Fair Game, and it's designed as a digital safeguard."

"We know that much from Pseudomics's list of classified programs. Can you tell us anything else?" Robert asked with a calming smile.

This impressed John, and he made a mental note of his boss's people skills.

Luther thought for a moment. "What's your need to know?"

"We have reason to believe this program is not what it seems," Robert continued.

"Hmm, an illegal or unethical DOS project? What else is new? My God, the DOS is in the news every week," Luther joked.

John and Robert laughed, attempting to bond with the little man. It seemed to work; Luther was almost completely at ease now.

"I can tell you the program is designed to allow a component to increase incoming results."

"Why would anyone want a program like that?" John asked.

Luther almost physically withdrew into himself. "I have no idea. It's a secret project, so the purpose is unknown to me. That's all I can and will tell you," he said nervously.

"Well, thank you, Luther. Can I come back if I have other questions?" Robert asked with a million-dollar smile.

"Maybe, but I can't tell you anything else—because that's all I know." Luther's gaze moved from John to Robert.

"Thank you, Mr. East," Robert said, standing and shaking the programmer's hand.

John took the cue and stood up as well, looming above Luther. He smiled and extended his hand. The little man's hand disappeared into John's. John shook his hand gently, which still appeared to hurt Luther's small fingers.

They walked out, and Luther nervously closed the door behind them.

John said, "Boss, I'm sorry I shut the conversation down by interjecting. You established a rapport with him, and I screwed it up."

Robert chuckled and said, "You scare me too. No big deal; that's all he was going to tell us anyway."

"I'm not so sure. Once again, sorry."

"No problem. Let's talk over lunch, then get back to work. We both have too much to do to focus on this anymore right now."

"Agreed, and great, I'm starving. I'll buy."

"Semper Fi," Robert responded.

John tried to think of an army mantra but couldn't. "Be all you can be," he said instead.

"That's the air force," Robert laughed.

"Oh… what's an army slogan?" John asked, embarrassed that he insulted Robert's army career yet again.

"I think the army says, 'Marines are idiots.' "

"You may be right, boss."

Robert slapped John on the back, and John bought him a nice meal at lunch, hoping to make up for his latest army gaffe. It worked; Robert showed no animosity. All was forgiven and, John hoped, forgotten.

Later that night as John lay in bed, his mind raced. The design for project

Fair Game was based upon a patent of Joie's father, Ray August. How was he going to broach the subject with Joie? He suddenly had a headache.

**

Chester, Joie's teammate, drove home after work. He ate dinner and went to bed after an exhausting day investigating Cyber-Hider and Dreams International. It was past midnight when a sound woke him up. It appeared to come from within the house—maybe even inside his bedroom. He also smelled smoke. Chester sat up and looked around the room.

A shadowy figure sat in the leather easy chair in the corner. A glowing red spot hovered in the air. Gavin puffed on his cigarette, and the red spot grew brighter. Chester reached into the top drawer of his bedside table. No gun. He panicked and said, "Who's there?"

"Your worst nightmare," Gavin growled in an evil voice.

Chester heard the click of his own .45 caliber Glock coming from the corner.

"What do you want?" Chester asked, panicking and quickly thinking of his options.

"I want you to die." Gavin pulled the trigger. The bullet ripped into Chester's chest, spewing blood onto the headboard.

Gavin fired again, hitting Chester between the eyes. His head jerked back, sending brains, blood, and hair onto the headboard and wall. Chester fell dead onto the bed.

Gavin walked to the bed and turned the lamp on. He admired his handiwork. No one would believe that this was a suicide because of the second shot. That was fine; he wanted the FBI to know it was a murder. He was sending them a message: *Leave Senator Adams alone. The Hillton Boys are watching.*

He turned the light off, walked back through the house, opened the front door with gloved hands, and disappeared into the night.

Chapter 12 ★ The Call

JOIE MET MIKE IN HIS office one day early in August. While they waited for Greg and Chester, they began talking.

"Have you heard the news today about the association between Senator Adams's documents and Dreams International?" Joie asked.

"No, what happened?" asked Mike.

"Judicial Watch obtained newly released documents that reveal more instances of foreign powers making donations to Dreams International immediately after military favors."

"Like who?"

"Like the His Royal Highness Prince Percheron bin Isa Al Adichie, crown prince of Bahrain."

"Wow, now that's a title. However, such practices may be unethical, but they are not illegal. Was there quid pro quo?"

"Not as far as I know. However, there are many other examples of quid pro quo. For instance, Blackstone asked Senator Adams for military favors they couldn't acquire through proper means. So, they donated something between two hundred fifty and five hundred thousand dollars to Dreams International, and they got the military support," Joie said.

"That's just one case, though, and not very compelling in a criminal investigation."

"How's this for further proof? Since Senator Adams's past schedule is public record, one of our agents found that eighty-five of the one hundred fifty-four people from private interests who met or had phone conversations scheduled with Senator Adams donated to Dreams International or pledged commitments to its international programs, according to documents obtained by the AP."

"How much was donated?"

"Get this: the eighty-five donors contributed as much as a hundred fifty-six million dollars altogether, and at least forty donated more than a hundred thousand dollars each, while twenty gave more than one million dollars."

"Damn. We still must prove Dreams International funneled funds to Senator Adams. However, it still goes in the file!" Mike said.

A knock at the door preceded Greg, who walked in with a white face. "What's wrong?" Mike asked.

"I have sad news."

"I can tell by your face. What's wrong?" Jopie asked.

Greg sat and continued speaking slowly, "The police just found Chester dead from shots to the head and chest. Police don't know how the perpetrator got in and out. His security system was still on!"

"Chester—dead?" Joie asked, eyes widening.

Greg nodded as Mike said, "Damn, I can't believe it!"

"Believe it. It was a professional job," Greg replied, stupefied.

Mike thought for a moment. "I'll call his wife right away with our condolences and offer to help her deal with it all. Chester was a valuable member of the team. That clinches it. Someone knows we're investigating Cyber-Hider and Dreams International."

"Agreed," Greg said.

Joie said, "But how? We only began yesterday!"

"No, Chester's been working on this for months. However, this does mean we need more security," Mike replied.

Mike picked up the phone and called the security chief and arranged for police protection for Greg, Joie, and himself. He hung up and said, "Done. We'll have police protection to and from work. They'll also check our home for intruders before we lock the doors and set the alarm."

"I'm sad about Chester. I just met him, but he was a great guy," Joie said.

"Yes, he was. We can grieve later. For now, let's continue," Mike instructed.

Greg and Joie looked at each other, surprised at his apparent callousness. After a moment of silence, Greg said, "There're more documents coming soon."

"More? What do you mean?" Mike asked, trying to concentrate despite the news.

"I spoke with a friend of mine at the NSA. They have almost all the deleted thirty-three thousand documents," Greg responded.

"Are they going to release them to us?"

"Soon. But we have a more pressing issue to discuss."

"What's that?" Mike said, doubting that it could be more important.

"Per your suggestion, I spoke to Deputy Director Clark Hermenez," Greg said, brightening up a little.

Mike exclaimed, "Shit, that was fast! I know you're connected, but how did you get an appointment with the deputy director in one day? His schedule books out for weeks, maybe months!"

"He called me!"

"Now I know you're kidding." Joie smiled.

"Nope, he called me at home after work."

"OK, joke's over," Mike said.

"No joke, and I have proof." Greg pulled a small tape recorder from his pocket.

"You recorded the conversation?" Joie asked.

"I record everything on my home phone. It's a habit I started when we began this investigation. The files down the hall indicate that when anyone investigates Senator Adams, death follows."

"Good point," Mike said, shaking his head in agreement and thinking about Chester.

"I've got this cued to the part you'd be interested in," Greg said, pressing the play button.

The recording played. "Agent Elgen, I know you worked on our investigation of Senator Adams's deletion of classified documents. You and the other agents did an excellent job. There's something you must know: the director changed the end of his press statement for a reason, and it's not because he's protecting Senator Adams. He had orders from his boss to drop the investigation. However, he has a plan to 'get' Senator Adams another way. Agent Elgen, you're going to help us indict Senator Adams. Trust me. I'll be contacting you again when I can tell you more."

Greg stopped the tape. Mike leaned back in his chair, shocked. "Holy crap!"

Joie said, "Did I hear that right? The FBI director's boss is involved? That's the attorney general. I don't believe it."

"Believe it," Greg responded, putting the tape recorder back in his coat pocket.

***

In Northern Virginia, another meeting began with Scarlett Schuller, Fred Reider, Todd Shamer, Lizzy Warden, Gavin Principle, and several other members of the team.

Scarlett spoke first. "I'm the only one that calls meetings. Todd, you scheduled this without my permission. I don't answer to you—you answer to me!"

Trying to ignore Gavin's menacing look, Todd said, "Sorry, Scarlett, but I have news I thought you'd want to know right away."

"What's that?"

"There are now eleven battleground states. Senator Adams is polling ahead in another state!"

"Which one?" Scarlett asked, thinking about forgiving him.

"We can add North Carolina to the other ten."

"Frickin' awesome," Lizzy said.

Scarlett looked at Lizzy and back at Todd before saying, "So what are you going to do about it?"

"I've already taken action and found wardens in many of the top ten largest precincts in North Carolina."

"Good. I'll increase the budget and clear it with Senator Adams. Anything else?"

"Yes. Out of the one hundred ten largest precincts in the eleven battleground states, I now have eighty-five wardens in place!"

"Excellent. The election is now ninety days away, so it sounds like you're going to make it."

Gavin, disappointed that Scarlett forgave Todd, turned his attention elsewhere. Scarlett continued, "Well since we're all here, have you made any progress, Fred?"

Fred, surprised he had to speak, said, "Yes. The first virus is in Todd's hands, and it can be sent to his precinct wardens whenever he's ready."

"OK, we already know that. What about the second virus that intercepts and changes scanned voting results?"

Fred glanced at Gavin, who was eyeing him with interest. He'd love to satisfy his "need" with this little man. He smiled at Fred, noticing that the sling was gone, the black eye almost healed. Was it time for another consultation?

"A little progress, but no breakthroughs yet," Fred responded nervously.

"That's disappointing. When do you expect a 'breakthrough'?" she asked patronizingly.

"Give me two weeks."

"You have one. Senator Adams wants to see progress."

"OK, you'll have it," Fred replied grimly.

"Meeting adjourned." Scarlett winked at Gavin.

Later that day, Gavin visited Fred again. He now needed crutches.

***

That night John called Joie at home. "Are you OK, Joie? I worry about you. You're working on a dangerous case."

"I'm fine, John. I can control myself. It's nice to know you care about me, though."

"Can't help it—you're my lady. Anything new?"

"No, not really," she replied, choosing not to tell him about the police escorts and Chester's death. He'd just worry more about her.

"Good. Stay safe. Can I ask you a question?"

"Yes," Joie said, hoping it was personal.

"Your dad had a patent on one of his office walls. It's an electronic device that counts signals."

"Yes. Why?" Joie said, disappointed that it was work related.

"I'm investigating something here called Fair Game. There's something crooked about it."

"How do you know it's crooked?"

"I don't know for sure. It's just a feeling. The patent on your dad's wall reminds me of it."

"What are you saying? You think my dad did something illegal?"

"No, Joie. Your dad was a great man and inventor. I just wish I could talk with him about this."

"My dad had a lot of faults, but he was honest."

"I know, Joie. Please, just forget it."

"I'll try."

"Thanks. Let's talk about something else."

"I already told you, things are fine," Joie snapped, still peeved.

"Good to hear. I'm working lots of hours. All I do is work, exercise, and sleep."

"Good. No time for other women, then."

"That's the farthest thing from my mind, Joie," John sighed. "I caught my limit—the beautiful, intelligent, sexy, and talented FBI agent Joie August!"

"Glad you know you're a lucky man!"

As they talked a little longer, John sensed she was worried about something but didn't press her for details. They hung up, and John went to sleep dreaming of Joie.

***

A dark sedan sat outside of Joie's DC apartment. Two men smoked and waited. Her lights went out. They waited another hour, then silently exited their car, heading for a back window they'd unlocked earlier. They remained undetected on their mission thus far.

Senator Adams wanted to send another message.

Chapter 13 ★ Success

IN LATE AUGUST, THE LAST formal cyber voting strategy meeting began in Northern Virginia with the same attendees.

"OK, Todd, where are we on the state weakness strategy?" Scarlett asked, expecting positive results.

"I now have a hundred and five out of a hundred and ten wardens in place and on the payroll. I'll have the other five by this weekend."

"Now that's progress. Email me when you have the last five for sure. Excellent job," Scarlett praised, looking from Todd to Gavin. Todd's relief showed on his face. Gavin's disappointment was apparent. He couldn't relieve Todd of his life—yet.

"Fred, how about you? You have a hard act to follow," Scarlett asked in a tone that indicated her displeasure with Fred.

"Well, although Todd is *almost* there, I am there!" Fred retorted.

Scarlett, surprised, asked, "How so?"

"Both viruses work. I've already demonstrated Virus A and tested it over a hundred times. It worked each time."

"OK, but what about Virus B?"

Fred smiled and pressed the intercom button on the conference phone in the center of the large conference table. "The warden from the largest North Carolina precinct is on the phone. He will remain anonymous for obvious reasons. Are you there?" he asked into the phone.

"Yes, here," came the man's voice across the intercom.

"You have the NC scanned results from the last presidential general election ready?" Fred asked.

"Yes."

"Please send them to my computer now."

The sound of keystrokes came across the intercom as the warden said, "Sending."

After two seconds, Fred's computer dinged. Fred opened the file as people gathered around his computer. Fred showed the first few hundred rows of a spreadsheet containing millions of rows. At the top was a row counter and summary table displaying:

Candidate	Party	%	# of Votes	Electoral Votes
Trump	GOP	50.60%	2,275,853	15
Clinton	Dem	48.40%	2,178,388	0
G. Johnson	Lib	1.00%	44,798	0

"OK, so what? That's just election results," Scarlett said flatly.

"So, this! I'm now executing Virus B on the sending and receiving computers," Fred said, typing a few strokes on the keyboard. Scarlett watched with great interest as Fred said, "OK, send the results again."

"Done," the voice on the intercom said.

After another two-second delay, Fred's computer dinged again. He opened the file. The people moved closer to his computer. Once again Fred showed the first few hundred rows, but this time the table on top displayed slightly different results:

Candidate	Party	%	# of Votes	Electoral Votes
Clinton	Dem	50.64%	2,278,158	15
Trump	GOP	48.37%	2,176,083	0
G. Johnson	Lib	1.00%	44,798	0

The group examined both tables closely. They were speechless. Finally, Scarlett said, "I'm impressed, but the change in votes is too dramatic. Since the paper trail won't agree with the digital results, we need a smaller modification of votes."

"Absolutely. I made the virus change about four percent of the votes so you could see it worked. In this case, it changed who won the NC race and who received the fifteen electoral votes. The actual virus will change less than 0.5 percent, or one out of every two hundred votes. Even a detailed audit may not find the changed votes," Fred explained, smiling.

"Prove it. Replicate the demonstration again set at a 0.5 percent change in votes," Scarlett said, still not believing that a virus so magical could work.

Fred hit some more keys and repeated the demonstration with the warden from NC. The results showed a 0.05 percent change, which meant Clinton still won the state. Now Scarlett was impressed. "Now the million-dollar question: Can you set the virus percentage based on the actual returns coming from the precincts when they're up to about ninety-five percent and there's little likelihood of a substantial percentage change? In other words, can you set it at the percentage needed to reverse the outcome?"

"Yes, of course. But once again, I wouldn't suggest setting the virus percentage at more than one percent because then it's changing one out of every hundred votes. It's likely an audit would detect the changes."

"Agreed. Very well done! It looks like we're set," she said, looking at Fred and Todd.

They both beamed, while Gavin showed his displeasure. Gavin wanted Senator Adams to win, of course, but he harbored just as strong a desire to kill. His hunger burned.

The meeting adjourned, and Scarlett later met with Gavin. "Don't take any action with Fred or Todd until after the election. The day after the election, release the Hillton Boys on them. They know too much to walk around free. Besides, they could blackmail Senator Adams for millions in exchange for their silence. You need to silence them—but later."

Gavin walked away, ecstatic.

*　*　*

The two large men slipped quietly behind Joie's building to her apartment on the bottom floor. One reached for the unlocked window and lifted it.

The leader of the assassin team whispered, "Remember, we have thirty seconds before the alarm sounds. We must move fast." The second man nodded without a word.

The window raised silently. With it halfway open, they crept inside one at a time with the stealth of deadly panthers. Within seconds their eyes adjusted to the darkness. They walked swiftly and silently through the apartment to the closed bedroom door. They paused, listening. They still had twenty seconds when the first man turned the knob and entered the bedroom swiftly. They walked to the bed and saw the bulge under the covers. They lowered their silencer-equipped weapons as one pointed at the pillow. The other pointed at the covers at waist level. They both fired simultaneously. The lump moved, then remained still.

The closest man pulled the blankets back, revealing a lifeless body. He turned on the lamp beside the bed and saw an FBI dummy—the ones used on the firing range. Suddenly, the realization hit them like a train.

Joie stepped from behind the closet door and kicked the closest one hard between the legs, leaving him doubled over in pain. She shot him with her .45 in the top of his bowed head. Blood and brains spewed out of his mouth, nose, and eyes. As the other intruder turned, raising his weapon toward Joie, two shots hit him between the eyes and in the chest so fast that he never even heard the first blast. An enormous discharge of blood splattered across the bedroom wall. They fell to the floor within one second of each other. Pools of blood began to form beneath them.

Joie breathed for the first time in seconds. A voice said from behind her, "Babe, remind me not to piss you off."

She holstered her .45 caliber weapon and quickly turned, running toward the voice. John stowed his enormous .50 caliber Desert Eagle handheld weapon and wrapped her in his strong arms.

"Just remember this the next time we argue," Joie said, kissing John passionately.

He squeezed her tight. Her forced grin slowly disappeared, and her lips began quivering. She held back the tears as John held her closer. She put one hand on his chest and the other on his back. She felt his strength, and his protection. She felt safe. Joie could take care of herself and certainly didn't need a man to defend her, but she loved John for wanting to do so anyway.

He carried her into the living room and held her tenderly until she regained composure.

John set her down, and she reached for the phone on the coffee table. She hit number three on the auto-dial list.

Mike Lundberg answered. "Yes?"

"It worked. The firing range dummy is officially dead, but I'm alive," Joie said calmly.

"Impressive. Good agents are hard to replace. Besides, I never trusted that dummy," Mike returned.

Joie chuckled and said, "Better him than me. By the way, would you call the police? We have two bodies here to explain."

"Of course. See you in the morning," Mike said flatly, hanging up.

John and Joie left the window open, turned off the alarm, and stayed out of the bedroom crime scene. Within minutes, the sound of sirens broke the silence and drew closer. Soon the room reflected blue, red, and white lights swirling outside from the five police and two sheriff cruisers outside the front door.

There was a loud knock at the door, and a deep voice said, "Police—open up." John and Joie retrieved their weapons, switched the safety on, and laid them side by side on a coffee table in clear view of the front door.

John cracked open the door and demanded, "Show your ID."

A detective showed his ID and badge. John examined it closely, then opened the door. SWAT, police, and a large deputy sheriff entered the room with weapons raised.

The lead policeman asked, "Are you armed?"

"No," Joie said, glancing at the table.

The SWAT team entered and quickly checked the four-room apartment. "Clear," they yelled after checking each room, closet, and potential hiding place. A policeman searched John, and a policewoman searched Joie. Another picked up their weapons with gloved hands and put them in separate baggies. The officer admired the .50 Cal pistol and winked at John in approval.

The SWAT leader yelled from the bedroom, "They're in here!"

One police officer stayed with John and Joie while the others entered the blood-shrouded bedroom. A tall and squinty-eyed detective entered the apartment and asked immediately, "Let's see IDs and weapon licenses."

Joie pointed to her FBI badge and agency-issued weapon license on the table beside her weapon. The detective checked her picture against the ID, taking time examining her skimpy pajamas. John pulled his weapon license and retired US Marine ID out of his wallet, stepping between the detective and Joie. The detective seemed displeased and checked his credentials even closer.

"You don't think .45 and .50 caliber weapons are slightly overkill?" the detective asked with a smirk.

"The FBI lets me carry a .45 Cal because of a dangerous case I'm investigating," Joie responded calmly.

"And you?" the detective asked John, taking in his size.

"I carry a weapon equal to my Special Forces training and arm size. What do you carry, a .38?" John asked, smiling at the much smaller man.

Joie rolled her eyes as the detective ignored John's remark, shrugged his shoulders, and said, "OK, sit down and tell me what happened."

They sat beside each other. Joie described the encounter, including the open window, the alarm, the fatal shots, and the call to Mike. She also explained the unclassified portion of her FBI investigation, being careful to omit any reference to Senator Adams. His connection with the authorities was legendary. John explained his visit to DC to see his fiancée. The detective took notes. When the coroner arrived, the detective pointed toward the bedroom and the coroner headed that way.

Within fifteen minutes, two bulging black body bags passed by on carts, headed for the morgue. Joie thought how close she and John came to death in this manner. She looked away from them to clear her mind.

The detective finished his interview, and police began vacating the crime scene after fingerprinting the weapons and returning them to John and Joie. Within three hours of the attack, John and Joie were alone again. Joie reset the alarm, closed the window, unfolded the living room couch, turned off the lights, and fell into John's arms. Exhausted as they were, they made love for an hour. They had to make up for the planned two-month hiatus.

***

On the other side of town, Hillton Boy Gavin answered his phone. He listened to a man speaking then said, "Are you shitting me? *Both?* Damn, they were two of our best. OK, here's the plan…"

PART III ★ BATTLEGROUND STATES

Chapter 14 ★ Florida

FRED REIDER, THE CYBER APPROACH leader, and Todd Shamer, the state weakness leader, met again in a conference room in northern Virginia. They sat and checked their notes before beginning the first conference call to one of the largest battleground states—Florida.

"Tell me again why we're beginning with Florida?" Fred asked.

"Because it's huge, average in voter fraud protection, and I'm familiar with Florida voting laws, practices, and rules," Todd responded.

"OK, makes sense. Hey, before we begin, did you hear the latest about Senator Adams's debacle with charitable gifts to Dreams International, allegedly gained in exchange for favors?"

"Yeah, it's all over conservative TV, radio, and newspapers. Of course, the liberal press won't touch it," Todd said, chuckling.

"What about it?" Gavin said, standing in the doorway. His evil grin chilled their very souls. "I think you'd better begin the call. Scarlett sent me to listen in. It had better be compelling stuff."

"It will be," Todd answered, dialing the conference call number and trying to slow his heart. There were several beeps as wardens joined the call from the ten largest precincts in Florida.

"Welcome to the call. You're Senator Adams's first line of offense in winning this election. Although he's leading in the polls, you're part of the noble cause to ensure a win. Let me congratulate you."

Sounds of thanks came across the intercom.

Todd continued, "As of today, you, clerks and inspectors, are on our payroll. Much of what we're discussing today needs to be executed right away. We can't afford to wait until Election Day. Some of the methodologies discussed will take time to implement. As you know, Florida polls open at seven a.m. and close at seven p.m. Florida is a battleground state, so the eyes of the press, Florida voters, and millions of Americans will follow the voting results. We're here to discuss both generic and Florida-specific voting practices we'll take advantage of. I'll introduce Fred Reider, our cyber approach leader, later. Are you ready?"

Several attendees on the call replied simultaneously, "Yes." "Yep." "Ready."

"First, let's discuss who can vote in Florida general elections. Voters must be US citizens, Florida residents, at least eighteen years old, not adjudicated mentally incapacitated, not a felon, and must provide an acceptable voter ID. Most states have less voter registration requirements."

"You mean Florida voter registration requirements makes voter fraud more difficult than other states?" one warden asked.

Todd answered, "Yes, but as you'll see, Florida has other weaknesses we'll cover later. Since Florida requires a voter ID, some of the non-voter-ID strategies we'll use in other battleground states are precluded. However, there is a weakness in the Florida voter ID practices. The preferred voter ID has a photo and a signature, like the Florida driver's license, the Florida ID card, the US passport, a debit or credit card, a military ID, a student ID, a retirement ID, a neighborhood association ID, a public assistance ID, a Veteran Affairs ID, a concealed weapon ID, or any federal, state, county, or municipality ID. The Florida DOS website indicates the types of voter ID needed in Florida in case there's doubt."

"That doesn't sound like a weakness," one of the call attendees said.

"I agree, but wait—the Florida DOS website specifies that if the ID with signature contains no photo, then the Florida voter must provide the last four digits of their Social Security Number."

"That sounds like a foolproof system," another attendee said.

"Yes, it does. However, the Florida DOS website also indicates that if a voter has no ID with a photo or signature, they can still vote by entering 'none' in the box or field."

"You're frickin' kidding!" someone interjected.

"Nope, look it up. It's right there on the Florida DOS website. So, the first strategy we'll use is to deploy a limited number of illegal aliens, felons, refugees, and voters with no IDs. Questions?"

There were none, so Todd continued. "Let's discuss Florida voting machines. According to the Florida DOS website, a voting system partially or totally is constituted of electromechanical components, sometimes in conjunction with 'marksense' ballots. Florida uses a paper-based voting system that complies with the HAVA provisions for accessibility voting. The voting system consists of an EMS, two types of optical scan precinct count tabulators—the ICP and the ICE—and a digital scan central count tabulator, the ICC. This introduces a modified lineup of modems for precinct reporting, a more robust environment for the standard configuration of the EMS, and other enhancements to improve performance. Therefore, almost all Florida voting machines possess a paper trail."

"A paper trail makes voter fraud more difficult, right?" a warden asked.

Todd responded, "Yes. However, the electronic voting systems in forty-three states, including Florida, are at least twenty years old. These systems, both the hardware and the software, are approaching or have already exceeded their lifespan. The potential for mechanical breakdown and technological failure possibly compromising the voting process and/or election results is great. This is the conclusion of an extensive report recently released by the Brennan Center for Justice."

Another warden pointed out, "So, the machines are old and subject to failure. But there's still a paper trail with most voting machines."

"Yes, but if a voter machine breaks down, most backup machines do not have a paper trail. Since their own report indicates they expect voter machine failure, guess what? We'll help them break down. We'll replace them with Dominion voting machines and other old voting machines. In case you don't know, Dominion voting machines…" Todd filled in the wardens on Dominion's history in elections.

"Besides Dominion, we replace them with voter machines without a paper trail. Beautiful—I like it," said one warden.

"Exactly, you catch on quick. Before we continue, we have two approaches toward changing votes in Florida. With that in mind, let me introduce Fred Reider, who will explain further. Mr. Reider, you have the floor."

Fred began, saying, "Thank you, Mr. Shamer. It's my job to explain two cyber-virus approaches we'll be using. For those few Florida voting machines without a paper trail, we use Virus A. You will install it on a few machines in your precincts."

"We're not installing it on all Florida voting machines without a paper trail?" an attendee asked.

"NO! We don't want it on all machines without a paper trail. That's too many machines and therefore more easily detectable. I've faxed the procedure for installing the virus and removing it since it's technical. Follow the instructions carefully. We'll limit it to one or two machines in each voter place within your precincts. Keep in mind that Senator Adams is ahead in the polls in Florida, so we just need a little help. If we're too aggressive, the likelihood of voter fraud detection increases dramatically. Understood?" Fred asked.

"Yes." "Yep." "Understood."

Fred continued, "Now, let's talk about the main cyber virus we'll use in Florida due to the high number of voting machines with a paper trail. Virus B intercepts the scanned votes sent from the precincts to the state collection point. It simply changes a small percentage of the votes for Ronald Jackson into votes for Senator Adams."

"Won't this be obvious if auditing the results? The digital results won't match the paper results," an attendee pointed out.

"Yes, that's why Virus B changes a small percentage of the votes out of millions in random patterns so even detailed audits probably won't catch it. Keep in mind we're only targeting the most populated precincts in Florida, so they're already heavily liberal and strongly favor Senator Adams. Therefore, audits are less likely to happen. If audits do occur, the local politicians and the press who support Senator Adams will suppress, cover up, and deny any such accusation, et cetera. Agreed?"

There was a murmur of assent.

Fred asked if there were any questions. There were none. "That's our two cyber virus strategies. Back to you, Mr. Shamer."

Todd took over. "Now let's talk about the precincts we'll focus on. Precincts do not align with counties. However, the precincts involved fall into the following counties and cities. This list includes the population by county. These counties contain almost twelve million potential voters!

"They are as follows: Miami-Dade County, Miami, 2,662,874; Broward County, Fort Lauderdale, 1,780,172; Palm Beach County, West Palm Beach, 1,335,187; Hillsborough County, Tampa, 1,267,775; Orange County, Orlando, 1,169,107; Pinellas County, Clearwater, 917,398; Duval County, Jacksonville, 870,709 774; Lee County, Fort Myers, 631,330; Polk County, Bartow, 609,492; and Brevard County, Titusville, 543,566."

"Wow," an attendee said excitedly.

"Yes. Wow is right—Florida is ours!" Todd replied.

"Agreed," another attendee responded.

"Now that we've discussed specific strategies to win the election in Florida, let's discuss the general actions we'll take. These have literally changed the outcome of general elections in the US several times. First, let's discuss provisional ballots. They're used to record a vote when there are questions about a given voter's eligibility. A provisional ballot is cast when: one, the voter refuses to show a photo ID in regions that require one; two, the voter's name does not appear on the electoral roll for the given precinct; three, the voter's registration contains inaccurate or outdated information such as a wrong address or a misspelled name; and four, the voter's ballot records."

"Yes, but they're not counted, right?" a warden asked.

"That depends. Whether a provisional ballot is counted depends upon the verification of the voter's eligibility. A voter can cast a provisional ballot if he or she believes that they qualify to vote; this was one of the guarantees of the HAVA of 2002. In other words, we'll fool as many oblivious voters as possible who support Ronald Jackson to use a provisional ballot instead of a normal ballot. This means their votes won't be counted. Inversely, we'll include a small number of provisional ballots for Senator Adams when the other side isn't watching."

"Is that possible?" someone asked.

"Absolutely. In the 2004 election, at least 1.9 million provisional ballots were cast, and six hundred seventy-six thousand weren't counted, meaning only 1.2 million ballots were counted. This is an extreme example, but it is applicable to our case. Studies of the use of provisional ballots in the 2006 general election in the United States show only twenty-one percent rejection of provisional ballots. Most rejected ballots cast by registered voters were preventable."

"Damn," a warden said aloud.

"Yep, provisional ballot abuse is important. However, there's another method that's just as easy to implement."

Another warden asked, "What's that?"

"It's the misuse of proxy votes."

"Oh, I read about that. There's a famous case about the misuse of proxy votes at retirement homes," a warden replied.

"Yep, and it wasn't prosecuted. Here's how it works: You approach registered voters who are homebound, in nursing homes, or just apathetic. You get them to sign a proxy promising to vote for the candidate of their choice. Then, of course, you vote for Senator Adams."

"It's that easy?" a warden asked.

"Yep. Now on to the next method we'll use. It's one of the most pervasive voting fraud techniques used in America. We vote for known inactive voters."

"How does that work?" a warden asked.

Todd answered, "It's so frickin' easy. We all know the disenfranchised, apathetic, or plain fed-up voters. All we do is use liberal voters, felons, illegal aliens, or refugees to vote for them. All they need to do is to know the inactive voter's name and address. There are millions of inactive voters. Get busy and check your roles for inactive voters. You wardens, clerks, and inspectors will know hundreds of such voters personally. Besides, you're going to have access to the records and can give the bogus voters the appropriate name and address of the inactive voters."

"I love it," a warden responded, and there was chatter among the others discussing their approach.

Todd continued, "Let me have your attention again. Another customary practice to influence elections is to disrupt polling places. Senator Adams has close ties to aggressive groups who will protest at polling places. They've been instructed to focus on precincts favoring Ronald Jackson. Plus, they'll intimidate those voters wearing hats or shirts supporting Jackson. If we can dissuade the other party voters from voting for fear of their safety, we can alter the outcome of the election!"

"Cool." "Wow!" "Impressive," came replies from the wardens.

"Finally, there are less invasive practices we'll use, like vote buying in economically depressed areas, spreading misinformation to confuse voters, and manipulating the votes of the blind, mentally disabled, elderly, drunk, et cetera."

"I don't know if I could vote improperly for a blind person," one of the wardens said.

"If you don't, I'll find someone who will," Todd retorted coldly.

There was momentary silence. Then someone else asked, "What about absentee and early voting ballots?"

"Great question. That's an important aspect of our strategy. First, let me describe the difference. Thirty-seven states, including Florida and almost all the battleground states, allow early voting. This includes the states that mail ballots to all voters."

"Which states are those?" a warden asked.

"Well, Oregon went to all mail-in balloting. Other states, including Colorado, Florida, Kansas, Minnesota, Missouri, Montana, Nevada, New Mexico, North Dakota, and Washington State, allow mail-in voting at one level or another."

"Interesting. So, this applies to Florida as well?" a warden asked.

"Yes, and the District of Columbia allows any qualified voter to cast a ballot in person during a designated period prior to Election Day. No excuse or justification required."

"So how does that differ from absentee voting?" the same warden asked.

"To be honest, it's mostly just semantics."

"How so?" someone asked curiously.

"You see, all states will mail an absentee ballot to certain voters who request one. The voter may return the ballot by mail or in person. In twenty states, an excuse is required. Some states offer a permanent absentee ballot list. If a voter asks us to add them to the list, he or she will automatically receive an absentee ballot for all future elections."

"I still don't see the difference," a warden responded, confused.

"Don't you see? That's part of our strategy. Absentee and early voting ballots do not require an ID. It's all electronic or done via mail. Many states do not even check the mail-in or absentee ballot signature against the voting roll signature. My God, in those states we'll mail thousands of them. Many states just happen to find an unmarked box of mail-in ballots toward the end of the day, with almost all of them for the losing candidate! Lastly, whether it's an early ballot or an absentee ballot, we count all of Senator Adam's votes and lose as many of Ronald Jackson's ballots as we can," Todd replied.

"Ah, OK." "Oh, makes sense." "Love it," many wardens responded.

"OK, another key component of our strategy is voting more than once. Are you aware there are over 2.5 million voters register in more than one state? There's over sixty-eight thousand people registered in more than two states. Neither is legal since a voter cannot register in more than one state at a time."

"That many register in more than one state? That can't be true," a warden said.

"Look it up. It's true. Most voters do this in error. For instance, the voter moves, and either the voter or the state election authority fails to remove them from the vacated state. Many of them are in the military, and they vote in the state they're stationed in yet their names are still on the voter rolls of the state in which they joined."

"So, most of these lapses are innocent mistakes?" a warden asked.

"Yes. However, here's our plan: Check the voting rolls and contact those from our party appearing more than once. Call them and tell them they're registered more than once and inform them we know this is unintentional. Also tell them that voting more than once is illegal but rarely detected unless they use the same social security number."

Someone chimed in, "What good will that do?"

"The honest ones will either fix the double registration or only vote once. The dishonest ones will vote multiple times and use their names but with a different social security number."

Intrigued responses of assent rang out from the intercom.

Another warden replied, "The one aspect of this you didn't cover at all is the other party voting officers and staff. You know they'll be watching us like hawks since the large precincts favor our side."

Todd replied, "That's true, but the precincts we're targeting strongly favor Senator Adams, so most volunteers and staff will look the other way. Just so we don't get too sloppy, we need to remember that Florida takes voting fraud seriously. Several voters have faced prosecution for fraud recently. There is no known database of all convicted voter fraud in the US available to the public. Of course, if so, the FBI would have access to it. However, one website lists many of them, along with dates.

"For example: Annique Lesage Newton was convicted in 2015 for registering to vote without informing election officials she was a convicted felon. William Hazard pleaded guilty in 2015 to one felony voter registration charge and three misdemeanor charges of attempting to submit false voter registration information. James Webb Baker pleaded guilty to ID fraud, intimidating voters, and creating fake county election documents in Palm Beach County. Deisy Penton de Cabrera was convicted in 2013 of being an absentee ballot broker as part of a massive absentee voter fraud scheme. Jeffrey Garcia pleaded guilty to orchestrating a plot involving the submission of hundreds of fraudulent absentee ballot requests during the primary in 2012.

"Josef Sever was charged and convicted of illegal voting. Sever was a Canadian citizen who, nonetheless, cast a ballot in two presidential elections. Sergio Robaina, uncle of the former Hialeah mayor, was charged with illegally collecting absentee ballots, a misdemeanor, and with felony voter fraud charges for allegedly filling out a ballot against the wishes of two voters, one of them a woman with dementia. Greg 'Charlie' Burke was found guilty of voter fraud of the third degree—a felony—for living and voting in one county while holding an elected post in another. And lastly, Rafael Antonio Velasquez, a former candidate for the Florida House, was convicted in 2003 for having voted twice before he became a US citizen."

Stunned silence came from wardens, faced with the real possibility of voter fraud charges against them.

"Therefore, be careful. But remember, the local press, authorities, and constituents are on our side. Remember, the only way to prosecute us is to prosecute Senator Adams. Hell, he's suspected of several felonies, and some go back decades! However, the FBI won't do a thing. So, if they catch us at a few things, who cares? Nothing will happen. So, don't worry."

There was no response, so Todd continued, "So let's recap. One, we use a limited number of illegal aliens, felons, and refugees with no valid ID. Two, we'll use Virus A on one or two machines that contain paper trails and Virus B on the scanned votes. Three, we'll count some provisional ballots on our side and eliminate the other side's. Four, we'll arrange attacks on polling places. Five, we'll buy votes. Six, we'll use misinformation to confuse voters. And seven, we'll lose as many of the other side's absentee and early voting ballots as we can. Questions?"

"This is a lot to remember. Can you send us an outline of all that we've discussed?"

"Yes, innovative idea. We'll do that," Todd responded, making a note.

"So far, everything you've covered is what *we'll* do. What is Senator Adams doing at his level?" someone asked.

Todd answered excitedly, "I'm happy to report that in almost every battleground state, local politicians on Senator Adams's side are manipulating the outcome by moving precinct boundaries to include inner cities with more rural precincts, thus increasing the amount of liberal votes. They're also disenfranchising voters by removing the other party's voters from registered rolls. Lastly, they're busy creating ballots that are misleading and/or confusing. Hell, California and New York do all three of these before every general election. Ya gotta love it!"

There were indistinct murmurs of approval and even cheers from some of the wardens.

"Any questions?"

"Yes, what about evidence?" a warden asked.

"I'm glad you asked. This was the last point on my list. This is of paramount importance," Todd said ominously. "You must destroy the outline I send you and remove the two viruses from the systems before you leave your precinct on Election Day! Understood?"

"Understood." "Yep. "Clever idea."

Todd and Fred answered a few more questions one by one over the course of another hour. With all questions answered, Todd and Fred gave the attendees their cell phone numbers so that they could text additional questions before Election Day. After the meeting concluded, Todd and Fred sent an outline of the voter fraud techniques they discussed, while the precinct wardens excitedly began the task of committing voter fraud in Florida.

Todd and Fred glanced at Gavin, hoping he was pleased. His grin betrayed his approval of the call. However, they still wondered if he forgave them for discussing Senator Adams earlier.

Only time would tell.

Chapter 15 ★ Fred Who?

"I JUST LOVE SEPTEMBER IN Washington. The foliage changes color to gorgeous hues, and there's a chill in the air," Joie said dreamily to Mike Lundberg.

"Spring is my favorite season in DC. I like the cherry trees blooming along the mall area," he responded, sipping his coffee.

Joie said in a depressed tone, "I wish it was spring. That would mean we had over six months to investigate Senator Adams. We're running out of time. The election is less than two months away."

There was a knock at the door, and in walked Greg Elgen.

"Good, let's get started," Mike said as Greg took a seat. "Where are we?"

"Well, besides the evidence we've already discussed and added to the investigation file, there's late-breaking news about Senator Adams," Greg began, opening a folder.

"What's that?" Mike asked as he took the folder.

"Just this morning, many networks are reporting that the Austrian bank CBA, one of the biggest and most powerful financial institutions in the world, has a shady relationship with Senator Adams. According to sources, Senator Adams intervened to help CBA out with the IRS. Soon after, the bank paid Senator Adams 1.5 million dollars for speaking gigs."

"It must be nice to be the ranking member of the US Senate's Appropriations Committee."

"Not really. I would not trade places with him; he's going down," Greg retorted.

Mike continued, "Yes, I heard about the bank, but we need a lot more than that in this environment. Hell, Senator Adams remained unscathed after our investigation of his blatant deletion of classified documents from a government mainframe. Anyone else would have been in prison."

"Well, how about this," Joie chimed in. "Bloomberg Politics reported that a judge squashed Dreams International's refusal to release the identities of the over one thousand one hundred donors, most of whom are not US citizens. They just released the list."

The three of them scrutinized the list, shocked at the lengthy list of terrorist countries and individuals known to covet the death of America.

"These individuals gave to Dreams International?" Mike asked.

"Yep, and many of them either received favors from Senator Adams or received an appointment with him. The meetings occurred behind closed doors, so there's no telling what agreements were made," Greg said sadly.

Mike glumly replied, "Senator Adams is basically selling out America for profit. He does more harm daily than Benedict Arnold did in a lifetime."

"Good point. It's disheartening that our country now ignores such illegal behavior for political reasons," Joie said.

"Agreed," Mike said. "By the way, Judicial Watch was successful in using the Freedom of Information Act to acquire a judge's permission to release a batch of two hundred ninety-six pages of Senator Adams's documents. They confirm the relationship between Cyber-Hider and Dreams International. One of them yields evidence that he's granted favors to Stephen Warrants, a Columbian billionaire, in exchange for donations to Dreams International worth between one million and five million dollars!"

"True, but we still don't have ironclad proof that Senator Adams receives payments from Dreams International," Joie replied.

Greg responded, "Well said, Joie. Another related issue is whether Dreams International meets charity organization standards. Charity Navigator, one of the largest lists and auditors of charitable organizations, said yesterday,

'We previously evaluated this organization but have since determined that this charity's atypical business model cannot be accurately captured in our current rating methodology.' In other words, the charity won't agree to outside scrutiny, and its practices are questionable."

"Holy crap! I quote a famous FBI agent," Mike said, smiling at Joie.

Joie blushed. "I guess I should use more intelligent exclamations."

"On the contrary, 'crap' and 'Senator Adams' belong in the same sentence," Greg said, still reading articles. "Here's another article about one of Senator Adams's staffers with ties to terrorism. He set up meetings with Senator Adams for people from the Middle East who made donations to Dreams International. In each case, favors followed."

Greg handed the article to Mike. While he read, Joie said, "There're two more deaths potentially related to Senator Adams. They're a stretch, but Seth Rich, a political data analyst, was working on voting rights issues. They gunned him down in an unsolved shoot-out on a street in Washington DC. He lived in a violent neighborhood, so it may just have been unrelated gun violence. However, Shawn Lucas filed a lawsuit against Senator Adams for voter fraud and rigging the primary election just last month. Guess what? He died in his bathroom last week under suspicious circumstances."

Mike replied, "The trail of death that followed Senator Adams for over thirty years just grew longer. Joie, find out what the authorities have on the two murders and open an FBI investigation. However, I'll tell you there were two thousand eight hundred shootings in Chicago alone this year. Getting interested in just two that may be related to Senator Adams is not very promising."

"Will do," Joie replied, making notes.

"Greg, you follow up on the articles we just read and inform the FBI team investigating Dreams International."

"Done."

"Any word from Deputy Director Hermenez? The recording you played for us about the director's plans was astonishing," Mike said.

"No, but I have an appointment with him next week," Greg replied.

"Holy crap!" Joie exclaimed, then hung her head realizing she said it again.

"Next week?" Mike asked Greg, smiling at Joie.

"Yep, he's focused on this investigation and keeping the director informed."

"We need to get back to work—time is running out." Mike turned back to his papers. He began scribbling quickly, and beads of sweat appeared on his brow.

**

John met with Robert Beyer over coffee in the breakroom. Robert said, "John, your department is performing well, sales are climbing, and profits are up. Keep up the splendid work, and you'll soon have my job!"

"Thanks for the positive feedback, boss, but I don't want your job. I love mine. I want to stay close to the work," John replied respectfully.

"Too bad. Corporate talked to me about a job at headquarters. I put your name on the short list to replace me if the promotion comes through," Robert shared, watching John's response.

"Wow. I'm honored. I'd probably accept if you stayed long enough to mentor me. It's funny—corporate talked to me about a position in DC as well. I wonder if they're just yanking our chain."

"No problem. Training one's replacement is expected of management."

John, uncomfortable with the conversation, switched to another topic. "Have you heard anything from Luther East, the Fair Game programmer?"

"No, I haven't. Maybe it's time for an update. Let's go to my office and make a call."

Within minutes, back in his office, Robert had Luther on the phone.

"How is your project Fair Game coming along?" he asked.

"I'm done. It worked, and I turned the final product over to the customer. He doesn't think I know his name, but I'm a professional hacker. His name is Fred Reider," Luther replied with pride.

"Did you ever find out what it was for?" Robert asked pleasantly, trying to put Luther at ease.

"Well, no, not specifically. He didn't say much other than thanks."

"Thanks, Luther, I appreciate your time."

"No problem. Sorry I shut you down so quickly the last time we talked, but that John Jacobson fellow scares me," Luther replied sheepishly.

"He scares us all," Robert said, smiling at John.

John smiled back but whispered, "Ask him about a diagram with a patent owned by a Mr. Ray August."

"Why?" Robert whispered back.

"Please just ask," John whispered a little louder.

Robert nodded his head. "Luther, what can you tell me about a diagram you may be using with a patent owned by Mr. Ray August?"

"Why do you want to know?" Luther asked warily.

"It's part of an investigation I'm pursuing."

"Well, there's not much to tell. I based the part on an old patent owned by Mr. August. However, the older technology was replaced with more modern technology. Mr. August's original diagram was just a framework, nothing more." John sighed with relief as Luther said, "Talk to you later, Mr. Beyer. I've got to go."

"Goodbye, Luther," Robert said, hanging up.

"What was that all about John? Why were you asking about Ray August?"

"It's nothing," John said and quickly changed the subject. "It's a shame we didn't learn much."

"That's where you're wrong. Luther just gave us a huge clue!"

"What's that?"

"The name, Fred Reider," Robert said, opening his browser. He entered "Fred Reider" and obtained 1,587 hits. Most of them were Facebook or LinkedIn pages and personal websites. He scanned down the first several pages of hit results. Then a title stood out. His eyes grew large, and he pointed it out for John. John read it aloud: "Fred Reider, DNC Political Advisor, Declares He'll Do Anything to Help Elect Senator Adams."

They opened the link to a *Washington Post* article. The short article described Fred Reider's recent post within the DNC. An excerpt read: "Senator Adams's staff hired Reider due to his knowledge of digital tools used in general elections. Fred Reider insists that modern elections use highly sophisticated voting machines and insight into their workings is essential for success."

After they read the article, John returned to his office and closed the door. He dialed a number, but the call went into voicemail. After the beep, John said, "Joie, this is John. Calling for two reasons. First, I love you. Thanks for the exciting time in DC during my last visit. It was a *blast*. Sorry for the pun, but glad I was there to help you—not that you need me to protect you, you're a badass. And yes, I mean that in two ways. Secondly, have you heard of a guy named Fred Reider? After you look him up, call me. We need to talk. I believe he's related to your investigation. Bye, love ya."

Ten minutes later, John's phone rang. He recognized the number and answered, saying, "That was fast."

"I'll always *cum* back to you fast," Joie replied.

"Well thank you, ma'am. I aim to please. You sure please me. So, what did you find out about Mr. Fred Reider?"

"He doesn't have a record in federal or state criminal databases."

"You already looked him up?"

"You know I work for the FBI, right?"

"Good point. Did you find anything else about him?"

"Not really. I read some articles about him, but there's nothing indicating any illegal action. Why? Do you suspect him of foul play?"

"Do you remember what I told you about the program Fair Game?"

"Yes."

"Well, Reider was the customer. He received the program and said it worked. You may want to keep your ears open about Fair Game and Fred Reider."

"Will do. Gotta go. Love ya."

"Wow, you do *cum* and go fast," John replied, snickering.

"You are such a bad boy. See you soon." Joie blushed as she hung up.

***

Fred Reider's private cell phone rang. He recognized the number and took the call. "Fred, you know who this is. I don't want to say my name on a cell phone."

"Yes, I know you. Go ahead."

"As you know, I work for Scarlett. One of my tasks is to track Google searches of you, Todd Shamer, Scarlett Schuller, and Lizzy Warden."

"Yes, what about it?" Fred asked.

"Get this. A Mr. Robert Beyer in Fort Worth, Texas, AND a federal agency in DC both looked you up and read several online articles about you. Any reason why?"

"No, I don't know any reason they would. By the way, which federal agency?"

"I can't tell. But I suspect it's either the CIA, the FBI, or the NSA. They have privacy protection on their search engine lookups."

"Hmm. Robert Beyer… find out what you can about him and get back to me," Fred said, concerned.

"When I find out, I'll call you second."

"Who are you going to tell first?" Fred asked, even more concerned now.

"Scarlett!"

Chapter 16 ★ Ready on the Firing Line

ON OCTOBER 1, A SPECIAL voting strategy meeting began in Northern Virginia. Scarlett opened the meeting, asking abruptly, "Where are we, Todd?"

Todd stood with a confident smile plastered on his face. "I have an encouraging update. I've conducted conference calls with all the battleground states."

"You mean *we* conducted conference calls with all battleground states," Fred interjected.

"We'll get to you in a minute," Scarlett said, glaring at Fred.

Fred looked at the floor. Gavin eyed him, waiting for Scarlett's order.

Todd continued, "Yes, Fred and I hired over one hundred wardens from each state and gave them instructions on how to secure more votes. They'll hire at least one clerk and inspector in each precinct."

"What was your general guidance?" Scarlett asked curiously.

"We covered their specific state voting weaknesses. You can find this in my report."

Scarlett looked down and scanned the report. Her smile broadened as she read. "Nice. Well done!" Todd sat down, glowing. She continued, "We'll know how effective your measures are when we compare this year's election results against previous years. As you know, our party won all but two battleground states in the last general election. I want a clean sweep this time!"

Fred replied, "That's not a fair measure. Each election is different, just as the candidates differ. You're comparing apples and oranges."

"No, I'm quoting Senator Adams. Do you want to speak to him about it?"

"No," Fred said, looking away.

"Wise move. Let's continue, Fred. How's your portion of this operation proceeding?" Scarlett asked in a mocking tone.

Fred stood up, nervously glancing at Gavin, then said, "Both viruses work. We'll use Virus A on the voting machines with a paper trail and Virus B on scanned data from voting machines without a paper trail. We've instructed the wardens about which voting machines the virus applies to."

"OK, sounds good." Just as Fred was sitting, Scarlett asked, "What's this I hear about a federal agency looking you up on the internet?"

Fred, surprised she already knew, replied, "I don't know."

People in the room moved away from him as if he had a contagious disease. Gavin glared, Scarlett scowled, and Todd stared.

Fred looked toward the door. He wondered how long he had to live. People around whispered and pointed. Scarlett interrupted the murmurs, saying, "I want to see Todd and Gavin after the meeting. Meeting adjourned." She motioned for Todd and Gavin to follow her.

They met down the hall behind closed doors. Scarlett said, "I have one question, Todd."

"Yes?" he asked fearfully.

"If Lizzy helps you, can you manage Fred's part of this?"

He thought briefly, then said, "Yes, the viruses are programmed, functioning properly, and already in the wardens' possession."

"Good. Take over. The project is officially yours. I'll notify Senator Adams of the change. Don't let me down," Scarlett said with a wicked smile.

"What about Fred?" Todd asked, afraid of the answer.

"Let me take care of that." Scarlett nodded to Gavin.

Gavin's wicked smile brightened. Todd left the meeting as Scarlett and Gavin discussed their plan.

Todd liked Fred. He was a good guy; just caught in a bad spot. Todd found an empty office and called him.

Fred answered, recognizing the number. "Yes, Todd?"

Todd whispered, "Run!"

Todd hung up and wondered when Scarlett and Gavin would discuss him in the future. They needed him for now, so he went back to work, safe for the moment.

***

Joie worked in her office when the phone rang. "Agent August speaking. How can I help you?"

"Agent August. This is Agent Burris. I have a Fred Reider on the phone. I know you're investigating Senator Adams. He says he has information you need."

"My God! I was just thinking about him. Put him through immediately."

"Here you go," Agent Burris said, connecting them and hanging up.

"Agent August," came a tense voice over the phone. "My name is Fred Reider. We need to talk. My life is in danger. If you put me in protective custody and give me immunity, I'll tell you everything you need to know to bring Senator Adams down."

"Holy crap! Start talking! But first, tell me how you got my name."

"A Mr. Beyer looked me up on the internet. I called him. He gave me John Jacobson's name, and Jacobson gave me yours."

"You spoke to John and his boss?"

"Yes."

"OK, go ahead."

"I'm working with Senator Adams's secret team dedicated to win the election through voter fraud. I'm also working on a program called Fair Game. But I won't tell you more unless you put me in protective custody AND give me full immunity!"

"Understood. Hold on," Joie said excitedly. She put him on hold and called Mike.

"Mike, this is Joie. I have a Fred Reider on the phone. He says his life is in danger and wants protective custody and immunity from all charges.

In exchange, he'll give us information on voting fraud methods about to be used by Senator Adams."

"How do you know he's for real?" Mike asked.

"It's a long story, but his name came up earlier linked to project Fair Game. He's the one John told me about, remember? We suspected it had to do with voting fraud, and now he just called me unexpectedly. What do I do?"

"Tell him we'll put him in protective custody and grant immunity based upon the information he has. Where is he? Can you bring him in?"

"I don't know where he is, but I'll pick him up in a squad car and bring him right to your office," she said, clicking back to Fred's line.

"Fred?"

No answer. "Fred, are you there?" Joie asked.

The line was dead.

Chapter 17 ★ Pre-Election Foci

JOIE STOOD IN MIKE'S OFFICE almost at attention in front of his desk. "When I switched over to Fred's line after talking to you, he was gone."

Mike was not happy. "Gone? Damn. We gotta find him. Did he say anything besides wanting protective custody and immunity?"

"Not much."

"A more experienced agent would have kept him on the line without promising him anything, to find out what he wanted and where he was. We don't know if he hung up or someone got him."

"You're right. I'm sorry. I'm the least experienced agent on the team."

"It's OK. I knew you needed training when I transferred you here. We'll recover somehow."

Joie lowered her head in shame. She decided to make up for the mistake.

That night, she called John when she got home. "John, I wish you were here."

"Me too. What's wrong, babe?"

"I screwed up today."

"What happened?"

"I let Fred get away. I don't know if he's alive or dead."

"You spoke to Fred? So did I. I gave him your number. Joie, I'm here, and I will help."

"How?"

"I have a few ideas. Let me get back to you. Love ya, Joie."

"Love you too, John. Bye."

John knew she was depressed when she called him by name, rather than "lug," "idiot," or, her favorite, "Neanderthal." When she didn't tease him, she was off her game.

He picked up the phone and went to work with zeal.

. . . .

Two days later in Mike's office, Greg said to the regular team members, "Did you hear the late-breaking story this morning about Senator Adams?"

"What now?" Mike asked.

"We can strengthen the Cyber-Hider case with new felony charges thanks to newly released documents."

"What's the news?" Joie asked.

"There's several documents clearly showing several counts of perjury by Senator Adams to Congress and the FBI!"

"How so?" Mike asked curiously.

"The documents reveal that Senator Adams lied about the contents of government documents in his files on a mainframe. They dealt with Senate Appropriations Committee issues and, even more damning, additional Dreams International appointments with large donors."

"Damn!" Joie cursed.

"Oh, but there's more!" Greg announced.

"You're kidding! What other gifts do you bring?" Mike asked, intrigued.

"We can add three counts of the felony. Obstruction of justice."

"No way," Joie gasped.

"Way. Other documents newly released by Judicial Watch revealed that Senator Adams planted questions with Senator Adams's party members before congressional investigations. Senator Adams deleted documents after the FBI told him of the investigation and destroyed fourteen phones, one laptop, two memory sticks, and five iPads after receiving notification of the investigation."

"Wow! That's huge!" Joie replied, taking notes. "Yes, definitely new foci."

"Foci?" Mike asked, raising his eyebrows, and everyone looked at her enquiringly.

"Yes, you know—new emphasis, applications, et cetera."

"Right! I knew that, but was just testing you," Mike retorted with a smirk.

"Good, I'd hate to think I'm working for an unlearned man. I already have one in my life—John."

Everyone smiled—except Mike, who responded, "Calling me 'unlearned' is not a smart career move for a subordinate."

Joie quickly retorted, "Oh, Most Learned One, thanks for sharing your abundant wisdom with your humble servants."

This time everyone laughed, including Mike. If offended, all appeared forgiven. However, she decided to be more careful and respectful for a while.

At noon, Mike turned on the news. The team continued their work until another late-breaking story announcement popped up. "Hackers are behind two recent attempts to breach state voter registration databases, fueling concerns that the Russian government may be trying to interfere in the US presidential election, US intelligence officials tell NBC News."

Mike turned up the volume. "Listen to this!" he called to the team.

The reporter continued, "The breaches included the theft of data from as many as two hundred thousand voter records in Illinois alone, officials say. The incidents led the FBI to send a 'flash alert' earlier this month to election officials nationwide, asking them to be on the lookout for any similar cyber intrusions."

"Damn!" Greg exclaimed.

The team shushed him as the reporter continued, "The FBI is requesting that states contact their Board of Elections and determine if any similar activity to their logs, both inbound and outbound, have been detected."

Joie asked, "I wonder which group in the FBI is working on this. How do we contact them?"

Greg responded, "I know them well. I'm already working with them, and they're keeping me updated."

"Excellent, but when were you going to tell me about the other team? As the team lead, I should have known," Mike retorted with a frown.

Greg nervously responded, "Sorry, boss. With all that's going on, it slipped my mind."

Mike, not happy, chided, "No harm done. But we need to link the hacks of voter registration rolls to Senator Adams. That won't be easy. Keep us informed."

"Will do, boss," Greg answered, somewhat relieved.

The reporter continued, "The bulletin does not identify all the targeted states, but officials told NBC News that those affected include Illinois and Arizona. Illinois officials said in July they shut down their state's voter registration system after a hack. In Arizona, officials said hackers got in using malicious software. These incidents led Homeland Security Secretary Johnson to host a call earlier this month with state election officials to talk about cybersecurity and election infrastructure. Independent assessments found that many state and local voting systems are extremely vulnerable to hacking."

"Is this for real?" Joie asked.

"It appears so," Mike commented.

"We only have days before the election. How do we investigate it all?" Joie asked.

Mike thought for a moment. "We can't. I'll bring in more agents. In the meantime, do the best you can and focus on Cyber-Hider, Dreams International, and voter fraud. And by all means, foci!"

"Will do, boss. Foci it is!" Joie responded, and Greg nodded his agreement.

The days passed quickly, yet the investigations proceeded slowly. Senator Adams and Ronald Jackson debated, and each party walked away claiming their candidate won. Both parties had no choice but to wait with bated breath for Election Day.

PART IV ★ ELECTION DAY

Chapter 18 ★ Eastern Time Zone

NOVEMBER 3 WAS A BEAUTIFUL fall day in North Carolina. Voting places had low voting day turnout because 60 percent of North Carolina voters voted early. Many of the ballots supporting Ronald Jackson in the battleground states were already destroyed, just as they were in the other twenty-seven states allowing large numbers of early, mail-in, and absentee voting.

Ryan Bloke, a recent graduate from a local university, drove excitedly down to the voting poll location closest to his house in Charlotte. Ryan would do his part for Senator Adams. A website, sponsored by Senator Adams, instructed him on the steps he would have to follow. He wondered if it was true; could he actually vote for an inactive voter due to the lack of voter ID laws in North Carolina? He decided it was worth the risk.

Ryan memorized the first name on the sheet of paper he drew out of his pocket. It listed several inactive voters. He folded it and put it in his golf shirt pocket. He parked in the lot, joined the short queue, and reached the voting check-in table in minutes. He moved into the line for people with last names starting with *A* through *F* and listened carefully to the poll worker talking to voters ahead in line. Ryan looked at his paper one last time.

Up ahead, the poll worker asked mechanically, "Name? Address? Here's your ballot, Mr.…. Name? Address? Here's your ballot, Mrs.…."

Ryan was next in line. He smiled and said, "Good morning."

The poll worker mechanically replied, "Good morning. Name?"

"Bill Clowers."

"Address?"

Ryan thought for a moment and responded, "411 Elm Street, Charlotte, 28078."

The poll worker found the name in the register and flatly said, "Here's your ballot."

Ryan nervously took the ballot as the poll worker robotically looked at the next person in line and said, "Next. Name?"

Ryan voted within two minutes, exited the polling place, and headed for the next one located in Charlotte. In a few hours, Ryan also voted for three dead voters and voted by mail-in ballot three times. He memorized the next name and address on his list of ten inactive voters in Charlotte.

"I'll be done in time to watch the poll returns with the family," Ryan whispered to himself, pulling into the next polling place parking lot. He was only one of almost seven thousand others doing the same thing across North Carolina. Senator Adams would be proud.

***

Tom Gent made one more pass through the Miami retirement village picking up proxy votes. He stopped in front of a house and knocked at the door. An elderly man opened the door and said, "Yes, can I help you?"

Tom gave a friendly smile and replied, "Hello, I'm here to pick up your proxy vote form."

"Oh, yes, my wife and I both filled one out. Thanks for making this year's vote easy for us. This is a great service. You're a nice young man to do this."

"It's a pleasure to assist you. I feel it's my civic duty as a patriotic and politically active American."

The man handed Tom the two proxy voting forms. Tom looked at the man's name on the form and said, "Thanks, Mr. Edwards."

"You're welcome, young man," the older man replied, smiling.

Tom shook his hand and headed for the next apartment in the upscale retirement village. After collecting another twenty proxy votes, he drove to the entrance of the village and waited. Three other cars pulled up behind him. The drivers got out and handed him their stacks of forms, a total of seventy-five proxy votes they picked up from their assigned portion of the enormous retirement village.

"Thanks, guys. Senator Adams thanks you," Tom said, waving goodbye and heading for the local polling place. Of course, he'd only turn in the proxy ballots for Senator Adams and throw the others away. He smiled, knowing he helped Senator Adams and his party.

* * *

It was a gorgeous crisp day in Concord, New Hampshire, as Charlene Baker headed for her local polling place. She fought her nerves as she arrived. She believed her parole officer voted on the other side of town, so it was probably safe for her to come here. Thankfully, the parole board reduced her jail time for good behavior.

She pulled into the parking lot of a large church. Could she really vote as a convicted felon? She filed into the building to find out. Within minutes, she was inside the fellowship hall where the voting was taking place. When she was close to the check-in table, she listened in on the dialogue. Soon it was her turn.

"ID, please?" the poll worker asked.

"Sorry, I can't find mine," she said apologetically. "I think it was stolen."

"You don't have any photo ID? A driver's license? Anything?"

"No."

"Not even a federal or state ID without a photo?"

"Nope, sorry."

"Did you drive here?" the worker asked suspiciously.

"No, I live just a few blocks from here. I walked. I can't afford a car. I take a bus to work."

The worker scrunched up her face and said, "OK, here's a provisional ballot. If you return with an ID, we can use it to verify your identity and we'll count it."

"Understood. Thank you," Charlene responded, relieved that she made it through. She took the provisional ballot, voted, and returned it to the inspector in the back of the fellowship hall. The inspector took it, looked at how she voted, and winked. He whispered, "Good job. Trust me, your vote will count."

Since the polling place included almost all liberal party supporters, they counted over half of the provisional ballots while the other side wasn't looking. It was a piece of cake.

Charlene was halfway to her car when she walked back inside, went to a confessional booth and said, "Forgive me, Father. I have sinned…"

***

Phil Tanner, once a stock broker but now living in a nursing home for the insane, walked to his local polling place in Philadelphia and joined a long queue. "This can't be true. It can't be this easy," he said to himself.

"What can't be this easy?" the person in front of him said.

"Voting for the aliens."

"Voting for aliens? Do you mean illegal aliens voting?" the person replied.

"No, voting for the aliens who are taking over the planet. They abducted me last year. They're here and running for political offices all over the country. It's OK, though. They're peaceful aliens and just want us to protect our planet through more ecological and environmentally friendly practices."

The person smiled, thinking he was kidding, and said, "Good one. I needed a joke today. I lost my job when my manufacturing plant closed and moved to Mexico."

Phil grinned witlessly, looked both ways, and replied, "Sorry to hear about that. But it's OK. The aliens told me they're striking Mexico with lasers soon because of their pollution. Your plant may come back here shortly."

The person's smile disappeared and he awkwardly turned away, hoping this stranger wasn't dangerous. They stopped talking and soon arrived at the check-in desk.

"Name and address?" the poll worker asked.

"Phil Tanner and I live at 718 Main Street," Phil responded

"ID?"

"I don't have any. The judge took away my right to vote. He thinks I'm crazy. He doesn't know they're already here—"

The poll worker looked confused and interrupted him, "That's OK. Luckily for you, Pennsylvania is not strict about ID. You have the right to vote without showing an ID, and your vote will still not be a provisional ballot."

"You mean I get a normal ballot?" he asked.

"Yep," she said, handing him an official ballot.

"Thanks, I'll tell them you were very helpful," Phil said, walking to the voting machine.

"Them?" she asked.

"The aliens," he replied in a paranoid tone.

"No problem. Next?" she replied, rolling her eyes.

***

Earl Killman left home after lunch and headed to the local voting place in Norfolk, Virginia. He found a place in the queue and pulled out his Virginia driver's license and "the paper" he needed to vote. Soon, he was at the check-in desk.

"Name and address?" the poll worker asked.

"Earl Killman, 1114 Harbor Circle."

"I'm sorry, but you're not in the list of registered voters," the poll worker replied courteously after going through his list.

"I don't need to be."

"Why's that?

"Because of this!" Earl handed the poll worker the paper containing the governor of Virginia's letterhead.

She perused it, saw Governor Terry McAuliffe's signature, and replied, "You're right. Here's your ballot."

The poll worker put the paper on a separate stack. Later, the warden saw the growing stack and asked the clerk, "What are those?"

"It's Governor Terry McAuliffe's 'Restoration of Felon Voting Rights' letters."

"Oh, yes. When the federal court rejected his executive order restoring voting rights to felons, he committed to hand-sign over two hundred thousand such letters."

"You're kidding."

"Nope. He decided he needed felon votes to ensure his party's victory. Therefore, he pardoned convicted felons so they could vote."

"Is that legal?"

"It hasn't been challenged yet."

"Damn politicians."

"Yep, Florida is doing the same thing. Conservative candidates don't stand a chance."

"Hell, who cares? I've stopped caring. It hurts too much."

"Me too. Maybe conservative candidates will win other battleground states!"

"Whatever," she replied before turning and saying, "Next in line, please."

***

"There're way too many damn conservative voters here," a clerk said to the warden at a polling place in Queens, New York.

"Hell yes. We'll fix that," the warden replied with a smile.

The warden found the contact in his cell phone and called right away. When the person answered, he said, "This is Kent Simpler in polling place 103 in Southern Queens. We need help. There's a bunch of people outside wearing Ronald Jackson hats and shirts. In addition, I'm seeing far too many votes for the other side. It's early, so we need to take action to reverse the trend."

After a pause, Kent said, "Look, we need them all. This is the largest polling place in Queens and one of the largest in NYC." He waited for the reply. "Thanks. How long will it take them to get here?" After hearing the response, Kent said, "That fast? Impressive!"

Kent hung up and called out, "They're on their way!"

"Who?" the clerk asked.

"The cavalry!"

"I don't understand," the clerk replied.

"I just called an 800 number a guy named Todd Shamer gave me. He's a bigwig in the party. Anyway, the number provides paid protesters who demonstrate and scare away voters of the other party. They'll be as aggressive as needed, just like they were when Ronald Jackson spoke at large conservative speaking engagements. Remember, New York is Ronald Jackson's home state, so he may sway the voters on the fence."

"Cool," the clerk replied as they both went back to work overseeing the large crowd of voters. Within an hour, paid protesters filled the parking lot and sidewalks. They wore regalia from many liberal social and political groups. Within an hour, the protest turned violent, and voters for Ronald Jackson left for other polling places or went home.

Senator Adams smiled watching the protest on live TV. "Way to go, Scarlett," he whispered with a hiss.

***

Ismael Khouri and Abdul Fakhoury, refugees from Syria, drove down to their local polling place in the Bronx.

"It's great living in America!" Ismael said.

"Yes, Allah be praised," Abdul replied.

They pulled into the parking lot as Ismael asked, "Do you think it's as easy as we heard?"

"We're about to find out."

They joined the long queue stretching around the block. While they waited and moved forward slowly, they started speaking to each other in Arabic.

"Salam! [سلام]"

"Kaifa haloka/haloki. [كيف حالك؟]"

"Ana bekhair, shokran! [أنا بخير شكراً]"

Those around them in line responded with complaints such as "Speak in English!" and "If you live here, learn our language or go home!"

Undaunted by the chatter, they continued. "Jayed/'aadee. [جيد/عادي]"

"Shokran. [شكراً (ج) الجزيل]"

"Al'afw. [عفواً]"

Within thirty minutes, they were at the check-in desk. The poll worker said, "Name and address, please?"

"Ismael Khouri, 21117 Island Avenue."

"ID, please?

"What, just because I'm a Muslim you don't think I have an ID?" Ismael asked loudly.

"No, I didn't mean anything like that. I ask everyone for—"

"Oh, sure, you're just another one of those American Islamophobic rednecks the President talks about."

"Sir, it's not that at all. Some of my friends are—"

"Oh, but not your *good* friends, I bet," Abdul almost screamed.

By now, almost everyone in the queue was staring at them. Ismael shouted at the poll worker, "We came to America to escape hatred and persecution, you American hypocrite! You talk about freedom and race blindness, but you're just another Anglophile or xenophobe who hates anyone who doesn't look like you!"

"Gentlemen, please. I apologize. I'm as politically correct as they come. Here's your ballots," the poll worker acquiesced.

Ismael and Abdul jerked the ballots out of his hand and walked toward the voting machines indignantly. The poll worker felt relieved and said, "Next."

After Ismael and Abdul voted for Senator Adams, they left while saying, "It's great living in America! Yes, Allah be praised."

They drove to the bank, cashed their welfare checks, drove to the grocery store, and used their state-provided food stamps, then disappeared into their urban NYC tax-free government subsidized environment.

***

Barbara Tucker of Columbus, Ohio, drove to her local polling place. The line was long, so she struck up a conversation with two other women named Cynthia Blank and Elvira Matthews. They exchanged pleasantries and spoke of family, the weather, and recent local news. They even swapped business cards.

"Can I ask you two a personal question?" Barbara asked.

"Sure," Cynthia said. Elvira nodded.

"We're probably not supposed to ask, but since we've kind of become friends and we're fellow Ohioans, I feel comfortable asking."

"You're among friends," Elvira replied, and Cynthia smiled in agreement.

"Since John Kasich ran in the Republican primaries and came close to winning, do you think the Republicans will win Ohio? I hope so."

"I hope so, too," Cynthia replied.

"I hope not," Elvira replied, still in a friendly tone.

"Thanks for answering. Still friends?" Barbara asked.

"Of course," Cynthia replied.

"Women have to stick together," Elvira said, smiling.

Soon they reached the head of the line and gave the check-in desk worker their names, addresses, and photo IDs. They voted in just ten minutes on DRE touchscreen voting machines. Unbeknownst to the women, Virus A within the machines swapped the two votes for Ronald Jackson to Senator Adams. Scarlett would be proud.

***

In Broward County, Florida, the warden and henchmen busily counted provisional and absentee votes for Adams and destroyed opposing votes. They stuffed boxes, suddenly found and counted thousands of questionable votes, and conducted an assortment of other voter fraud activities. A bonus was on the way!

Not related to Fred's virus activities, other local hackers, who were active in every election, busily switched votes. One in NYC defaulted ballots to select one party only. The voter had to deselect them, then choose the candidate of their choice. Another ballot in PA chose one candidate no matter what the voter selected. The only option to cancel the virus was not to vote. A third switched votes when making the last choice. Unless the voter reviewed all previous selections and changed them, the virus worked.

These and other local viruses did their dirty work in every battleground state. Many voters captured these viruses on YouTube to warn others. Doubters watched the hundreds of YouTube videos of the damning evidence and heard reports on the local news. The Dominion voting machines reversed votes in Adam's favor. Virus A and B did their thing effectively, and mail-in votes without signatures or address verifications counted for Adams, while opposing ballots thrown away—sometimes by the box. Memory cards favoring the opponent made their way into trash cans.

Senator Adams watched the reports with immense pleasure as networks released post-voting polls in the Eastern Time Zone. It was a close race.

***

Joie and Mike watched the returns in disgust when Joie's cell phone rang. She answered, and the voice on the other end of the line said, "Agent August, this is Fred Reider."

Joie put her phone on speaker and asked feverishly, "Fred, where are you? Are you safe? Why did you hang up?"

"I have work to do, and I can't do it in protective custody."

"But we can't protect you if you're out there alone."

"What I must do, the FBI can't be involved in. I must clean up my own mess."

Mike dialed a number and whispered to Joie, "Keep him on the line. I'll trace the call."

While Mike traced the call on the other line, Joie continued, "Fred, we won't put you in protective custody then. We'll assign agents and local authorities to protect you where you are."

"No way, I don't know who to trust anymore. Besides, Senator Adams would know you're protecting me. I need to catch them in the act. No deal."

Mike indicated the trace was ongoing and whispered, "Keep stalling. We almost have the number."

Joie nodded, and Fred continued, "I need help and protection from someone, though. It's scary out here alone."

"Maybe we can help you do what you have to do in an unofficial capacity…"

In another ten seconds, Mike whispered, "Got him. He's in Fort Worth, at 817-567-8913."

"Fort Worth? Are you sure about the number?" Joie whispered to Mike, starting to feel sick.

Fred heard her and immediately hung up. Mike immediately sent agents to the address corresponding to the phone number.

Fred looked up from the phone and said to John, "Let's go. We have work to do!"

Chapter 19 ★ Central Time Zone

IN DES MOINES, IOWA, TWO voters left the voting booth and walked back to their car.

"Billy, did you understand that frickin' ballot? Everything was backward."

"What do you mean?" Bubba asked.

"I mean the ballot was stated in the negative, so a 'yes' vote was voting against the candidate or proposition. I read about it in a conservative article in *The Journal*. The ballot explained that in small print at the bottom."

"You mean I just voted for Senator Adams when I thought I selected the other guy?"

"Yep."

"Why didn't you tell me, Billy?"

"Because I knew you were voting for Jackson, and I wanted you to vote for Senator Adams."

"Damn. Well, it's just one vote."

"Not really. There'll be hundreds of other confused voters in Des Moines, not to mention in California, the mother of ambiguous and inverse ballots. That reduces some of the twenty-five percent conservative vote out there."

"Son of a bitch! No wonder you guys win elections!"

"All's fair in love, war and politics," Billy said as they drove back to work.

**

In Detroit, Michigan, a blind man made his way to the front of the line with his cane. He was a friendly man, easy to assist. After he registered, the clerk said, "I'll be happy to help you vote."

"The local news said this polling place was set up to accommodate the blind."

"Well, we are. But I'm sorry to say the 'special assistance' voting machine is out of order."

"How do I know you'll vote the way I want?"

"Because you have my word as an official voting place volunteer."

"No offense, but I want another witness."

"No problem. I'll get the warden, the highest officer at this voting place."

"OK, as long as there are two witnesses."

"You got it," the clerk said, waving the warden over.

"Can I help you?" the warden asked, seeing that the voter was blind.

"Yes. I'd like the clerk's help voting, and I need you as a witness that she enters my choices correctly."

"I'd be happy to assist you," the warden replied in a helpful, courteous tone.

They made their way over to a voting machine and began the voting process. The voter specified his choice for each candidate, and the clerk chose Senator Adams's party each time regardless of the voter's choice. Finally, they were at the last choice—the choice for US president.

"Do you want Senator Adams or Ronald Jackson?" the clerk asked quietly.

"Ronald Jackson."

The clerk chose Senator Adams instead. They concluded the voting process and the voter said, "Thank you for your kindness. Can I get a hard copy of the vote please?"

"I'm sorry, but this voting machine does not provide one."

"Hmm, well, I guess I'll have to trust you. Besides, I doubt you'd both lie to me. Thanks again." The man readied his cane and headed toward the exit.

"It's our duty and pleasure," the warden replied, winking at the clerk.

"That was a lot of work for one vote," the clerk said once the man was out of earshot.

"Are you kidding? We have wardens, clerks, and inspectors at the largest precincts in the country duplicating this process with all those who are incapable of voting by themselves, such as the elderly or even the drunk. By the end of the day, you can multiply this vote by at least twenty-five thousand."

"Will twenty-five thousand really make a difference?"

"Every little bit helps. Plus, you add in the millions we'll get from all the other voting fraud methods our party is using, and we're home free!"

"We'd better get back to work," the clerk said, looking at the long queues.

"Yep," the warden replied, whistling as he walked away.

***

In Milwaukee, Wisconsin, voters lined up all along a city block. Thankfully, the polling place was efficient, so voters moved through the process relatively quickly. A city bus pulled up out front and almost fifty voters piled out and staggered into the lengthy line so that one in every four voters in the queue belonged to a unique group. Each of them carried a small card with the name and address of an inactive Milwaukee voter. It also contained instructions on how to vote, taking advantage of a newly enacted Wisconsin voting law.

Within fifteen minutes, the first voter of the group arrived at the check-in desk.

"Name and address, please?" the poll worker asked.

"Tanya Bollivar, 8762 Fairway Drive."

"ID, please?"

"I don't have one, so I'd like to sign the state-approved affidavit form stipulating my identity."

"No problem," the clerk said, handing the voter the form.

"Tanya" signed the form, and the clerk presented her with a ballot.

After about twenty people fumbled through their names and addresses, the clerk called the warden over. "I don't like this," he said. "There are way too many people in line having to think too hard about their name and address, and then choosing an affidavit certifying their identity rather than presenting a photo ID."

"It's Wisconsin law. There's nothing we can do about it."

"But you know they're just taking advantage of this voter ID flaw."

"We're just here to ensure people obey voting laws and regulations. It's comical that liberal states claim voter ID checks are racist—not so, since government voter IDs are free. Oh well, let's go back to work and not worry about it," the warden replied, walking away.

"Will do," the clerk said grudgingly.

This very process occurred in other polling places as well in Milwaukee, Madison, Green Bay, Kenosha, Racine, Appleton, Waukesha, and Oshkosh, tilting Wisconsin toward Senator Adams. However, almost all Michigan voting machines used optical scan ballot systems, so at least there was a paper trail there unlike many other states that strictly used hackable digital voting systems. Luckily for Senator Adams, Virus B was busy converting scanned voter data sent to the state collection point. Michigan was in the bag!

***

In Houston, Texas, loyal liberals, illegal aliens, felons, and refugees used inactive voter IDs and 15 percent made it through the check-in desks, giving Senator Adams over one thousand votes in Houston alone. San Antonio and Dallas followed suit, adding thousands more. Texas was in the top three states using absentee and early voting ballots. In addition, there were more military ballots filed in Texas than in any other state. Therefore, inspectors loyal to Senator Adams busily destroyed, lost, and disqualified the absentee and early votes as well as the military ballots when the other side wasn't watching. This helped Senator Adams only a little, but it did change the outcome of several down-ticket races.

***

In Chicago, Illinois, two women made their way through the two-block-long line. While they waited their turn, they passed the time talking.

"How many kids do you have?" one of them asked.

"Six. You?" the other replied.

"Five."

"Do you work?"

"No. Neither did my mom or grandma. You?"

"No, with just a GED and six kids under ten, I can't afford childcare."

"Same here."

"I don't like our liberal-run city or our sanctuary city policies, or the violence towards Blacks."

"I know, the police are killing us like animals."

"That damn Fox channel interviewed a black PhD who said that Blacks kill more Blacks than the police by a factor of ten."

"Do you believe that propaganda?"

"No, I don't care what his stats or credentials say. The police are the criminals. I loved the way our party's national conference invited speakers like the mothers of people killed at the hands of the police."

"Me too. Damn the police!"

"Besides, we must vote for Senator Adams. The other side may not give us welfare for having kids and not able to work. What would we do then?"

"You're right. The president's entitlement programs are a lifesaver! Of course, he doubled the US debt, but that's rich people's problem. We're just fighting to survive."

They nodded in agreement as they finally reached the check-in desk, got their ballots, and voted for Senator Adams. Similar conversations occurred in inner-city voting booths in almost every state in the country.

* * *

Mike, Agent Greg Elgen, and Joie sat in an FBI conference room watching network news voting returns. The numbers were discouraging.

Mike asked, "So, where are we on Cyber-Hider and Dreams International? We can't change the outcome of the election anymore, but we can indict Senator Adams if we have enough evidence."

Joie answered first, "There are a multitude of potential Cyber-Hider charges we've considered. However, here are the charges for which we have enough substantial evidence to move forward with: The two misdemeanors are giving classified documents to unauthorized personnel and deleting government documents without authority. However, the felony is conspiracy to conceal documents from government officials. This comes with a three-year sentence. The latter would also disqualify Senator Adams from becoming president."

"Excellent! Please document the charges and attach the associated evidence. Excellent job, Joie!"

"Will do, boss."

Greg spoke next. "As far as Dreams International is concerned, we have a weak case because Senator Adams evades questions from the press and investigators. Also, judges won't issue a subpoena without more evidence. So, we can't examine charity documents. Thus, the charges on which we have some supporting evidence to act upon are: nondisclosure of foreign fund donations, bribery, criminal racketeering, charity acting in the best interest of a business or individual, incomplete disclosure of recipients, and misuse of charitable donations."

"Holy crap! That's great news!" Joie replied.

"Are you aware you say 'Holy crap' a lot?" Mike teased.

"OK, holy shit!" Joie grinned.

"You're right, go back to the former. Although these seven potential charges are serious, and most of them are felonies, the evidence is weak. Keep digging!"

"I agree, Mike." Greg continued studying the evidence.

"You got it, boss. I'll go deeper," Joie responded, shuffling papers.

Chapter 20 ★ Mountain Time Zone

IN DENVER, COLORADO, EVERY VOTING booth faced long queues. A clerk called the warden over and said, "Colorado's voter ID requirements are a joke."

"What's the problem?"

"Let me show you. So far, I have seen seventy-five Colorado driver's licenses, fifty-eight US passports, forty-nine employee photo IDs, forty-two IDs from other US and Colorado departments, thirty-four Colorado Department of Revenue IDs, twenty-two US military photo IDs, nineteen veteran photo IDs, and fourteen student photo IDs."

"What's wrong with those? They all contain a photo ID."

"They are fine. I shook the hand of everyone who provided a proper ID. It's the rest of the list I have a problem with."

"Why?"

"Because the other voter IDs I've received this morning are all problematic in some way or another. As many as two hundred twenty-five provided a current utility bill, a bank statement, a government check, a paycheck, or some other such government document that shows the name and address of the voter but does not include a photo. In addition, one hundred sixteen people submitted county and municipality IDs that may not be legit; fifty-six submitted board, authority, or Colorado political subdivisions, whatever they are. Also, forty-nine were Medicare or Medicaid cards, most of which don't have a photo, and thirty-five were certified copies of a US birth certificate, which also don't have a photo. Fourteen were Certificates of Degree of Indian Blood, which once again don't provide photos, twelve were certified documents of naturalization, and, unbelievably, eight were tribal membership cards."

"They're all acceptable according to the Colorado Department of State website."

"I know, but I wonder, how many are fraudulent?"

"That's not our concern. All we can do is follow the law."

"OK, I just thought I'd share my concerns."

"Thanks. Just do the best you can."

"Will do," the clerk said, reaching for the next ID. It was a card stipulating that the bearer was an Alaskan Native. It contained no photo. She rolled her eyes and checked him in.

***

In Las Vegas, a lengthy queue at a voting booth on Las Vegas Boulevard contained hundreds of voters. Fred's wardens identified voters in Senator Adams's party and sent them a $50 chip from their favorite casino if they provided proof that they voted. A bus on the corner made round trips from the polling place to the major casinos. All the voters received $50 chips.

***

In Phoenix, long lines included illegal aliens voting with the names and addresses of inactive voters. Meanwhile, wardens on Todd's payroll were in back rooms destroying and invalidating the other party's ballots. Virus A changed votes on voting machines without a paper trail, and Virus B converted votes sent to the state voting board. Todd and Scarlett ecstatically received the wardens' texts about the good news!

***

Fred and John hid on the fourth floor of John's workplace in a vacant office. It was in the interior of the building, so the room had no windows. "John, I have proof of the illegal voting practices used by a secret committee working for Senator Adams."

"What proof do you have?" John asked, intrigued.

"First, I want assurance I have immunity. My conversation with Agent Joie August cut short."

"We'll clear that up right now," John said, dialing a number in his cell phone. "Joie, this is John. You'll never guess who's with me right now!"

"Ah, is it Fred Reider?"

"Yes, but how did you know that?"

"Because he called from a number located inside your building. John, you're in serious trouble for aiding and abetting a criminal. My boss is talking about pressing other charges as well. What have you done?"

"I'm trying to help you. I'm also trying to make the election process fair! I would think you—"

Down the hall, the security door blew open by a small explosion, interrupting John. He opened the office door and peered down the hall in the direction of the explosion. Men in black suits and thick bulletproof jackets ran down the hall toward him, bearing the FBI insignia on their helmets and jackets. However, John wasn't buying it; Adams had the connections to send fakes.

He pulled out a concealed 9 mm with a silencer from a shoulder holster, then slammed the door shut, locked it, turned over a desk, and dragged Fred behind it. Suddenly the office door crashed open. A tear gas container hit the floor, spewing its contents into the room in less than a second. Simultaneously, a flashbang detonated, deafening them both. John and Fred struggled for breath, dazed by the shock of the explosion. They fell to the ground, neutralized. Seconds later, men covered with gas protective gear ran in. One stepped on John's chest and grabbed his weapon. Another dove onto Fred, trapping him on the floor.

Another man in black entered the room and picked up John's phone, reporting to Joie, who was still on the line, "We got 'em, Agent August. Thanks for the heads-up about Mr. Jacobson's military training. We took aggressive measures, but they're both fine. More importantly, so are we."

After a pause, the man in black said, "Sure, he's right here."

He handed the phone to John, and the other man removed his foot from John's chest. John put the phone to his still-ringing ear and choked, "Joie, what the hell?"

Mike Lundberg said, "This isn't Joie. Mr. Jacobson, I'll see you and Mr. Reider in my office in three hours. A chopper is on your roof. It will take you to Meacham Field. An FBI Learjet will bring you to Washington National Airport. Agents will bring you here to my office. Mr. Jacobson, you're in serious trouble. Don't add to it by resisting arrest!"

Agents read Fred and John their rights, put them in handcuffs, and walked them down the hall to the elevator. Employees peered out of offices and down the hall as the small army walked by. One spectator was John's boss, Robert Beyer. He came out of his office and demanded, "What the hell is going on, John?"

An agent looked at him blankly and said, "Mr. Jacobson is under arrest and has no comment."

They were soon inside the elevator and gone. Robert looked at the destroyed security door and the demolished office and wondered what the hell just happened to his best employee.

Chapter 21 ★ The Left Coast

THE GORGEOUS SUNSET OVER THE ocean west of San Francisco Bay went almost unnoticed as voters headed to the polls in record numbers. Two strangers stood in a queue in a precinct between Frisco and Oakland.

"Thank God California voters understand the issues and nullify the redneck states. Why can't they see the truth? We're the party of the people, not the rich," said one of them.

"Agreed, brother. The states that require IDs are bigots. Don't they know America is a great melting pot and includes those down on their luck, including illegal aliens, refugees, felons, the poor not trained to work, and so on? They need a helping hand."

"You're right. California's fifty-five electoral votes send a message to those conservative backward states. Putting entitlements over the deficit is the right thing to do."

"Couldn't agree more. San Francisco's progressive nature is the way of the future. As a proud sanctuary city, we set the trend."

"That's so true! Even the Kate Steinle verdict sent a message that illegal aliens have rights. They ought to have as many rights as US citizens!"

"I'm glad you know the truth. I belong to a national group representing the downtrodden. This morning, sanctuary cities such as LA, New York, Chicago, Baltimore, Miami, San Antonio, Phoenix, Denver, San Diego, and the inner cities of almost all the top twenty-five most populated cities sent a message through their votes that Senator Adams represents our noble cause."

"I know we're a sanctuary city, but I'm a little embarrassed that I don't know more about what that means."

"No reason to be embarrassed. I love telling others about it. 'Sanctuary city' is the name given to a city in the United States that shelters illegal immigrants. The procedures we use are laws and policies. We also block municipal funds applied to the enforcement of federal immigration laws."

"Huh? What does that mean?"

"Simply put, we don't permit authorities to inquire about a person's immigration status. You see, in 1996, Congress passed the Illegal Immigration Reform and Immigrant Responsibility Act requires local governments to cooperate with Department of Homeland Security's Immigration and Customs Enforcement Agency. However, we have hundreds of urban, sub-urban, and even some rural communities gallantly ignoring this legislation out of regard for the plight of our demoralized and oppressed illegal aliens."

"What about the argument that the very illegal immigrants, refugees, and felons we're protecting lead to the highest crime per capita in the country? In San Fran and Chicago, for instance. Not to mention we're being overrun with the homeless and drug addicts."

"That's just propaganda. However, even if it is true, doing the right thing is often difficult and worth the death of a few citizens for a virtuous purpose. Our cause is just like the Revolutionary War against the oppression of pow-ers trying to control us."

"Oh! In that case, I support our sanctuary city stance, too."

"Awesome. I've educated one more citizen concerning our mission."

Meanwhile, Los Angeles's polling places contained long lines of illegal aliens, thanks to the state policy that did not require voter IDs. There were also too many voters for Ronald Jackson in one large LA county precinct, so the warden called the provided 800 number and within thirty minutes the parking lot filled with violent organizations. Patches on their shoulders adorned with names such as the American Civil Liberties Union, the Anti-Defamation League, the Council for Secular Humanism, the Mainstream Coalition, and United for Peace and Justice.

Fred's wardens in the cities of San Diego and San Jose, the eighth and tenth largest cities in the US, used every voter fraud practice on the list—and a few more—and it all went unnoticed due to the predominant support for Senator Adams.

In Oregon and Washington, Virus A, Virus B, and the lack of voter ID restrictions worked exactly as designed. Alaska's three electoral votes succumbed to California's smallest cities, and Hawaii's conservative voters stayed home because the election was over before their voting places even opened.

Polling locations in all four time zones busily counted absentee and early voting ballots not requiring an ID. Many states did not check the mail-in or absentee ballot signatures against the voting roll signatures. Hundreds of thousands came from Senator Adams's henchman, who voted many times. Several states just happened to find unmarked boxes of mail-in ballots toward the end of the day in states where Adams was behind. Behind closed doors, ballots for Ronald Jackson were destroyed, and millions of illegal aliens with newly printed IDs voted in almost every state. The master plan worked!

***

Three hours after their arrest, John and Fred walked down the hall of FBI headquarters in handcuffs. Curious agents and staff watched them walk by surrounded by heavily armed police and FBI agents. Fred's fear and John's anger were each evident.

An FBI agent poked John to stop walking, and John's muscles flexed uncontrollably. He looked at the agent with such fury that the man backed off. Fred stopped, obeying the agent closest to him. The lead agent knocked on a door with the sign that read Sr. Special Agent Mike Lundberg. Moments later the door opened, and Agent Greg Elgen motioned for them to enter. The small army of agents, military weapons, and protective gear soon filled the office.

John looked for Joie, but she wasn't visible. Mike looked at the name tag of the agent who brought them in and calmly said, "You can remove the handcuffs, Agent Roberts."

"Are you sure?" Agent Roberts asked, looking at John's size and angry face.

"Yes, I'm sure. I have his kryptonite right over there," Mike said, pointing to the corner.

The sea of agents parted. There a woman stood dwarfed by nearby agents. She smiled at John, and John's anger diminished. His arms stopped flexing as his head lowered toward the floor.

"My God, she is Delilah to this Samson!" an agent joked, and every man laughed except for John and Fred.

Agent Roberts removed John's handcuffs and waited for an aggressive move. It didn't come. Another agent removed Fred's handcuffs, who sat down, wanting to get his jail sentence started. At least he might be safe from Gavin and the Hillton Boys this way.

The agents began filing out as Mike said, "I need you to remain, Agent Roberts, just in case."

Within moments, the only people in the room were Mike, Joie, Greg, Roberts, John, and Fred.

Mike spoke first. "Everyone sit down."

Everyone followed his direction except for Agent Roberts, who stood behind John ready to respond to unwanted hostility. He knew John's size, strength, and Special Forces training would allow him to eliminate everyone in the room in seconds—including him. Mike nodded to Agent Roberts in approval of his vigilant stance.

He then looked at John and Fred, saying, "Welcome to Washington, gentlemen. You've brought quite a bit of excitement to the election as well as to our lives. First, you're still under arrest, so anything you say can and will be used…"

By the time Mike finished reading their rights for the second time, John's devastation and feelings of betrayal overcame him. He looked at Joie several times, but she avoided eye contact.

"Do you both understand the rights I just read?" They nodded. "I need you to say yes or no out loud."

Fred and John simultaneously said, "Yes."

"OK, let's get started. I'll get to you in a moment, Mr. Reider. I'm going to begin with you, Mr. Jacobson."

John looked up in partial submission. "Yes?"

"What the hell were you thinking, aiding and abetting a known fugitive of the law?"

With his head still lowered, John said, "I was trying to do the right thing. I have information—"

Mike cut him off, saying, "Breaking several laws is not the way to do the right thing! You're facing serious charges now! I'll get back to you in a minute." He turned his attention to Fred. "Now let's talk about you."

Fred looked up, almost in tears, as Mike continued, "I understand you asked Agent August for protective custody and immunity from laws you've broken. I suppose you want this in exchange for information you have on bigger fish."

"Yes," Fred answered, shaking.

"And what is this supposed valuable information?"

"Evidence of several counts of voter fraud by Senator Adams."

"We've been after Senator Adams for years. What's this evidence that is so compelling that I would drop the many charges against you?"

"Can I reach into my pants pocket?" Fred asked sheepishly.

"Yes," Mike answered, motioning for Agent Roberts to watch him closely.

Agent Roberts put his hand on his weapon as Fred reached into his front left pocket. He withdrew a memory stick. Agent Roberts relaxed, and Fred handed it to Mike.

"What's this?" Mike asked curiously.

"It's two executable files."

"What kind of files?"

"They are viruses designed to change votes within voting machines all over America. I can prove what they're designed to do, and that they did, in fact, change votes in favor of Senator Adams."

"Holy crap," Joie whispered.

John smiled for the first time since the arrest.

"Can I reach into my other shirt pocket?" Fred asked again.

This time, Agent Roberts didn't flinch and seemed as curious as Mike was. Fred pulled out several sheets of paper folded in two. He handed it to

Mike. Joie and Greg leaned in closer. Whatever it was, John hoped it helped drop the charges against him.

"What's this?" Mike asked excitedly.

"They're outlines of the over twenty-five voting fraud methods used against specific weaknesses within state voting systems."

"Which states?"

"The twelve battleground states of Arizona, Colorado, Florida, Pennsylvania, New Hampshire, Ohio, Iowa, Virginia, Michigan, Minnesota, Nevada, and Wisconsin!"

It was Mike's turn to exclaim, "Holy crap!" He looked at the sheets and, without even looking up, said, "You may leave, Agent Roberts."

"Are you sure?" he asked, looking again at the huge John Jacobson.

"We'll be OK. We have Agent August, aka Delilah, aka Kryptonite, aka fiancée extraordinaire."

Agent Roberts looked at Joie. "I see your point. She can control me anytime."

John looked up at him with contempt. Agent Roberts noticed John's scowl, nodded at Mike, and left the room, glad to escape John's proximity.

Mike looked at Fred again. "You can prove these two digital viruses and eleven pages of voting fraud methods were actually used?"

"Absolutely."

"If you can prove it, you have your protective custody and immunity from all laws you broke related to the election. However, if you lie to me, or this evidence proves false, the deal is off. I'll personally prosecute you to the fullest extent of the law. Understood?

"Understood," Fred responded, calming down for the first time since his arrest, now four hours old.

"Let's discuss this in detail," Mike said to Fred.

"What about me? What about the charges against me?" John asked.

"If this stuff is for real, you'll receive thanks from a grateful nation. If not, you'll be getting out of jail sometime before your seventieth birthday," Mike said, not bothering to look up from the outlines.

Agent Elgen walked over to Mike and studied the pages as well. He asked, "Are you certain these voting fraud methods worked?"

"Sadly, yes. Most of the methods occur in every election, but we added a few more, including the two vote-swapping viruses. As far as I know, this is the first time a candidate led the process so overtly." Fred suddenly felt guilty for having taken part in them.

Mike, still not looking up, said, "Agent August. Please take Mr. Jacobson into your protective custody. You probably have things to discuss. Mr. Jacobson, you can't leave this building until I release you. Understood?"

"Yes," John responded, avoiding Joie's eyes.

Joie stood and took John by the hand, and he followed her toward the door like a one-ton bull led by a ten-year-old 4-H member. Agent Elgen couldn't help but snicker. John couldn't care less as he hopefully got closer to getting some answers.

* * *

The voter fraud committee gathered for the final time. The meeting took place in Scarlett's home in a remote upscale gated Leesburg community. The typical attendees were almost all present with the addition of a new guest—Luther East, the Virus B programmer. The only regular member missing was Fred.

They sat at a massive banquet table drinking expensive champagne and eating caviar, lobster, steak, and other delicacies prepared by a famous DC chef who served them personally before leaving the room.

At the end of the meal and the joyful celebration, Scarlett stood up. "I want to congratulate you all. I'm happy to say the viruses and voting fraud methods were so successful that we won almost all the battleground states! Therefore, Senator Adams asked me to pass on accolades. To show his appreciation, Senator Adams brought you all here for this feast at great expense, to reward you for your hard work and devotion to this critical project. When Senator Adams takes office, you'll know you played a significant role in the victory. America owes you a debt of gratitude. With that in mind, Senator Adams has a gift for each of you."

Scarlett stepped back as Gavin stepped forward with an automatic AR-15 and began firing. Bullets ripped through flesh like a knife slicing through a cantaloupe. The execution took less than ten seconds. No one escaped.

After the gory massacre, Scarlett told Gavin, fresh blood dripping from her hair and clothes, "Good job. Now find Fred. We must thank him too."

Gavin's bloodstained face took on a malicious smile, a combination of Heath Ledger's Joker and Jack Nicholson in *The Shining*. The demented smile even frightened Scarlett. *Will he ever smile over my corpse like that?* she wondered.

***

News services reported cases of voter fraud in all fifty states, but especially the battleground states. By midnight on the east coast, news services around the world announced Senator Adams as the president-elect. Half of them displayed the new title in lower case, as they believed it had perhaps been acquired through alleged voter fraud and not won fairly. They knew it but just couldn't prove it.

Liberal news networks ignored the voter fraud reports and joyfully announced Senator Adams as the winner and next president of the United States. However, conservative reporters hoping for a Pulitzer went to work in earnest!

PART V ★ LOSING GROUND

Chapter 22 ★ Poof

JOIE LED JOHN DOWN THE hall to a vacant office, turned on the light, and closed the door. As soon as it clicked shut, she dove into his arms. He pushed her away, saying, "Bringing us in like common criminals was a little uncalled for, wasn't it?"

"John, you *are* a criminal in the eyes of the law! We went easy on you. Agent Lundberg offers you immunity for prosecuting the president-elect. But so many things could go wrong, and you face many serious charges."

"I agree, but how were you easy on me? Your agents tear-gassed me and dragged me here in handcuffs. He either drops the charges, or I won't tell him what I know."

"John, sweetie, regardless of what you think, you're not able to bargain. The FBI has the power to put you in jail for the rest of your life."

She kissed him softly, and his rough exterior softened a little. He kissed her back, and soon they were in a passionate embrace. She reached down and felt his hardness, then began stroking him. He reached inside her blouse, feeling her firm breasts and hardening nipples. Within seconds, John was compliant.

"I have a question," John said, panting.

"Yes?" Joie asked, stroking him faster and breathing heavy. This continued until he exploded in climax, and she slowly regained composure.

John's breathing slowed enough to ask, "How did you know about Fred? I thought I was ahead of you."

Joie buttoned her blouse, saying, "Well, besides the obvious answer—*I'm with the FBI*—you gave us Luther East's name, the Fair Game programmer. We pressured him, threatening prosecution for vote fixing. Of course, it was a bluff, because he didn't really know what the virus was for. Fred called me soon after. From there it took us two seconds to find him via his phone's GPS. Now, let me ask you a question: How did Fred end up with you?"

"Pretty much the same way. Luther East told Fred about me and my suspicions about the program, so he called me. He flew down to DFW, and we went back to my office. Then your goons brought us here."

"John, they're not goons. They're FBI agents."

"They could have talked to us rather than assault and arrest us."

"I know you, John. If they just interviewed you, you would have told them just enough to appease them. Then you and Fred would try to take on the world by yourselves. You're not one to play it safe. But John, this isn't a game."

"To me, it is," John replied flatly.

"Well, it's not. Besides serious charges against you, murders occur when people challenge Senator Adams."

"OK, Joie. I'll back off since you're asking, not because I'm scared."

Joie rolled her eyes in resignation. "OK, Mr. Neanderthal, let's go back to Agent Lundberg's office."

"OK, but our session is not over. I plan on satisfying you physically like you just did for me," John said seductively.

"It's a date, John," she replied as they entered Mike's office. Mike, Greg, and Fred were talking about the evidence Fred provided. The two of them sat down and listened.

Mike was asking, "So, the ten largest counties in the twelve battleground states each had a warden on the payroll, right?"

"Yes."

"Did the clerks and inspectors know about this?"

Fred responded, "Only a few in each precinct knew. Wardens handpicked them. We instructed the wardens about what to do and to direct their staff to accomplish the task in such a way that most didn't know about our voter fraud activities."

"Well, that's too bad. But we still have a hundred wardens, and many clerks and inspectors who can testify, right?"

"Yes. However, I told them to destroy the outlines and the envelopes they came in. They also should have removed the two viruses from the systems and gotten rid of the memory sticks they came on."

"So, what proof do we have, other than your testimony, your outlines, and your memory stick with the viruses?"

"We can get the testimony of Todd Shamer, the state weakness approach designer. We can also force a confession out of Lizzy Warden, the polling expert for the president-elect."

Mike printed their names and handed the note to Greg Elgen so he could track them down.

"What else do you have as evidence?"

"You heard about the supposed Russian hack of voter databases?"

"Yes, we listened to the live report."

"Well, it wasn't the Russians. It was me."

Mike, looking confused, asked, "You breached the state systems and stole two hundred thousand voter records in Illinois and Arizona?"

"Yes, but we also stole millions more from other states."

"With what purpose?"

"Simple. We give the voter fraud methods to those favoring Senator Adams. For instance, voters could use the data to vote for inactive voters in all states without strict voter ID laws."

"Shit. How much of the data did you use?" Greg asked.

"There's no way to tell. That's the beauty of the methods we put in place—they're virtually undetectable. Of course, the lack of voter ID laws in many of the states allows, if not encourages, voter fraud. Mail-in votes are a joke. There's no way to verify ID."

"Damn! That's unreal. So, if we can't use that as evidence, what else do you have?" Mike asked, sounding despondent.

"My cell phone has proof of the phone calls with the wardens."

"Where is it?"

"It's back in John's office. You guys dragged me here before I could grab it."

Mike commanded, "Greg, call the FBI in Dallas. Have them go to Fort Worth and get Debbie Stevens, John's secretary, to let them into John's office to fetch Fred's phone."

"You know my secretary's name?" John asked.

"We know everything about you, John. Not only did we investigate you, but I believe you know your fiancée works for me," Mike said with a smug smile.

"Good point." John looked at Joie, betrayed. Joie frowned and looked away.

"What else do we have?" Mike asked Fred.

"We also have the testimony of Luther East, the Virus B programmer."

"Right. Greg, get the FBI agents who go to John's office to also interview Mr. East about what he knows."

"He didn't know what the virus was for," Fred said, and John nodded in agreement.

"No, but it's just one more piece of the puzzle. The more we have, the more compelling the case is to the courts."

"Do we have anything else?" Mike asked Fred, John, and Joie.

Fred replied, "We can't prove anything about Virus A, because we only put it on the voting machines without a paper trail to indicate who the voter actually voted for. So, if the wardens removed it as instructed, there's no proof. However, Virus B converts a small percentage of the votes in favor of the president-elect. We can compare the original scanned voter data with the voter data received at the state level."

"Does that really prove a virus did it? Wouldn't it just look like a computer glitch?"

"Yes! That was the objective of the virus! It's based upon a design from an old patent used in the oil field. A Mr. Ray August owned it, but we updated it with modern technology." Fred smiled in response.

Joie stood up. "Ray August? Are you sure?"

"Yes, I'm sure. Luther East brought it to my attention. He also mentioned he discussed it with John's boss."

"Oh really?" Joie said, putting her hands on her hips and glaring at John.

"Babe, let's talk about that later. OK?"

"Trust me, we will."

Mike cut in. "Mr. Reider! You frickin' conspired to manipulate voter results, potentially affecting the outcome of the general election race. Are you pleased with yourself? Wipe that smile off your face!" he roared.

"No, I'm ashamed. That's why I'm here."

"No, you're here because you tried to escape the animals searching for you! You're here because I sent agents to drag your sorry ass here in hand-cuffs," Mike thundered.

Fred hung his head, and Mike looked at John. "That goes for you too. Understood?"

John clenched his fist, and Joie put her hand on his shoulder. She was still mad but knew she had to calm him down. He acquiesced and looked down at the floor.

Mike, confident that his prisoners were under control, continued, "Do we have anything else?"

Fred thought for a moment and said, "I have emails and other documents on my computer in my DC office just across the river."

Mike looked at Greg, who made a note to pick it up.

Greg looked at his notes. "We have Fred's phone and computer. We can probably get the wardens and Luther East to confess in exchange for immunity if they testify against the designers of the plan. We may be able to prosecute Scarlett Schuller, Todd Shamer, and Lizzy Warden. However, the outlines and viruses may no longer exist in the precincts."

Joie stood up abruptly and looked down at Greg's notes. She read them slowly before saying, "Scarlett Schuller? Are you sure of the name?"

Fred answered for Greg, "Yeah, that's her name. Why?"

Joie looked at John, then over to Mike before saying, "Mike, we need to talk in the hall."

Mike walked into the hall with Joie, closing the door behind them. Joie looked up and down the hall before saying, "Mike, I need to disclose that I know Scarlett Schuller."

"How do you know her?"

Joie whispered into Mike's ear, and his expression turned to one of shock.

"She's your what?!" Mike practically screamed.

Joie nodded slowly.

Mike thought for a moment before saying, "OK. OK. You need to recuse yourself from the aspects of the case that have dealings with her. Let the rest of the team oversee her."

"Will do, boss. Can we go back to the meeting?"

"Yes, we better. But first, what was the conversation about Ray August?"

"He's my father. But I assure you, just like Fred said, the new component was just based upon one of his old patents. He died when I was young. He has nothing to do with this—I promise!"

"Any other revelations?" Mike asked, half afraid of the answer.

"No! I swear."

"I hope not," Mike said as he opened the door, still in shock.

They walked back in just as John was asking, "What's the challenge of prosecuting Senator Adams?"

"It depends on tying all this to the president-elect," Mike responded, sitting again behind his desk.

After a few moments of contemplation, Mike said, "Greg, put Fred in protective custody and start the paperwork on Fred's and John's immunity in exchange for their testimony. John, you are in Joie's custody. I assume that meets with your approval?"

"Yes," John said with a smirk.

This annoyed Mike. "Am I going to have any trouble with you, big boy? If you show any resistance or attitude, I'll put you in jail until you testify. Do I make myself clear?"

"Yes, sir," John replied, dropping the smile in sincere submission.

"Is there anything else?" Mike asked looking at the others.

"Yes. What about Gavin Principle?" Fred asked.

"Who?" Mike asked.

"He's Scarlett's muscle. He killed a few members of the team and terrorized the rest of us to comply with her orders."

He made a note of the name and handed it to Greg, saying, "Get all the information you can on Mr. Principle before our next meeting."

"Anything else?" Mike asked once again, looking at them all. Everyone shook their heads. "Get to work, then."

Greg led Fred away, John left with Joie, and Mike made notes about next moves.

* * *

Scarlett met Gavin in her DC office. "The FBI arrested Fred Reider and John Jacobson in Fort Worth. They're here in DC now. Find and eliminate them. We can't have them walking around," she instructed, tense.

"That's a tall order if they're in the custody of the FBI," Gavin said impassively.

"Do what you can. You have the Hillton Boys at your disposal."

"OK. What about the wardens? They know about the voter fraud as well."

"That's taken care of. I paid them double to deny everything. They also know that if they fail to comply, you'll pay them a visit. They confirmed they destroyed the outlines and viruses."

"Cool. Seems like you've thought of everything."

"I hope so."

Gavin looked at her through lifeless eyes and warned, "By the way, if you plan on 'taking care' of me, too, just remember I've got the Hillton Boys under my charge. They only obey me. If I disappear, so will you. Got it?"

Scarlett responded without batting an eyelid, "And I have the president-elect on my side. They work for him, just like you. Do you think they'd side with you if President-Elect Adams offered one of them a million to take you out? No, you'd be dead in hours no matter how far you run. Got it?"

Gavin grinned. "I'll kill Reider and Jacobson. Don't make it a bonus by tempting me to kill you too."

"It's fair to say we're in this together and don't need to threaten each other. We're partners," Scarlett said, forcing a smile.

Gavin nodded and walked out of her office to pursue his mission. Scarlett got on the phone to take care of other loose ends. She hoped Gavin wouldn't be one of them.

***

Two days later—most of which John and Joie spent in bed while Greg spent it conducting the various points of the investigation—the team met again in Mike's office. In addition to Mike, Greg, Fred, Joie, and John, another agent was also present.

"Let's get started. First, who's our guest?" Mike asked, looking at the stranger.

Greg said, "This is Agent Baker. He has information for us—bad information."

"What's that?" Mike asked, shaking his hand.

Agent Baker replied, "Agent Elgen gave me instructions after your last meeting. I called the FBI in Dallas to acquire Mr. Reider's phone in Mr. Jacobson's office. It's gone!"

"Gone? It was on my desk," John said emphatically.

"It's gone, and your office is trashed," Agent Baker replied calmly.

"Damn!" John whispered.

"Also, agents here in DC went to Mr. Reider's office to get his computer. It's gone, too, and the office demolished."

"What?" Fred asked in shock.

"Yep. We also called half of the wardens on the list, and all of them denied any knowledge of Mr. Reider or his plans."

"The sons of bitches!" Mike replied.

"Ready for the really shocking news?" Agent Baker asked.

"Holy crap, what else could possibly go wrong?" Joie asked.

"Yesterday, local authorities found the bodies of Lizzy Warden, Todd Shamer, Luther East, and four others in a dumpster just off VA-7 in Sterling, Virginia."

"Shit!" Mike cursed under his breath.

"Where's Sterling, Virginia?" John asked.

"Halfway between Leesburg and DC," Joie replied.

He shot back, "Where does Scarlett live?"

"We don't know," Greg replied, making a note to check.

"I know where she lives," Joie added softly.

"Where?" Mike demanded.

"Leesburg."

"How do you know that?" John asked, shocked.

She whispered, "I'll tell you later."

"Any more unwelcome news?" Mike asked, afraid of the answer.

"Just one more tidbit. We identified Gavin Principle."

"Who is he?"

"He's an ex-CIA operative. He used to do wet work for the agency."

"Wet work?" Joie asked.

"Assassination," John responded, deep in thought.

"Good God! An assassin? That's all we need. Do we have anything left of value in our voter fraud investigation?"

"Can't think of a thing," Greg responded.

Chapter 23 ★ The Case

"YOU'LL STAY WITH ME TWENTY-FOUR seven. It'll be too easy for the Hillton Boys to kill you in jail," Greg said to Fred.

"Sounds good to me. But you know I live in DC, right? I could stay at home. I doubt they know where I live."

"Just how stupid are you? Of course, they know where you live," Greg said, shocked at his naiveté. "It's going to be tough to keep you alive unless you listen to me. There's a trail of death following President-Elect Adams. Hell, we have two file cabinets full of victims. I don't want to add you to those."

"Me neither. I'll do what you say."

"Good. You may just make it out of this alive. Don't forget Lizzy Warden, Todd Shamer, and Luther East. You would've been in that dumpster, too, if we hadn't protected you."

They drove to Agent Greg Elgen's house at eight p.m. Greg parked in the driveway and said, "Wait here. Don't get out of the car for any reason. I'll be right back."

A policeman and Greg walked through the dark to his front door. Greg unlocked the front door, and the police officer slipped in the front door without a sound. Fred watched from the car and saw lights come on one room at a time. Fred watched cars drive by and ensured none stopped. One drove by slowly but kept moving. The driver was a medium-sized person looking at each house slowly. *Maybe they're just looking for a friend's house*, Fred thought. He hoped so.

The police officer gave a thumbs-up, and Greg walked out to the car and motioned for Fred to follow. Greg looked up and down the street once again as they walked in the house. The police officer left. Greg took Fred to a hall and opened the second door.

"You stay in here. If you're hungry, there are leftovers in the fridge. I think they're still good," Greg said, pointing toward the kitchen.

"Thanks, Agent Elgen. I'm just tired. I'm not used to this secret agent stuff. I'm going to bed."

"OK, I'm in the room right next to you. If you need anything, just knock on the wall or come over. Knock on the door, though. If you charge in, I may shoot you if I'm half asleep."

"I'll try to remember that. OK, night. Thanks for everything."

"You're welcome. It's part of the job."

They went into their separate rooms and closed the doors. Fred heard Greg's TV at a low volume and slipped under the covers. He was asleep in minutes. It was the end of a long day.

Fred woke with a start around two a.m. Had he heard a shot? Something was wrong. The window was partially open. The curtains blew in the light breeze. He nervously looked around the room trying to make out each shadow and piece of furniture. Fred sat up and knocked on the wall. He didn't hear movement in the next room.

Fred heard fighting outside his window. He got out of bed and looked outside to see two men trading punches and kicks. He couldn't tell who was prevailing. One man was larger, but the other was faster. The large man hit the smaller man hard, and he went down before coming up with a knife. The smaller man lunged, and the larger man kicked the knife out of his hand. The smaller man jumped in the air and kicked the larger man in the face. He went down hard.

Suddenly a third person sprinted toward them from the flank and drew a black Glock .45 Cal. It fired, and the smaller man flew backward. However, he got up and ran for the road. The gun went off again as he disappeared into the night.

Fred turned on the lights and opened the door just as a huge man limped to the front door holding his stomach and bleeding from his nose, mouth, and left ear.

The large man gathered himself and grabbed Fred, mumbling, "Let's go!"

Fred resisted until he finally recognized John in the light of the hall. Joie was at the front door.

"What's going on?" Fred asked, stressed out of his mind.

"I'll tell you after we're out of here," John returned, looking in every direction.

Joie opened the door and peered outside with her .45 Cal drawn. John covered her from behind. "It's clear. Follow me," Joie said calmly.

"To the ends of the earth, babe," John responded, equally calm.

They made their way to a car in front of the house on the road. John opened the back door for Fred. There was a large lump in the back seat under a cover. John ran around the car to the driver's door. Joie jumped in the passenger side, and they were gone.

Joie pulled a siren out of her purse, reached through the open window, and placed it on the hood. As it sounded, blue and red lights began to rotate. Fred looked at the lump beside him—it was Greg. His eyes closed and breathed heavily through his mouth. He was alive.

"What happened back there?" Fred asked loudly above the blaring siren.

John replied, "Gavin tried to kill you. He was almost inside your window when I grabbed him. We fought. Agent Elgen came outside to help and caught a kick in the face. I think he'll be OK."

"Why were you there?" Fred asked.

"To save your frickin' ass! It was Mike's idea to stake out the house. Gavin got away, though. He's skilled to escape Joie and I. Gavin's a fast little bastard. When we fought, I could feel his flak jacket. The two bullets struck him in the chest, so he'll hurt like hell, but the bullets probably didn't seriously wound him. He was like a ghost. I hit him hard, though. He'll have a shiner in the morning," John said quietly.

They drove to the hospital and dropped off Agent Elgen, who was still struggling to breathe. Next, they drove to Joie's apartment and put Fred on the couch, heading for the bedroom themselves to get a few hours' sleep.

"Will I be OK out here?" Fred asked.

"We gotcha. This is our domicile. The last two guys who tried something here are in the morgue," John responded nonchalantly.

It bothered Joie that John still saw all this as a game, but at the same time, it was one of the reasons she loved him.

They slept three hours before going back to the FBI building. John, Joie, and Fred went to Mike's office, and hot coffee was waiting for them. Agent Stevens sat in the corner as Mike asked everyone, "How was last night?"

"It was fine," John answered quickly.

"That's not what I heard," Mike responded, unsatisfied with the answer.

"Fred is OK, as you can see, and Agent Elgen should be fine," Joie responded quietly.

"How the hell did Gavin get away?"

John replied, "Because he's a trained frickin' CIA assassin with Army Ranger training. He's as good as me. Maybe better!"

The concern on John's face betrayed his anxiety. He finally faced a man with his level of skills.

Mike took note of his demeanor and decided to get down to work. "Alright, we have three cases against President-Elect Adams. We have Cyber-Hider, Dreams International, and Fair Game. Joie, let's start with you on Cyber-Hider. You've been investigating for weeks. What do you have?"

"As you know, there are a multitude of potential Cyber-Hider charges we considered. But the only charges we have enough evidence to move forward with are two misdemeanors including mishandling of classified documents and deleting government documents without authority. President-Elect Adams clearly broke those two laws. But, being misdemeanors, would the AG be interested in spending time and taxes pursuing them? I doubt it."

"I agree," Mike said, and Greg nodded.

"However, the felony charge of conspiracy to conceal documents from government computers is much more serious. We also have the evidence necessary to file the charge with the DOJ. This comes with a three-year jail sentence and would disqualify the candidate from taking office."

"Excellent! Prepare the charges and attach the associated evidence.

Excellent job, Joie. You have earned the title of Madam Foci."

"You got it, boss," Joie responded, silently regretting ever using the term.

As Joie finished briefing progress on Cyber-Hider, Greg knocked and slowly walked in. His swollen face bore a distended and covered nose, and he sported bandages on his jaw and puffy eyes. The others stared at him as he found a chair and breathed through his mouth with a grimace.

"Damn, Greg. What are you doing here? You look like shit," Mike said, his face twisting in empathy.

"You should see the other guy," Greg said, attempting a smile and jerking from the pain.

"Unless he's dead, he won," Joie returned.

Greg smirked and once again immediately stopped due to the pain in his swollen face.

John put his hand on his shoulder and said, "He got the best of me, too. Don't let these idiots get to you."

Fred simply said, "Thanks, Greg. I'd be dead without you."

"You're welcome," Greg responded nasally.

Mike asked Greg, "What's your condition? How did you get out of the hospital?"

"I have a broken nose, fractured jaw, and damaged left eye. I got out because I left between nursing shifts and after the doctor left for golf."

"In all seriousness, my friend, no one would blame you to take a few days off," Mike said compassionately.

"No, I want to be part of the team that finally brings justice to President-Elect Adams."

"In that case, can you brief us on Dreams International?" Mike asked.

"You bet," Greg said, pulling a file out of his briefcase.

He continued despite his obvious pain and clenched-shut jaw. It affected his voice and movements, but he began, "Our case is growing stronger because the press and Congress are pressing the president-elect harder. We may have enough for a supine for some of the charges. First, I think we can forget the charges involving tax evasion, nondisclosure of foreign fund donation, and incomplete disclosure of recipients. The president-elect closed those potential areas of illegality through data released to the press and smart lawyers. Besides, it's difficult to prove because Dreams International is not releasing data on funds they gave to the president-elect."

"Agreed. Go on."

"However, the four charges I recommend we move forward with are bribery, criminal racketeering, charity not acting in the best interest of a business or individual, and misuse of charitable donations. I believe we can prove those with further investigation and a supine of Dream International's records."

"Isn't 'charity acting in the best interest of a business or individual' a misdemeanor and the others, felonies?"

"Yes."

"Then drop the misdemeanor and pursue the three felonies."

"Makes sense. Will do, boss."

"Excellent, Greg and Joie. I think we're ready to prepare charges for Cyber-Hider and Dreams International. Please take the lead on that. Greg, pass off as much as you need to heal."

"Will do, Mike," Greg said, breathing through his mouth.

"That brings us to you, Fred. Let's review what we have on Fair Game."

Taking a deep breath, Fred said, "Well, I'm not an attorney, so I'll need help knowing what we can prosecute or not. However, here goes: The evidence we lost are my phone, computer, and witnesses Lizzy Warden, Todd Shamer, Luther East. Also, the wardens destroyed their copies of the outlines and viruses. In addition, they must have accepted a bribe. They all said they don't know anything about it. Finally, there's no proof of Virus A in voter data because it was only on computers without a paper trail."

"Damn. Is there any good news?" Mike asked.

"Kind of. We have *my* copies of the outlines and two virus files. Also, remember we only used Virus B on scanned data from the battleground state precincts into each state election headquarters."

"How does that help?" Mike asked. Agent Stevens leaned forward with interest.

"Because we used that virus only in the states of Arizona, Colorado, Florida, Pennsylvania, New Hampshire, Ohio, Iowa, Virginia, Michigan, Minnesota, Nevada, and Wisconsin."

"So?" Agent Stevens prompted.

"Because I bet the percentage of votes not agreeing with the paper trail is three to four percent higher than in the other thirty-eight states, statistically speaking, the chances of only the states we worked with exceeding the other states in vote data discrepancies by that magnitude are millions to one."

"I like it," Mike said, and Agent Steven nodded in agreement.

"I'll begin working with state election headquarters to examine the data," Fred said.

"You'll need a warrant allowing you to look at the data. Agent Roberts, get one from Judge White. The conservative party appointed him, and he hates President-Elect Adams."

"You got it, boss," Agent Roberts answered, making a note.

At 4:25 sharp, John said, "I gotta go. I have something important to do."

"More important than the case?" Mike asked.

"No, but important to Joie and me," John said, standing and heading for the door. He winked at Joie, who nodded back in approval.

When John reached the hall, he pulled out his cell phone and called a number in his contacts. After a moment he said, "Boss, this is John. I'll be here in DC longer that I thought. I'm almost out of vacation, but I have critical tasks to accomplish. What do I do?"

Robert replied quickly, "John, you realize we work for a government contractor, right? Most of our contracts are with the DOD, DOS, DOJ, and DOC. When I told the president of the Aerospace Division what you were doing, he appeared stunned. He said it would be bad for business to take on President-Elect Adams and Washington insiders. You also left here in cuffs in front of the entire office. However, when I reminded him, we were also Americans trying to do the right thing for our country, he softened a little. I'm still working on him. In the meantime, charge your time to the division overhead account. I'll sign your time sheets. Let's see how that goes."

"Thanks, boss. I love my job and working for you. I want to retire with Pseudomics; I hope I have the opportunity. By the way, go navy!"

"Eat shit and die. Go army!" Robert returned.

John hung up smiling and headed for his second appointment. His life depended on it.

Chapter 24 ★ The Evidence

MIKE, GREG, JOIE, AND AGENT Baker reviewed the evidence before them. There were three neat piles on Mike's desk. "Let's summarize the evidence," he started.

"Already done," Joie said, connecting her computer to an overhead projector. Agent Baker dimmed the lights as Joie continued, "These bullet points encapsulate the evidence."

The slide read:

Cyber-Hider—

- Felony charge of *conspiracy to conceal documents from government computers*
- 35 counts of *perjury* to Congress and the FBI (separate charges documented in the evidence, including knowing what "C" meant in the header of documents)
- 3 counts of *obstruction of justice* for:
    - Planting questions with the congressional investigation
    - Deleting thousands of documents after the announcement of an FBI investigation
    - Destroying 14 phones, 1 laptop, 2 memory sticks, and 5 iPads after being notified about the FBI investigation

Dreams International—

- 3 felonies:
  - *Bribery*
  - *Criminal racketeering*
  - *Misuse of charitable donations*

Fair Game—

- 13 felonies:
  - Voter ID fraud
  - Tampering with voting machines
  - Misuse of proxy ballots
  - Misuse of provisional ballots
  - Misuse of absentee ballots
  - Misuse of early voting ballots
  - Voting for inactive voters
  - Illegal destruction of ballots
  - Illegal invalidation of ballots
  - Illegal protests at polling places
  - Vote buying
  - Misinformation to confuse voters
  - Voter manipulation

Staggered by the list of voter fraud felonies, Mike whistled. "Damn. I knew there were several potential charges, but when you see them together, it's stunning."

Greg continued, "You're right, boss, but now let's talk about which ones we can prove. With an unlimited budget, I believe we could prove them all by interviewing the one hundred counties we focused on. Keep in mind, they all had many polling places each, so we're talking about thousands of locations and tens of thousands poll place officers, wardens, clerks, inspectors, and volunteers."

"I see your point," Mike said.

"So, let's reduce the list to the ones we have the time and the budget to pursue. Let's take them up one at a time."

"Good idea. Proceed," Mike responded, ready to peruse the charges.

Greg began, "Voter ID fraud is too vague a charge and is hard to prove. I sincerely hope states will implement a stricter check on voter IDs. Tampering with voting machines is a go thanks to the copy of Virus B we have on my memory stick and the voting data I'll compare against the ballots. We can also use the evidence we have concerning Dominion voting machines."

"OK good. What's next?" Mike asked.

"Misuse of proxy ballots is hard to prove. I hope states are more careful about that in future elections. Misuse of provisional ballots is the same. Misuse of absentee ballots—same. Misuse of early voting ballots—same. Voting for inactive voters is a go. It was so pervasive in this election. We'll focus on the one hundred precincts with voters that haven't voted in more than ten years but magically showed up for this election. I know we can get thousands of statements from them."

"How do you contact them all?"

"Agents are already calling them one by one. We've covered hundreds already."

"Good job. What's next?"

"Illegal destruction of ballots is a *no*, because even if we email all the poll workers and ask if they saw this, it'll be one worker's word over another's. This would probably be expensive and unsuccessful. Illegal invalidation of ballots—same. Illegal protests at polling places are a go, because I already called the authorities in some of the larger precincts, and none of them gave permits for protests at polling places."

"Good, it sounds like you're proceeding with the charges we can prove. Any more charges to cover?" Mike asked.

"Just three. Vote buying is a *no* because the voters paid to vote would have to self-incriminate. Misinformation to confuse voters is too subjective and hard to prove; what's clear to one person may be confusing to another, so that's a no. Voter manipulation is too hard to prove. Thoughts?"

After a moment, Mike replied, "I believe your reasoning is sound, and you're the expert. I say we pursue the ones you suggest. What do you need?"

"I need at least ten junior agents to pursue three felony changes for tampering with voting machines, voting fraud, and illegal protests at polling places. We'll have to make a shitload of more calls and send emails to polling place personnel, and maybe even make a few trips to interview wardens willing to help us."

"You got it. Greg, do the paperwork needed to acquire additional junior agent assistance. I'll work on approving the budget. Fred, you just secured immunity. Excellent job, Greg and Fred!"

"Thanks, Mike. It's nice working for the good guys for a change," Fred responded.

"Welcome to the team, Fred. OK, everyone, get busy. We have a lot of work to do to acquire the evidence we need for each of these charges! Let's meet in my office every morning at eight thirty to discuss progress." Everyone nodded in agreement and headed out to do the work assigned to them.

Agents Greg and Roberts helped Fred with the legal points he wasn't familiar with. The hours and days slipped by in a flurry of activity. Powerful testimonies as well as evidence rolled in. The case against President-Elect Adams became more compelling by the hour, and the team met daily to discuss progress and share where they needed help. They built an undeniably formidable case—they had the president-elect dead to rights!

Every day at 4:30 p.m., John disappeared for about an hour. Only Joie seemed to know where he went. No one asked, but Mike's concern was obvious.

Two weeks later, the team reviewed the charges and spent time making their last-minute changes. After seeing the strength of the case, Mike said, "Greg, please make an appointment with Deputy Director Hermenez."

"I already have, knowing it would take weeks to get on his schedule. It's set for tomorrow," Greg answered.

"Tomorrow? My God! Why didn't you tell us?" Mike asked, panicking.

Greg smiled, still breathing through only one nostril. "Because I didn't want this reaction!"

Mike grinned, saw his point, and said, "OK, you son of a bitch."

"Takes one to know one," Greg retorted with a smirk.

"Everyone, take the afternoon off, get some sleep, and prepare yourselves to impress Deputy Director Hermenez."

Fred left with John and Joie, as he'd been staying with them ever since the incident with Gavin. Greg and Agent Baker left together to discuss their presentation one last time.

Still in his office, Mike examined the evidence again and used the "Notes View" to add comments, explanations, observations, and clarifications to the PowerPoint presentation. He worked until 9 p.m. and then finally left the office, satisfied they were ready.

Mike drove toward home and waved off the police escort car assigned to him. It followed anyway, as their superiors ordered. However, an armed robbery was soon in progress close by, and the escort ordered to respond. Another cruiser several miles away would take at least ten minutes to arrive.

Meanwhile, a dark sedan followed behind Mike and drew closer when the police cruiser left. After the third turn, Mike noticed the headlights in his rearview mirror. When just a mile from home, he turned away from his house, and the car followed closer.

Mike pressed the phone button on his steering wheel and said, "Call Agent August, home." The phone rang and went to voicemail. He hung up and pressed the button again. "Call Agent August, mobile."

The phone rang, and Joie finally answered. "Agent August. Can I help you?"

"Yes, you can. I'm being followed."

"Where are you?"

"Heading west on Constitutional Avenue, just two blocks from Fourteenth Street. I'm passing the Smithsonian Museum of Art."

"OK, I'll call the police. John and I are on our way. Are you in your Lexus GS?"

"Yes, but don't come. Protect Fred. This may be a ruse to get to him."

"He's with us. We're in the car and headed your way already. Be there in ten to twelve minutes."

"I said no! Just call the police."

"And I said I already called the police, and I'm on the way. Be there in nine minutes. Fire me tomorrow if you want. Can you lose them?"

"I'll try," Mike responded, knowing better than to argue with Agent August when she was determined.

Mike sped up, but the dark sedan stayed with him. He took three quick turns and the car continued to close on him. He called Joie again and said, "I'm on Independence Avenue."

"Go to Raoul Wallenberg Place and take a left between the two federal buildings."

"Will do. They're almost on my bumper, and I'm driving at fifty miles an hour through semi-dense traffic. I'll be there if I survive," Mike said, hoping his joke wasn't prophetic.

Three minutes later, Mike took the left Joie described. Up ahead there was a sea of police cars with their lights rotating. The sedan following his car slowed, then continued down to Raoul Wallenberg Place and disappeared. Mike pulled up to the first police car and got out. The officer asked, "Are you FBI Agent Lundberg?"

"Yes, thanks for the army," he said, looking at the host of local police, sheriff, and state police cars.

"No problem. Agent August filled us in. Happy to help."

"Where is Agent August?" Mike asked.

"Beats me. She asked us to meet you here. She didn't say where she'd be."

"Shit. I bet I know where she is!"

"Where's that?" the officer asked.

"Right behind the car that was following me!"

"Should we pursue?" the officer asked.

"No. A small army couldn't do what she and John can."

"John who?"

"John 'the frickin' Giant Killer' Jacobson. That's who."

The two officers looked at each other and shrugged. One asked, "Are you OK now? We've got a city to protect."

"Yep, I'm fine. Thanks, officer. Please thank the rest of them for me."

"Will do."

The police car pulled away and a voice came over its loudspeaker. "We can go now. The FBI can fend for itself for five minutes without us."

Mike laughed and gave him the finger in jest. The officer returned the gesture, only partially kidding.

***

The dark sedan drove onto Maine Avenue and headed southwest. Soon, they were on I-395 S. When they passed Crystal City, they pulled off on a side street and stopped to get orders from the boss. The driver dialed the dreaded person's number.

After they picked up, the driver said, "We tried taking out Agent Lundberg, but suddenly police cars surrounded us. He must have seen us."

The voice responded, "How could you blow that?"

The driver closed his eyes. "We'll have another chance. We'll get him."

"You had your chance! I should have done it myself, rather than send the second string."

"You want us to get Agent August instead?"

"No, go back to your other assignment. Agent August and her fiancé are mine," Gavin said, hanging up.

The driver hung up and looked at the passenger. Suddenly his eyes grew big. Outside the passenger window was a gun—a big handgun!

"Damn! What the hell?"

The gun tapped on the window. The passenger held up one hand and hit the electric window button with the other. As the window lowered, the gun pushed in and touched the man's temple. The driver slowly reached down to his weapon on the front seat. He heard a tap on his window and saw another handgun. This was even bigger than the first.

"Shit," he whispered, raising one hand and lowering his window with the other.

"Get out slowly," John said to the driver.

"You too, Tonto," Joie told the passenger.

They both slowly opened their doors and exited, hands in the air.

"Go to the hood," Joie commanded.

They leaned on the hood and spread their legs, knowing the routine.

Joie holstered her weapon and asked, "You got 'em, partner?"

"Yep," John replied, concentrating on the two hardened criminals in front of him.

Joie searched the first one, and he whispered, "Take your time on my crotch, honey."

"Hey," John warned, tapping his head with his .50 caliber Desert Eagle.

He quickly shut up, and Joie searched the second one. As she turned, he grabbed her, whipped her around, and trapped her in a perfect neck hold with his forearms.

"I'll snap her neck unless you drop the cannon," he threatened John.

John began lowering his weapon as the other man approached him. Just as he had his hand on John's weapon, Joie stamped on the driver's foot so hard that she heard his toes crunch. He doubled over, and Joie whirled around and kicked him in the nuts. He fell to his knees. Simultaneously, John brought the huge grip of his weapon up, hitting the other man in the jaw. Blood spurted from his broken jaw and smashed teeth. The man grabbed his bleeding jaw and fell to his knees as well.

Joie called 911, and sirens approached within minutes. Two police cars pulled up and officers jumped out. John and Joie set their weapons on the car hood, then Joie identified herself and showed her badge and FBI ID. In moments, they handcuffed and arrested the two injured men. While an officer put them in the back seat of a patrol car, the other officer pointed and said, "If you're Agent August, you must be John 'the frickin' Giant Killer' Jacobson."

Joie rolled her eyes as John said, "I like that title."

"Let's see your ID," the officer said seriously.

"I'm reaching in my pocket, OK, officer?" John asked solemnly.

"Sure, but go slow," he said, eyeing the big man.

John produced his driver's license and retired military ID. The officer inspected and returned them, saying, "So you are the two people who finished those two guys earlier this month. This is the second time in a month you two have either killed or maimed others. The first two arrived at the station with long wrap sheets, and by the looks of these two, they will too. But try not to kill anyone else this week, OK?"

"Will do, officers," Joie retorted with a smirk.

The officers left with their prisoners and Joie and John returned to their car. She let a pissed off Fred out of the trunk.

Joie called Mike on the way back. "We got 'em, boss."

"I heard on the police scanner," Mike said, disapproval in his tone.

"See you in the morning, Mike. I'm too tired to be chewed out right now," Joie said.

"I'll yell at you at eight a.m., before we brief Deputy Director Hermenez at nine."

"I look forward to it," she responded.

Chapter 25 ★ The Charges

AT 8:45 THE NEXT MORNING, Mike, Joie, Greg, John, and Fred sat in Deputy Director Clark F. Hermenez's reception area. They waited as the receptionist offered them coffee for a second time. They declined, and at 9 o'clock sharp the deputy director's doors swung open like in *The Wizard of Oz*.

"Am I the dimwitted scarecrow or the heartless tin man?" John whispered.

"You'll be crushed under the descending house like the Wicked Witch if you don't shut up and take this seriously," Joie scolded.

John's smile disappeared, and he succumbed to his Delilah. Mike couldn't help but smile.

Deputy Director Hermenez sat behind an enormous desk and motioned for them to enter. Seeing their apprehension, Hermenez stood up and walked around his desk. He approached Greg first and said, "Good to see you, Agent Elgen. We go way back. You can add this case to your illustrious career."

"Thank you, Deputy Director," Greg responded stiffly.

"For God's sake, relax. You're among friends here! Call me Clark."

"Sir, I don't know if I can do that, but I'll try."

"Relax, or call me Clark?" he asked.

"Both," Greg said, smiling and looking a little more at ease.

"I must say, the last time I saw you, you didn't have two black eyes and a swollen nose, though."

"It's been an interesting investigation thus far, Deputy—I mean Clark."

"Yes, I've heard about the team's escapades," Clark said, slapping him on the back before moving on to Mike.

"You must be Agent Lundberg?" he said, extending a hand.

"Yes, sir," Mike responded, shaking his hand firmly.

"It's a pleasure to meet you at last. Your accomplishments have been the subject of a few staff meetings."

"That's good to know, sir."

"It's Clark."

"Yes, sir, Clark."

He smiled and moved on to Joie. "You need no introduction. You're the talk of the agency."

"That's kind of you to say, sir," she answered.

"Are you guys learning impaired? It's Clark."

"Yes, Clark, sir," she responded with a nervous smile.

"OK, I guess I'll have to settle for 'Clark Sir,' " he said, moving on to John. "And you must be… hold on," he said, reaching into his shirt pocket. "You're John 'the frickin' Giant Killer' Jacobson."

John blushed. "You can just call me Frickin' John."

Joie shot him a look, and John cleared his throat, saying, "I meant to finish that sentence with 'Clark, Sir.' "

Clark laughed heartily. "I like your style, John. I was in the military as well but didn't make it into the Special Forces. You're a man that speaks his mind. Good."

"Well, I'd say you're doing OK now." John glanced around at the expensively decorated office and Clark's three-thousand-dollar suit and tie.

Joie rolled her eyes and shot him another look. John looked back at Joie and said, "He likes me. Leave me alone."

Joie mouthed the words, "Shut up!"

Seeing this, Clark laughed and said, "I'll let you two finish that later." He motioned for them to sit. "Let's get started. I have thirty minutes before my next appointment. I understand you have charges you want me to review."

"Yes, sir," Mike said, connecting a memory stick to the projector.

"Before we begin, I want to call someone who wanted to listen in," Clark said, pressing a button on his phone.

"Have you heard everything thus far, sir?"

The fact that the deputy director referred to the audio attendee as "sir" caused the entire team to tense up again.

Clark noticed the change. "I began this meeting telling you that you were among 'friends.' What did you think I meant when I pluralized the noun? Please proceed."

Mike began the presentation and went through the charges they had meticulously prepared against the president-elect. Clark stopped him a few times with comments and questions. Mike finished in twenty-five minutes.

Clark sat back in his chair and looked at the ceiling, thinking. Finally, he said, "I like it. We have nine felonies, all well-documented and defendable. Well done! But we must keep in mind the repercussions. President-Elect Adams seems to have the powers of darkness at his disposal. The political fallout will cascade on me. However, the president-elect's henchmen may come after you. Are you sure you want to proceed?"

"Sir, may I speak freely?" Mike asked.

"Of course."

"They've already come after every one of us. Your career may be in the balance, but our lives have been on the line ever since we began this investigation."

"You're right. Forgive me for my cavalier attitude toward your situations." Clark pressed the intercom button and repeated, "Still listening, sir?"

"Yes, I'll be right in."

Within three seconds, a side door opened and in walked the FBI director. Everyone stood up, including Clark.

The director walked right up to Mike with a stern face. He wore the same face previously seen in his numerous press conferences. There was no joy—no pride in their work, no apparent emotion at all. Mike had no idea what to do or say. The stoic man stared blankly at them one at a time. After what seemed like an hour of scrutiny, he looked back at Mike and stepped closer. Mike froze!

The director extended his hand and smiled, saying, "Good job! You've done excellent investigative work the bureau can be proud of."

"Thank you, sir," Mike responded, his voice trembling.

The director nodded to the rest of the team. Then he eyed John and said, "Are you sure you don't want to join my bureau?"

"Sir, I'm honored, but couldn't stand the pay decrease."

Joie closed her eyes, making a note to kill him later.

The director smiled brighter and said, "Yes, and I'd have to kick your ass for insubordination every week."

"You're probably right, sir."

Everyone chuckled except for Joie. He noticed and commented, "You must be Joie, the master of John 'the frickin' Giant Killer' Jacobson."

"Yes, sir. I'm going to kill him right after this meeting, sir," Joie responded, looking sternly at John.

"I'm sure you can do it."

Clark asked, "Director, do you want to proceed with the proposed charges against the president-elect?"

"Yes, send the file to my office, and I'll make a few changes before sending it to the AG."

Agent Elgen looked down in disappointment, remembering what had happened to the report he sent to the FBI director earlier. He took notice and approached Greg. "Agent Elgen—may I call you Greg?"

He stood at attention. "Of course, sir!"

"Greg, I apologize for what happened before. But if you remember, I went through the litany of charges so that Americans would know the irresponsible way the president-elect managed our nation's most secret information. That way, voters would remember on Election Day. The AG already decided she was going to drop any charges we sent to the Department of Justice; she's the one who asked me to change the text of my briefing. Hell, she met with the president-elect just days before the FBI interview. Who knows what they discussed? President-Elect Adams is a wily politician—but we'll get him one way or the other."

Agent Elgen relaxed a little with the man's explanation. He looked down and said, "Sir, I'm sorry I doubted you."

"No problem. It comes with the work we do."

"Sir?"

"Yes?" the director responded.

"May I?" Agent Elgen asked, extending his hand.

The director walked over to him, looked him directly in the eyes, and shook his hand, saying, "The honor is mine, Agent Elgen." Turning his attention back to the group, he added, "Just remember, no matter what happens, I know you all did your best. I also want you to know there's a backup plan in case the AG drops the charges again. It's been in the works for over a year. Now, get out of here and send Clark and me those charges today!"

"Yes, sir!" they all said, doing an about-face and leaving the office.

While Joie chewed out John, Mike and Greg finalized the necessary charges. Later that day, Mike carried them personally to Deputy Director Hermenez's executive secretary.

**

Two days later, the attorney general of the United States held a press conference. The press packed the room, but there were five vacant seats in the back with signs showing the names Lundberg, Elgen, August, Reider, and Jacobson. They took their seats and waited patiently for the AG. Thirty minutes later, the AG walked in and took her place behind the podium. She put on her glasses and took out a few pages of notes. She then drank some water and cleared her throat, making the audience wait longer.

Finally, she began reading a statement. "The press broke a story two days ago that the FBI sent nine felony charges to the US Department of Justice against President-Elect Adams. In addition, many conservative media reported accusations of voter fraud techniques due to lack of voter ID, non-paper-based voting machines, computer viruses, and abuse of ballots such as proxy, provisional, absentee and early voting."

She paused, shook her head, and smiled incredulously at the ridiculous allegations. "There's also claims of multiple voting from ballot box stuffing, voter impersonation, ballot harvesting, voting for inactive voters, and voting in more than one state. Even more ridiculous is the assertions of ineligible voting by unregistered voters, felons, refugees, and undocumented Americans."

The woman took a breath with a skeptical smile and continued, "Finally, there are accusations of destruction or invalidation of legitimate ballots, organized attacks on polling places, vote buying, misleading ballots, political misinformation, voter manipulation, and suppression. I take issue with these baseless complaints. Despite this lengthy list of allegations, allow me to summarize the few FBI charges.

"First, my office already dropped the charges against the president-elect relative to his use of classified information on a government mainframe last year. I see nothing new in this felony charge that the FBI didn't already consider when we dropped the charges the first time. Therefore, the DOJ chooses to do the same now. We will not be moving forward with the latest charges."

The press reacted with soft murmurs, speaking into tape recorders and calling their news desks in whispers. John and Joie looked at each other, then over to Mike, stunned.

"Allow me to continue. Secondly, the FBI charges the president-elect with three felony counts, including one falling under RICO, concerning a charity called Dreams International. However, there is no definitive proof that President-Elect Adams is associated with it. After carefully examining each one in terms of their legal merit, the Department of Justice feels these charges do not meet the standard of proof required by the associated criminal statutes. Therefore, the department chooses to drop these charges as well."

This time, the press reacted with louder murmurs and activity. John, Joie, Mike, Greg, and Fred looked at the floor, devastated that the AG so easily nullified their arduous work.

"Finally, each general election brings charges of voter fraud. The FBI charged the president-elect with only three counts of voter fraud. We, in the DOJ, take charges of voter fraud very seriously. When Americans vote, their voice should remain unfettered so that the will of the American people directs our nation's government."

She stopped to get a drink while the press core, agents, and the entire nation waited for her decision. She turned the page and continued. "However, these charges are circumstantial at best. They are not worth this court's time. I will not be filing criminal charges here, either."

She then calmly turned and left as reporters screamed questions like, "Can we see the actual charges?" "What is the wording of the charges?" "Why didn't you go through the actual charges in your address?" "Are you on the take again?" "Will you meet secretly again with President-Elect Adams?"

John, Joie, Mike, Greg, and Fred left after the unceremonious dismissal of the crimes committed, shattered. They returned to Mike's office, trying to encourage each other.

Mike noticed a fax from Deputy Director Hermenez. It read "We thought this might be the outcome, but we had to try. You did your best. We couldn't be prouder. Check the papers in the morning. The FBI director and I just released the actual charges to the AP through secret channels. That way the press will know the charge details. Go home—it's not over!"

PART VI ★ IMMINENT CLASHES

Chapter 26 ★ Congressional Investigation

A WEEK AFTER THE AG simply dropped all charges, Wayne Bonner, the chairman of the Judiciary Committee of the US House, sent a subpoena for President-Elect Jeffrey Adams to appear before them concerning his activities.

It was late November in the capital, the wind howled, and snow fell on the Capitol's steps. However, it was warm inside as politicians lined up for cameos and TV cameras rolled. America and much of the rest of the world prepared to watch the proceedings on live TV. The congressional panel included five Democrats and five Republicans. Chairman Wayne Bonner, Democratic congressman from Florida, presided. He knew President-Elect Jeffrey Adams from meetings on the Hill, party dinners, and now from several secret phone calls.

President-Elect Jeffrey Adams strolled into the halls of Congress without a care in the world. He was short for a future president, standing at just five feet ten, but by his swagger and haughty demeanor he appeared seven feet tall. His perfect hair, million-dollar smile, and boyish face made him look as innocent as Opie Taylor. Behind the virtuous façade, however, lay a monster. He looked at these mere US Representatives as peons, insects to squash if they stepped out of line. Besides, he knew they would never prosecute him. The Hillton Boys already talked to a few leading congressmen.

They could be as aggressive as they wanted in their questioning, but if they recommended any criminal charges, they were dead. This was in the bag!

After a series of commercials, commentator explanations of the proceedings, and a general welcome from the chair, the first to ask a question was a Democrat from a Southern state. "Can you summarize your illustrious career for the panel, so we get a sense of your selfless service to our country?"

Five members of the panel rolled their eyes as the president-elect pontificated about his work for ten minutes. Jeffrey Adams described his rise to power through the state legislature and the US House all the way to the Senate and finally to his current role as ranking member of the US Senate Appropriations Committee. His answer concluded with, "My role is defined by the US Constitution, requiring appropriations made by law prior to the expenditure of any money from the Treasury, and is therefore one of the most powerful committees in the Senate. It's been an honor to serve this great nation." Senator Adams tried to appear humble, yet his narcissism was clear to all.

Several members of the gallery applauded this great servant of the American people. The second question came from a Republican from a Northern state. "This panel wants to know why you chose to delete government-owned documents from a mainframe after notification of an FBI investigation. I have here before me forty-five of them, out of the thousands you deleted. The NSA recovered these. This is a felony for conspiracy to conceal documents from government computers. Many previous offenders charged with this felony are in prison, have lost their jobs, or barred from working for the government, et cetera. Your offense in this category is much more egregious. Why should we exonerate you for doing worse than most of them?"

The president-elect talked in circles for five minutes, again not answering the question. The congressman posed the question again, this time using specific examples. The answer was simply, "I've already answered the question."

The next question was from a West Coast Democrat. "Can you tell us about your admirable efforts in support of entitlement programs for the poor?"

Five members of the panel sat back, heaving sighs of frustration at the obvious attempt to skirt the real issue. The president-elect responded with five minutes of dancing around the question that would have made Fred Astaire proud.

A Republican congressman said, "As you know, the AP released the actual wording of the FBI charges after the AG dropped the charges. There were an astounding thirty-five documented counts of lying under oath concerning the destruction of government-owned classified documents! Do you really expect this panel, the FBI, and the American people to accept this behavior? Especially from a sitting US Senator and now president-elect?"

Adams responded, "I didn't attend confidential information training. So, I didn't know the proper procedure. Since they were on my mainframe, I thought I was free to delete them."

"Well, you are either lying or the most unqualified president-elect in American history. How can we trust you with confidential information to which you'll have access as our next president?"

"I know the proper procedure now."

"What about this document shown on the overhead with redacted information erased? You acknowledged this document as classified and referred to the *C* in the header."

"I don't remember."

"How can you not remember this?"

"I don't know."

The congressman yielded, rolling his eyes. The next Democrat asked, "Can you summarize your comprehensive national defense position?"

Almost everyone in the entire room murmured under their breath. The obviously prepared answer was so boring that commercials replaced most of his seven-minute response.

When the TV cameras were live again, a Republican asked, "I'd like to know about the charge concerning obstruction of justice. You deleted thirty-three thousand documents after notification from the FBI. You previously said they were all personal, but this document clearly instructs your assistants to delete them after the FBI investigation announcement."

"I choose not to answer," the President-Elect Adams answered, fidgeting slightly.

"What about the 'bleaching' of a government-owned mainframe so information would be irretrievable? If you had nothing to hide, why would you do that?"

"I don't recall that. If it was, as you say, 'bleached,' I know nothing about that nor the technology associated. I'm a politician, not an IT guru."

"OK, what about destroying fourteen phones, one laptop, two memory sticks, and five iPads after being notified about the FBI investigation?"

"I don't recall doing that. I've used many devices so I replace them often."

Exasperated, the congressman sat back and let the next Democrat take over. The latter asked, "Please tell us about your plans to bolster the economy."

Ten minutes of vague and ambiguous recitation ensued.

A Republican from the East Coast asked, "Please tell us about the charge of bribery relative to Dreams International. This document"—he pointed to the screen—"clearly shows a staffer granting access to a donor. It says right here," he explained, pointing at the specific line with a laser pointer, "that he paid millions to Dreams International. Afterward, you agreed to meet with him. Then you helped his corporation avoid millions in taxes. Soon after that, an equivalent size deposit to your personal bank account appeared. What about this?"

"I'm not associated with Dreams International. I meet many people. The fact I met with this person and then they just so happened to give a donation to a charity is purely coincidental."

"But President-Elect Adams, this is not the only person you gave favors to that happened to give funds to Dreams International. Are you saying they are *all* coincidental?"

"Yes," he responded, a little shaken.

"I have no more questions and yield to the chair. However, I and the American people see through this rouse," the congressman said with disgust.

The next Democrat asked, "Please tell us of your plans to heal the US, where nationality and race are such critical issues facing us all."

The president-elect spoke about poor criminals, foul police, more Blacks living in poverty than ever before, and new entitlement programs for refugees and the unemployed. Illegal immigrants listening in NYC, LA, and Chicago cheered!

A Republican from a conservative state started, "I want to continue the discussion about Dreams International. What about the charge of criminal racketeering associated with this now infamous charity? For instance, the political advocacy group Freedom Watch filed a racketeering lawsuit last month against you and this charity. You say you have nothing to do with Dreams International, yet this document clearly shows you receiving funds from this so-called 'charitable organization.'"

"This criminal charge is for failing to produce documents under the Freedom of Information Act. This civil suit accuses you of conducting a corrupt enterprise for more than ten years by using private documents to hide large donations to Dreams International, then receiving large payouts from this charity. These payouts came directly after you provided official government actions, policies, statements, military support, or arranged other political benefits using the leverage of your official position."

"I'm not aware of that."

"Not aware of the lawsuit or the accusations?"

"Neither. I'm too busy to focus on bogus charges and ridiculous accusations. I'm busy serving the American people!"

"Well, do you remember being dead broke in 2001? Yet you're now worth hundreds of millions? This money supposedly came from book deals and speaking fees."

"Yes, it did," Adams responded tensely.

"The numbers don't add up. Your speaking engagements total around fifteen million dollars, not hundreds of millions."

"I'm not an accountant but a servant of the American people."

The congressman continued, "I'd like to remind you about one case where a Mexican businessman purchased up to one-fifth of the US plutonium assets. An acquisition of this size and nature requires approval by you, and it just so happens that at the very same time, his firm made a 2.35-million-dollar donation to Dreams International. Also, the firm paid you five hundred thousand dollars for a single speaking engagement. Can you comment on this specific example out of the over thirty other documented cases of accusations of criminal racketeering?"

"Yes. I received monetary compensation for speaking and signing books, but I don't recall the specifics of this matter."

The congressman yielded back to the chair, who gave an almost indiscernible wink to Adams.

Another Democratic congressman asked the president-elect about his plans to deal with ISIS. The answer made terrorists around the globe celebrate.

A Republican congressman from the Midwest asked, "Can you tell us why Dreams International resists opening its finances, which would allow America to decide if the charge concerning misuse of charitable donations has merit?"

"As I've repeatedly said, I'm not associated with Dreams International. However, from what I've read, this wonderful charity benefits the needy around the world."

"Yes, but their work to benefit the needy only constitutes fifty percent of the documented donated amount. Where's the rest?"

"I don't know, because I'm not associated with them. However, it's probably for administrative, traveling, and overhead costs."

"Are you sure much of it didn't filter into your personal wealth, explaining your newfound prosperity?"

"No, it didn't," the president-elect responded uneasily.

"Where did the additional affluence derive from, if not from the Dreams International operation?"

"My tax records have been released."

"Yes, but they don't explain where your affluence came from in such a brief time."

"I don't know what else to say about this topic. I've answered your question."

"No, you haven't."

"Yes, I have. I choose not to make any further comment."

"I can understand why. I have no more questions. I believe America understands your reluctance to answer my questions. I yield the floor."

A Democrat asked, "Can you tell us about your proposed tax plan?" The answer made everyone worth over five hundred thousand dollars start packing their bags for Canada.

A Republican from the Southwest asked, "What is your knowledge of the charge of tampering with voting machines? This includes the use of Dominion voting machines, outlawed in many US states and foreign countries. The FBI charge also included documentation, pictures, diagrams, and testimony concerning a virus that increased votes for you in the scanned voting data sent from precincts to state election collection points. What do you know about this?"

"I have no knowledge of that."

"How do you explain the discrepancies between the paper ballots and the voting data?"

"It is not my job to explain this. I'm not a voting machine expert."

"According to sworn testimony and conclusive evidence, this virus appeared in the battleground states only. How do you explain that these discrepancies are one percent higher in the battleground states?

"I'm sure it's just a fluke."

"A fluke? Right! How about the other virus used only on voting machines without paper trails? Do you know anything about that?"

"No. Do you have proof of its existence?" the president-elect asked, afraid of the answer.

"No, but I have sworn testimony from a Mr. Fred Reider and several wardens that it did exist."

"Without proof of its existence, it's my word against theirs."

"Yes, it's the word of several credible witnesses, as well as several counts of perjury and other felonies!"

"That's your opinion."

"Yes, it is! Do you know the name Fred Reider?"

"No."

"Next question: Do you know anything about the charge that includes thousands of documented cases of voting for inactive and dead voters?"

"No."

"You don't read the papers or listen to the news?"

"It's just rumors and right-wing conspiracy theories," President-Elect Adams answered.

"What about the supposed Russian hack of voter databases? The charge includes evidence that a team working for you conducted the hack.

Furthermore, the hack was not just in Illinois and Arizona, as initially reported. The hack reportedly stole *millions* of voters' information with the intent of submitting early voting and absentee ballots favoring you. Also, the evidence indicates voters used the data to vote for inactive voters in all states without strict voter ID laws."

"I have no knowledge of this." Adams began squirming a little more.

"How about the illegal protesters magically appearing at polling places when needed to dissuade voters for the other party from voting?"

"I know nothing about that."

"You're aware of the many testimonies and the overwhelming documentation concerning this felony?"

"No."

"Do you know the name Todd Shamer?"

"No," he answered apprehensively.

"What about Scarlett Schuller or Lizzy Warden? Do you know them?"

Even more nervously, he replied, "No."

"That's funny, because the evidence shows emails between you and Scarlett Schuller in cryptic language dealing with the election."

"If it's cryptic, how do you know what the emails are about?"

"Let's see if we can be less cryptic. If you look at the screen, you'll see an outline. As you can clearly see, it gives specific guidance to wardens in the largest precincts in the great state of Virginia. This document plainly shows how to take advantage of voter ID laws, and how to take advantage of that state's voting machines. Mr. Fred Reider signed an affidavit with the FBI as to its validity."

"I know nothing about the document and have already testified that I don't know Mr. Fred Reider."

"I also draw your attention to the rest of this document. It visibly instructs polling personnel, called wardens, to violate voting fraud regulations. The instructions are specific and illegal! The entire document appears in Appendix A."

"As I previously testified, I know nothing about this document, the training of so-called 'wardens,' or this Fred Reider," the president-elect said, his voice slightly faltering.

"I don't believe you because of your former perjury. In addition, look at the last statement on this document: 'Be careful to avoid prosecution, but the only way to prosecute us is to prosecute President-Elect Jeffrey Adams.' "

"I can't control the actions of those supporting me. I have nothing more to say on the subject. I know nothing about voter fraud or any of the names you mentioned."

"Do you want to answer to the fact that there are eleven more of these outlines for each battleground state?"

"I'm not familiar with any of those documents. However, just because the documents mention my name doesn't mean I'm associated with them. There are many groups out there favoring both parties that may do such a thing, but it doesn't mean that I or my opponent know anything about it. It may be a frame job from the opposing party."

"That's a ridiculous accusation considering the sheer number of charges, counts, affidavits, statements, signed documents, and other overwhelming evidence against you."

"I'm innocent of all charges."

"Right! Let's move on. Finally, do you know the name Gavin Principle or 'the Hillton Boys'?"

"No."

"What if I told you there are emails between Mrs. Schuller and Mr. Principle referring to your election campaign?"

"I don't know their names or anything about their emails."

"What about the Hillton Boys?"

"I've never heard of them," he answered coldly.

"One last question, President-Elect Adams. What about the trail of over thirty years of murders following your career? It seems anyone bold enough to oppose or investigate you ends up in the grave."

Adams answered with a smirk, "Those deaths attribute to me by a conspiracy attempting to damage my ability to serve my country. There is no evidence I had anything to do with any of the deaths. I've been investigated most of my career due to the enemy on the other side of the political aisle targeting me. That's all there is to it."

The congressman said, "Mr. Chairman, I have no more questions for

President-Elect Adams, who doesn't seem to remember anything. I think the American people know more than the president-elect about these numerous documents and felonious activities. The president-elect's implausible answers further support the lengthy list of felonies. I yield to the chairman."

The chairman concluded the investigation by saying, "I want to thank the president-elect for answering our questions. I also want to thank my esteemed colleagues for their inquiries. Finally, I want to point out that the FBI dropped the charges initially, and the AG dropped the second wave of charges. This committee will further discuss the issues now that you've testified. However, we will probably come to the same conclusion."

"What? You're kidding? That's not what we agreed to!" a senior congressman shouted.

"I declare conclusion to this congressional investigation. This committee will discuss our next steps, but I, for one, am satisfied with President-Elect Adams's answers. We appreciate your willingness to appear before us," the chairman said, dropping his gavel heavily.

The press headed for the doors to report the news, telling two very different versions of the congressional investigation.

***

Mike, Greg, Joie, Fred, and John turned off their TV.

"The president-elect won again," Joie muttered.

"Not necessarily," Mike responded.

"What do you mean? The AG dropped the charges, and the congressional investigation ended without asking the AG to pursue charges, or even for FBI to investigate further," Greg responded.

"Remember, the director said there was a backup plan in case this happened," Mike said hopefully.

"Do you know what the plan is?" Joie asked.

"Not a clue, but he's a man of his word. I bet it's in motion already."

"I hope you're right, but I know what the president-elect's next plan is," John replied.

"What's that?" Mike asked, already knowing the answer.

"Eliminating the five of us!"

***

After taking a moment to collect himself after the disappointing proceedings, John called his supervisor. "Boss, how much longer do I have to work this case? It's not concluded yet."

"What do you mean? I just saw the congressional investigation on TV. It's over."

"No, it's not, boss. I can't explain the details, but I need at least two more weeks to clean things up."

"You have one week to come back, or I'll be forced to replace you."

"Please, boss. The FBI director has a plan and may need me to help carry it out."

"John, the president of our division already stipulated you have seven days to come back."

"OK, boss. I'll be there. Thanks for giving me time to finish this."

"See you on Monday. That's six days from now."

"Will do, boss. I'll be there."

"I hope so. You're my best employee. By the way, you and I have an appointment with many executives to explain why they drug you out of here in handcuffs. You had better have a great explanation, or you may not have a job anyway. Be in our conference room at nine a.m. next Monday."

"Yes sir. I'll be there at eight thirty to tell you the whole story before I give them the condensed version."

"I look forward to it. You never disappoint!"

"Bye, boss." With that, John hung up and headed for his secret 4:30 appointment.

Chapter 27 ★ The Showdown

AT 6 P.M., MIKE AND Greg followed a police escort to their respective homes for sweeps. Fred stayed with Greg one night, giving John and Joie a break. After the police left, each of them locked doors and windows, turned on the alarms, loaded their weapons, and protected their families.

John and Joie went to her apartment and did the same.

"I'm hungry. Let's go out to eat," John said, patting his stomach.

"Are you mentally impaired? You want us out in the open to be easily picked off? No, we're eating here. I'll make spaghetti."

"Impressive. That'll work."

John turned on the news while Joie began cooking. After some time, Joie said, "You know he's coming, right?"

"Yes. Gavin is not a man to give up." He tried ignoring the idea by concentrating on the news.

"I can call the FBI, and we'll have a car outside with trained agents."

"For how long? Even if they're here for weeks, he'd just wait until they left."

"At least we'd be safe."

"Joie, I have five days until I fly back to Texas. If I must stay longer and lose my job, so be it. But I'd rather have you *and* the job."

"I'm glad you put me first."

"Well, it's a toss-up, but you barely won out."

"Good to know, jerk."

"You're welcome, Madam Foci."

Joie smiled, loving the man in front of her for his strengths, drive, dreams, weaknesses, and crude sense of humor. But it was his devoted love that made her adore him.

After dinner, they went to bed and took turns keeping watch. No Gavin. In the morning, they planned their day inside the apartment while drinking coffee and yawning. They talked, played chess (Joie won each time), watched TV, and read.

John sat in the bedroom reading a book next to Joie. She looked over and asked, "How's your boring technology thriller?"

"Great! And how is your exciting FBI policy manual?"

"It's a page-turner," she replied, giving him the finger.

"I hope that sign is a precursor of things to come later tonight," John replied hopefully.

"Nope, I'm just sending an indication of my disdain."

"Hey, I've got an idea for an extracurricular activity." John smiled.

"Does it involve bodies writhing in pleasure?"

"Sure does," he said, motioning her over.

She walked over, anticipating an embrace. But John put his huge arm up on the table in an arm-wrestling position.

"This is your idea of writhing in pleasure? OK. Double or nothing?"

"Deal," John replied, smiling.

Joie used both arms in the standing and leaning position. "Ready, set, go," she announced, beginning between "set" and "go."

John yawned. "Let me know when you want to start." She leaned in harder, grunted, and put her shoulder on his arm, pushing with all her might. "Really, let me know when to begin."

"Neanderthal."

"Foci lover."

She started laughing and gave up. John teased, "Darn, you gave up just when you were getting the upper hand."

"Jerk!"

"Beautiful."

"You win, John."

"Yes, I do, as long as I get you for the rest of my life."

She melted and fell into his waiting embrace. They made love for hours.

At 2 a.m., she woke him for his turn to keep watch. He made coffee and returned to the bedroom. He thought she was asleep and sat down in the chair beside the bed vigilantly.

Without moving, Joie said, "John?"

"Yeah, babe?"

"I'm scared."

"Got news for you. Me too."

She turned over to look at him. "Really? I've never known you to be afraid of anything."

"Well, he's not a thing. He's a psychotic trained assassin."

"And as good a fighter as you?" she asked.

"Probably better," John replied calmly.

"You think so?"

"When we fought last, he was faster and hit almost as hard. He got in three licks to each one of mine."

"I believe in you, John."

"Thanks, babe. I believe in you, too," John responded, though with more uncertainty than she expected.

She got up and sat in his lap. He held her tight. "Tighter," she whispered.

He held her until she fell asleep. Then he laid her in bed and went back to his chair. He watched her breathe. Certain she was asleep, he whispered, "I am afraid. But not for me. I'm scared of losing you."

He drank his coffee and paced the apartment every fifteen minutes, checking the door, the windows, the alarm, and every possible hiding place. He woke her at 6 a.m.

"You were supposed to wake me at four to relieve you," she scolded.

"I lost track of time," he jested.

She made breakfast and the rest of the day shot by again, as did the next three days.

On the fifth evening Joie said, "Your plane leaves in the morning. I want you on it."

"Not a chance. You're my priority."

"John, I have the entire FBI protecting me. You're the vulnerable one. How do you know he's not waiting for you in Texas?"

"Because that wouldn't satisfy this sick son of a bitch. He'd want to maximize my suffering by killing you first."

"I don't think he's that much of a planner. He's just a sick bastard."

"He's here, Joie. I can feel him. I can't explain it, but I know he's coming here."

"And if he doesn't, will you get on the plane in the morning?"

"Let's cross that bridge when we come to it."

"Deal, but I plan to win this argument."

"You always do."

Joie smiled but then grew serious. She took John by the hands and looked deep into his eyes. John liked the affectionate gesture, but he could tell something was on her mind besides intimacy.

"John, I must tell you something. You're not going to like it."

"Nothing you say will change the way I feel about you."

"I'm not so sure."

"I am!"

"John, just listen. I was not totally honest with you about a question you asked me while driving back from my mom's house."

"Which question?" John asked, thinking back.

"You asked me if I had siblings, remember?"

"Yes, and you said no."

"That's not exactly what I said. I said my parents *together* had no other children."

"Huh? If your parents had no other children, then you have no siblings."

"Not necessarily. You see, they didn't have any other children together. However, my father had a daughter with another woman. I have a stepsister."

"Stepsister?"

"To cut a long story short, my dad had an affair with another woman, and she had a child. This is also partially why my mom is so bitter. The child's name was Scarlett."

It took a moment for this to sink in. "Scarlett Schuller?"

Joie looked at the floor and nodded.

"You lied to me! Don't you think I had the right to know Scarlett Schuller was your sister?"

"Stepsister," Joie corrected.

"OK, stepsister. What's the frickin' difference? You should have told me then so I would be more prepared for the danger we're in!"

"You're right, John. I'm so sorry. But honestly, I didn't know she was involved until Greg mentioned her name from his notes just days ago. I knew she was bad news years ago and distanced myself from her. I knew a relationship with her would hurt my chances of getting into the FBI."

"Damn! Anything else you haven't told me?"

"No, John. I've told you everything about my life now. However, before you get too mad at me, why didn't you tell me you discussed my father's old patent?"

John raised his voice, "Way to change the frickin' subject! However, I saw a diagram in Luther East's office, and we asked him later about it. He assured Robert and me that the original patent had nothing to do with the virus."

"I told you that already. My dad was a good, honest, and decent man. He made one serious mistake in his life and had an affair."

"I know, Joie. I honestly never suspected him of wrongdoing. But before you get holier-than-thou on me, you must admit, your family has a few characters!"

Joie responded quickly, fighting her anger, "Your dad is awesome, but your family history is awful, and I accept it because I love you. You must admit, besides your dad, your family is no prize, either."

He put his big arms around her. "It's OK. None of us choose our family. I agree, my family is a mess too."

"Alright, then. Shut up and hug me, you big lug." Joie sighed and gradually calmed down.

They went to bed, but there was no lovemaking. John needed time to process the latest information. Was there anything else she was hiding?

At 10 p.m., she began the first watch. At midnight, he took the second. At 2 a.m. she took the third. He tried to sleep but couldn't, knowing that he may be leaving without her in four hours. However, at around 2:45, he drifted off.

At 3:08 a.m., Joie heard a noise in the kitchen. She got up with her loaded .45 in hand. She aimed and walked out of the bedroom into the hall. She looked left and right—nothing. All the lights were on in the apartment, so there were no shadows to hide in. She checked the front closet—no one there. She looked behind the couch—nobody. She checked under tables—zilch.

Finally, she rounded the corner and peeked into the kitchen. The closed pantry door stood out as the only hiding place. *Did John close it?* she wondered. She thought it was open before. She crept over and slowly turned the door handle. It opened with a creak. The space slowly lit up—it was empty. She turned around, relieved, when suddenly she felt a brutal strike to the side of her head. She fell to her knees, coming up with her weapon ready, but a hard kick to her wrist sent it flying across the kitchen. She grabbed her broken wrist and jumped up, hoping to get a kick in. Another blinding-fast punch hit her jaw, sending her down for the last time. Her eyes began to dim as she saw a gun lower toward her forehead. She closed her eyes, waiting for the blast.

She heard a loud bang, expecting a bullet to pass through her head. However, the bang wasn't a gunshot—it was the table breaking in two as John threw Gavin across the room. Gavin crashed to the floor but was up in one fluid motion, his gun pointed at John's chest. Before he could fire, John knocked it away with his enormous hands, like a gorilla brushing away a banana.

John lost balance with the thrust as Gavin jumped in the air, kicking John in the face but narrowly missing his throat, his real target. John stumbled backward as Gavin threw three punches so fast that he could barely see them. John swung at Gavin, missing. The much faster Gavin answered with two more hard punches to the face.

John reeled to the right, trying to recover, but Gavin weaved left and caught him with another swift punch to the stomach. John barely felt it thanks to his thick abdominal muscles, but Gavin saw this and punched him twice more in the face. John fell to his knees, semiconscious. Gavin brought an elbow down at the base of his skull. John saw black. Gavin stood up, satisfied his prey would wait for the kill without resistance.

John slowly opened his eyes and saw Gavin kneeling beside Joie, his hands tightening around her throat. She was struggling and choking. A split second later, Gavin felt a blow to his head. He turned to see a dazed John barely standing erect, retracting his punch. Gavin stood up, unfazed by the strike. His face transformed into an evil grin, and he growled, "OK, let's end this."

He walked away from Joie and approached John like a panther. John stood straight and smiled back, surprising Gavin.

"You really don't think those love taps damaged me, do you?" John asked calmly.

"That was just the warm-up round," Gavin mocked.

"Come and get some!" John taunted.

"I think I will." Gavin practically flew forward, unleashing a torrent of punches. John blocked each one with ease.

Confused, Gavin soared in the air again, attempting two kicks before landing on the ground. John blocked one kick with his left arm and the other with his right leg. Perplexed, Gavin twirled in a roundhouse kick and John grabbed his foot in midair, stopping it instantly. John brought his arm down on the side of Gavin's extended leg at the knee. Gavin writhed in pain and retracted his injured leg, thankful it still functioned. Gavin's befuddled expression made John smile.

"What do you think I did every day at four thirty in preparation for this moment?"

"What's that, asshole?" Gavin retorted, a little afraid to find out.

"I trained with a sixth-degree FBI black belt just about your size."

"Did he teach you this?" Gavin asked, shifting to a karate stance.

"Teach me, oh wise one," John goaded.

Gavin, in a move that would have made Bruce Lee proud, delivered several rapid chops at John. The bigger man blocked each one with perfect counter moves.

"That's all you got?" taunted John.

Gavin lost it and lunged toward John. He caught John on the jaw with a solid punch, but John returned the favor twice, much harder. Gavin then attempted one more kick but seemingly in slow motion, John brought his elbow down on Gavin's awkwardly twisted leg, breaking his knee. Gavin went down screaming. John kicked him in the face, sending him flying backward. He fell beside Joie. Gavin looked up as Joie brought a heel down on his temple. Gavin rolled over, holding his leg, and mercifully passed out.

"Thanks for starting the fight, babe. You softened him up for me," John said, falling to the floor.

As he passed out from pain, a smile crossed his face knowing the love of his life was safe.

Joie called the police then arrested Gavin and took him to the hospital, where he slowly healed handcuffed to his bed. He developed decubitus sores from lying on his back continuously. No one cared.

Meanwhile, just down the hall, doctors set Joie's wrist and patched up John as best they could. His wounds were significant, and he would be sore for weeks.

The charges leveled against Gavin included assault with a deadly weapon against Fred Reider, Mike Lundberg, Greg Elgen, Joie August, and John Jacobson as well as the murder of Chester Hammond, Todd Shamer, Luther East, and Lizzy Warden. He would finally taste the justice he was willing to dispense to others.

**

Mike, Greg, Fred, and Joie flew to Texas on the FBI director's personal jet with the semi-comatose John for his 9 a.m. meeting with Pseudomics executives. They arrived five minutes early. The packed conference room included his secretary, Debbie; Robert, his boss; the president of the Aerospace Division; and even the president and CEO of Pseudomics. Many other senior executives packed the conference room as well, all wanting facetime with the CEO.

John hobbled in on crutches. The executives stood up and applauded. His traveling companions joined the cheers. When the roar died down, John said, "I don't know if I deserve this. I was just protecting my fiancée."

President and CEO Bob Bannister replied, "And you brought to light one of the most outrageous voting scandals in US history. And fought against a murderous group called the Hillton Boys. And brought honor to Pseudomics!"

Once again applause filled the room. Robert said, "John, I'm honored to inform you about a promotion. In two weeks—after a paid vacation, of course—you begin your new job as director of quality in our corporate head-quarters in Washington, DC. And it pains me as a retired army officer to say the following, but... go navy."

Laughter and applause filled the room. For the next hour, Mike, Greg, Fred, and Joie recounted the entire story of John's heroism. John blushed and looked at the floor throughout the account.

When it was over and the cheers died down, Bob Bannister stood. Everyone turned in his direction.

"Thanks for inviting me to this celebration. I just have one more thing to say: start your vacation, John. Rest up, because you have an important job waiting for you just down the hall from me. Let me welcome you to corporate. Your new office door has your name and title. I've also taken the liberty to print business cards for you. The official one is waiting for you in your office. The unofficial one is right here," he said, pulling a business card from his pocket.

He passed it around the room first, and everyone read it, laughed, and passed it on. It came to John last. The unofficial business card contained his new title, but his name appeared as "John 'the frickin' Giant Killer' Jacobson."

Chapter 28 ★ The Reckoning

PRESIDENT-ELECT ADAMS LISTENED TO ADVISORS in a conference room just outside of DC at a five-star resort. They couldn't care less that most of their party barely scraped by. The president-elect lived as a millionaire—protected and pampered. Despite the hundreds of millions in the bank, taxpayers paid for the retreat.

Adams said, "I want to thank this group. Despite charges against many others, I remain untouched."

One of his aides said, "Even though the US AG dropped all charges, there are many lawsuits filed in states demanding recounts due to potential voter fraud."

Adams replied coldly, "The lawsuits are frivolous, and they have no evidence. The courts will throw them out."

"Sir, Arizona, Georgia, Michigan, Pennsylvania, North Carolina, and Nevada all filed suits due to finding additional votes for your opponent. Some were on memory cards and some were in boxes of uncounted votes."

"The number of uncounted votes won't change the outcome."

"But sir, the lawsuits also include Republicans kicked out of crucial areas in several states. Also, the suits include state laws extending three days after the election as being unconstitutional."

"Our lawyers will fight and get the suits overturned. Besides, the media and large social media platforms deny these accusations. We'll be victori-ous."

"There's more, sir. Our opponents are throwing out ballots with incom-plete addresses, no signature, and over three thousand instances of ineligible individuals casting ballots. Sworn affidavits support these and other voting irregularities."

"I pay you to take care of these things. Get to it," Adams threatened.

"I will, sir, but there are other suits stating that several secretaries of state changed laws just before the election concerning counting mail-in ballots. Not only that, but the most damning lawsuit claims that Dominion voting machines change votes. They appear to have proof."

"Even if they reverse some votes, it won't be enough to change the out-come."

"Sir, there are millions of votes in question. If the lawsuits upholds, it will change the outcome!"

Now Adams was incensed at his aide's arguments. He closed the discus-sion, saying, "Then take care of it or you won't have a job, or things may end up even worse for you. Any last words you want to share?"

The aide shook his head and looked away from Adams's threatening icy stare.

The group, frozen with fear, said nothing. Adams cleared his throat. "Now to the subject at hand. Let's choose a state and city for my first presi-dent-elect speech."

An advisor said, "We need to choose one of the states we won with inner-city support. We bought their votes with welfare, free healthcare, food stamps, et cetera. They love us."

Another advisor replied, "I disagree. We already own those places. Let's gain support in an established conservative state. I like the city of Phoenix. Besides, President-Elect Adams has enough Secret Service protection to stave off a host of terrorists or aggressive zealots."

The conversation lasted another ten minutes, alternating between points and counterpoints. Finally, President-Elect Adams sat forward, and the room grew quiet. "Let's compromise. What's another conservative state in which we gained ground in this election and in which we want more support?"

An advisor said, "How about Texas or Georgia?"

There was chatter all around the room when Adams broke in, saying, "I like it. The only question is whether it's Atlanta, Houston, San Antonio, or Dallas."

One advisor argued, "I say Texas, because Houston, San Antonio, and Dallas are in the top ten most populated cities in America. Besides, it would be amazing to secure enough support from inner cities in Texas to finally win that frickin' redneck, backward, old-fashioned, traditional-value, military- and police-supporting state."

Restrained laughter erupted all over the room. "We already have great support in Houston and San Antonio thanks to illegal aliens, refugees, and the impoverished populations. They're also sanctuary cities. Dallas is on the fence. We're going there," Adams said authoritatively, ending the conversation.

"OK, I'll find an opening in your schedule and contact the Texas governor, state senators, the Dallas congressmen, and the mayor. I'll write a press release," an aide said.

"Make it so!" Adams said, and the meeting was over.

***

Over the next few months, the lawsuits failed, and President-Elect Adams became president. He conducted business, wrote executive orders, appointed liberal judges, and met with liberal senators, congressmen, governors, and mayors from most of the top twenty-five most populated cities. All was going well. Resisting Americans succumbed to heavier taxes and the apathetic despair and hopelessness that followed. Illegal aliens, refugees, felons, and welfare recipients rejoiced. Sanctuary cities prevailed through Adams's support. The wealthiest Americans and corporations began leaving the country, as did the jobs they provided. The stock market tanked, and unemployment climbed. Yet entitlement programs increased!

***

"It's amazing, isn't it?" Roger Chapman, a Secret Service agent, marveled.

"What's that?" Police Captain Patrick Griffin asked.

"This morning, President Adams boarded Air Force One at Andrews AFB and landed at DFW three hours later. Now Marine One is on its way here to the heliport on top of the Kay Bailey Hutchison Convention Center," Roger said, looking over the horizon.

"What's so amazing about that?"

"President Adams's trip is only four hours long, but I've been here ten hours. That doesn't seem fair," Roger replied, surveying nearby rooftops.

"That's the job!" Patrick said, looking at his watch.

"He'll be here in six minutes." Roger looked toward the DFW Airport. "We're ready."

"Better believe it," Roger said, winking at Patrick.

"This place is a madhouse. The president's entourage practically booked all the rooms at the adjacent Omni Convention Center."

"Your tax dollars at work," Roger said to Patrick while listening to his earpiece. "The Secret Service just confirmed he's almost here. Yep, there he is." Roger pointed toward the northwest.

Suddenly the rooftop filled with Secret Service agents, police, and President Adams's welcoming committee. Marine One slowed down and banked just above the roof. In seconds, it landed in the middle of the heliport. Secret Service surrounded the chopper as President Adams stepped out of Marine One without a word of thanks to the pilots, crew, or his staff or agents. Area news helicopters circled the building as reporters appeared on the street below, some rushing onto the rooftop. Cameras rolled.

President Adams ignored it all and followed his escort toward an elevator. The president drew ten feet from the elevator doors. Patrick looked at Roger and they almost undetectably parted, leaving a space about two feet wide behind the president. The press later called it a "penetrable path."

"What's that noise?" a Secret Service agent close to the edge of the heliport asked.

A police officer responded, "I'm not sure. It's a weird high-pitched buzzing sound. I can't quite figure out where it's coming from because of the noise coming from Marine One."

Suddenly, a five-foot-wide drone ascended from behind a neighboring building about two hundred yards away. One second after they spotted it, a loud deep shot rang from the drone. There was a sickening thud as President Adams went down. Blood spurted from his abdomen.

Patrick, Roger, and twenty other agents and police surrounded President Adams, looking outward.

"I got this sucker!" the captain of Marine One shouted. Five loud bangs rang out as he shot the drone out of the sky with .50 caliber rounds.

An agent opened the president's jacket and saw a quarter-inch hole squarely in the middle of the chest.

"Step back," a medically trained agent said, turning the president over to ascertain if the bullet passed through or was still inside. Blood poured from a three-inch hole in President Adams's back where the bullet exited the body. There was no breathing or heartbeat. The elevator and stairway door swung open and additional agents, police, press, and convention personnel flooded the landing port.

An agent shouted, "Where did the drone come from?"

Another agent pointed northeast toward downtown Dallas and the sea of buildings. Agents spoke into head-mounted radios, and the police headed downtown toward the site.

Shouts of "The president is down!" came across radios, and the news helicopters repeated the news in seconds. In real time, the entire world knew.

***

Mike, Greg, and Joie sat in Mike's office watching the coverage.

"A person that lives by the sword, dies by the sword," Greg said, watching the coverage in disbelief.

"I don't approve of murder, but if anyone deserved it, Adams did," Mike said in return.

"I wonder who did this," Joie thought aloud.

"Being that this is the murder of a president, we'll know soon," Greg responded, still in shock.

He was right. Within days, the press reported the full irony of the assassination.

NBC Nightly News Anchor Lester Holt reported, "Today, Secret

Service Agent Roger Chapman and Dallas Police Captain Patrick Griffin both arrested as conspirators in the assassination of President Jeffrey Adams. Witnesses stated they saw them step aside, allowing the .45 caliber bullet from a drone kill the president. More details to follow."

Hours later, a CBS National News correspondent reported, "Sources at the FBI and CIA concur that a Syrian refugee, whose name is not known, brought the drone across the Mexican border last month. He then received amnesty and stored it in the basement of a friend who is an illegal immigrant."

ABC News Anchor David Muir reported, "The CIA arrested an unnamed Iranian terrorist. He allegedly built the drone that shot the president. Ironically, President Adams released him from Guantanamo Bay Detention Center just months ago. According to our sources, the infamous Iranian terrorist network designed and built the drone from funds made available by the multibillion-dollar Iran nuclear deal. The terrorist knew where the president would be thanks to classified documents stored on a personal server, paid for by dissatisfied donors to Dreams International."

A FOX news anchor reported, "We have late breaking news. The FBI just released the details of the Iranian terrorist who operated the drone that shot President Adams. He's been detained in Istanbul by the CIA. Details are still coming in, but according to sources, on the day of the assassination of President Adams, he was roughly half a mile away operating the drone with a remote control. He was in a vacant southwest-facing apartment building in downtown Dallas off Wood Street. It provided perfect visibility to the heliport.

"He reportedly took the elevator down to the bottom floor, and witnesses say they saw him calmly but swiftly walk through Lenny's Sub Shop to his car parked on South Field Street. He took TX-366, just blocks from President Kennedy's assassination. He expected there to be coverage of the airport, bus, and train stations in the area by local, county, state, and federal authorities in minutes—and there was. Therefore, he drove on I-35 North, bound for Oklahoma City. He arrived four hours later and stayed a week in a thirty-nine dollar a day hotel just across from the Oklahoma government building. You'll remember this very building was blown to bits by

American-grown terrorists in 1995, Timothy McVeigh and Terry Nichols. Then the Iranian terrorist boarded a jet bound for Tehran, Iran, via New York, Frankfurt, and Istanbul."

There were hourly news bulletins on all the networks. One announcer said, "Breaking news: The FBI announced they're within minutes of apprehending additional suspects associated with the assassination of President Adams. We, of course, know about the Iranian terrorist connection, but there is now evidence that a group of alleged assassins known as 'the Hillton Boys' are involved."

In her Leesburg, Virginia, Scarlett Schuller heard the broadcast and frantically packed her personal belongings in three suitcases strewn across the bed. There was no time to take her lifelong belongings with her. She looked at the pictures of her posing with high-ranking politicians, the knickknacks she'd collected from around the world, and the gifts from the president-elect. She'd have to leave it all behind. Her eyes darted from her bags to the TV, which was showing footage of the president-elect's assassination and the ensuing investigation.

"Shit!" Scarlett screamed as she zipped her bags and grabbed her ticket to Bogota, Colombia. She was almost to the door when she heard sirens drawing closer by the second. Turning, she ran out of the back door to her waiting car. She was slipping the key in the lock when she heard a familiar female voice. "Going somewhere, sis?"

Scarlett whirled around to see Joie leaning against the back of the house in a relaxed posture.

"Joie? Is that you? I haven't seen you in years. What are you doing here?"

"Yep, it's me. No, we haven't seen each other since you decided crime was a suitable way of life. Where have I been? I've been busy climbing the ranks of the FBI."

Scarlett retorted, "I know you're an agent. I've kept up with you over the years. However, now is not the time to chitchat."

"I think now is the perfect time to talk, sis," Joie said calmly as the sirens drew closer.

Scarlett thought for a moment before saying, "Joie, I'd love to talk, but

I'm in a hurry right now. I must get to the airport."

"What's your hurry?"

"As you know, I work with several US senators and even cabinet members. I'm late for a meeting."

"You're going to have to miss your meeting, Scarlett."

"Why's that?" Scarlett asked, setting her bags down.

"Because of what you've done, the people you've murdered, and your association with the Hillton Boys."

"Hillton Boys? Who're they?"

"The assassins you've given orders to kill for you, and for the president-elect."

"I don't know what you're talking about. I gotta go."

"You're right. You do gotta go—to jail. I'm here to arrest you for murder, conspiracy to commit murder, assault, and bribery."

"That's ridiculous! I'm leaving."

Joie reached into her back pocket and pulled out handcuffs. She also opened her jacket, revealing the large .45 caliber pistol in her shoulder holster. Scarlett's face slowly transformed from the doting sister to her real self. An evil smile slowly appeared, and reached into her purse, she pulled out a .38 revolver.

"I'm packing too, sis," Scarlett said, aiming it at Joie's head, assuming a chest shot would hit a bullet-resistant vest. As she pulled the trigger, she felt an enormous impact to the side of her face. As she turned and began losing consciousness, she saw a large man standing over her. The last words she heard before she passed out were "You brought a .38 to the fight. I brought John 'the frickin' Giant Killer' Jacobson."

Scarlett woke up two days later with an enormous headache, handcuffed to a hospital bed with a police officer at her door.

Chapter 29 ★ Closure

JOIE FLEW TO DFW AND John picked her up as usual. But there was nothing usual about the circumstances.

"So, you have a week of well-deserved vacation with me?" John excitedly asked, loading her luggage in his car.

"Yes, I badly need some *R* and *R* in your arms," Joie said, patting him on the butt.

"I'll bring a whole new meaning to *R* and *R,* my lady," John returned, opening her door.

As he started driving for Fort Worth, Joie said, "You want the latest news?"

"Sure. Tell me now, because when we get home, they'll be no talking for hours—just touching."

"Deal," Joie said, moving closer to John. "Well, Gavin Principle, the leader of the Hillton Boys, escaped the death penalty by accepting a plea for life in prison without parole in exchange for testifying against my stepsister, Scarlett Schuller. She's still recovering from a concussion and a broken jaw, no thanks to you."

"She should not have resisted arrest compliments of FBI Agent Joie August. I know her personally; she's a badass."

"Don't you forget it. Anyway, Gavin testified against the other members of the Hillton Boys for their thirty-year killing spree. The older members were more than seventy years old but still plea-bargained for life sentences."

"Well deserved! I still ache from my little skirmish with Gavin."

"I know, sweetie. I wish I could have helped you more during that fight."

"Give me two hours in bed, and we'll call it even," John said with a smirk.

She leaned over and whispered, "Just two hours?"

"My heart probably couldn't manage more than that with your gorgeous body," John playfully whispered back.

The week passed all too quickly. Afterwards, Joie helped John pack for his move to DC.

Meanwhile in the Capitol, the US vice president resigned, which made Speaker of the House Lawrence Elkins the next president. They swore him in three days after the death of the president. President Elkins called the losing Republican candidate and the cheated Democratic nominee to the Oval Office.

"Gentlemen, thanks for coming," he began. "I want to be a president of the people. Therefore, I'm listening to the real votes in the primaries and the fraudulent general election. I'd like you both to serve in my cabinet. Mr. Larry Flanders, your party cheated you out of winning the Democratic primary, as indicated by the DNC email hack. Therefore, I'm offering you the position of vice president of the United States. Now, I'll be honest, you and I differ greatly in our political views. I mean, imagine—a staunch conservative serving with a democratic socialist! However, you'll be serving as VP, the least powerful office in the United States government," he said, laughing.

Larry Flanders simply replied, "I accept, President Elkins. Thank you for the honor."

"Great! Now that brings me to you, Ronald Jackson. You're a self-made billionaire and successful businessman. I need your financial expertise and leadership skills on my staff. I'm offering you a historical dual role as US director of commerce and US director of state. After six months, choose the role you want, and I'll fill the other. Do you accept?"

"Yes, Mr. President. I accept. Of course, I'd rather have your job."

"Denied," President Elkins answered, smiling. The three men went out for dinner and planned their administration.

As President Elkins began his administration, embracing both sides of the congressional aisle, the government worked together to obliterate the stifling regulations introduced by the previous government. They proposed plans for a healthcare act that made sense, reduced taxes, cut expenditures, reworked entitlement programs, reformed immigration laws, began to balance the budget, passed term limits, and "built the wall."

One day soon after President Elkins's administration was in position, a small group of strangers milled around on the steps of the Capitol. A mother of four with a new job said, "America, you are beautiful."

A construction worker from St. Louis stopped, looked up to the sky, and uttered slowly, "O beautiful for spacious skies."

Others stopped and approached him almost reverently. A high school teacher from Omaha faced west and declared, "For amber waves of grain."

A banker from Colorado Springs answered, "For purple mountain majesties."

An unemployed college graduate stated, "Above the fruited plain!"

Men, women, and children approached by the hundreds and sang together, "America! America! God shed His grace on thee, and crown thy good with brotherhood, from sea to shining sea!"

The unemployed college graduate left with the banker, fully employed.

In the following months, voter law reform swept the country. Before the next general election, all states required photo IDs. All voting machines contained a paper trail. Fred worked directly with the states, having known their weaknesses, drastically bolstering their defenses against voter fraud.

John and Joie scheduled their wedding the following summer. The invitations included Mrs. August, Mike, Greg, Fred, the president of Pseudomics, and the director of the FBI. However, one more guest was also coming—but that's another story for another time.

Appendix A – Voter-Fraud Methods List

Dr. Rob Bryant discovered over 25 current voter-fraud techniques currently used in US elections! Although 21 methods are listed below, a few contain more than one technique requiring different applications. For instance, voter impersonation and voting by unregistered voters contains voting by illegal immigrants, felons, refugees, and posing as another registered voter. This study includes all US states; however, it focuses upon Battleground (BG) states. Many state-election-laws and policies increase, encourage, and even protect voter-fraud.

The information below appears in official state-voting-law web sites, journals, verified web sites, videos, litigations and media reports.

The Voter-Fraud methods discussed include:

1. Lack of Voter ID
2. Non-paper-based Voting-Machines
3. Computer Viruses

Misuse of ballots such as:

4. Mail-in
5. Provisional
6. Absentee
7. Early
8. Proxy
9. Ballot box stuffing
10. Ballot harvesting
11. Voting for inactive voters
12. Voting in more than one state

13. Voter impersonation
14. Unregistered voters

Other Voter Fraud Methods:

15. Destruction or invalidation of legitimate ballots
16. Organized attacks on polling places
17. Vote buying
18. Misleading and/or confusing information
19. Vote manipulation of protected groups
20. Voter suppression
21. Politicians moving precinct boundaries to their benefit

Appendix B – Voter-Fraud Methods Detail

The Voter-Fraud methods discussed include:

1. Lack of Voter ID

Many states do not require a photo ID to vote, and some require no ID at all. Therefore, voters may vote multiple times when ID is not required or when mail-in ballots are allowed. All states provide free voter IDs to US citizens, negating argument that voter IDs should not be required. Retail establishments require an ID. Why not when voting?

The table below lists the top twenty-five states by electors. There are ten blue, 5 red, and ten BG (purple) states included. This indicates a red state disadvantage. The states that allow voting without an ID or mail-in voting contain 179 of 270 electors needed to win the presidency. Even more surprising is that the states allowing no-excuse mail-in votes contain 336 of 270 electors needed to win the presidency! Therefore, how can we say the election process is valid? We have no idea who really voted or how often. This is, of course, by design.

#	State	Electors	ID Req	Mail-In Allowed
1	California	55	None	
2	Texas	38	Photo ID	Excuse Req
3	Florida	29	Photo ID	
4	New York	29	None	Excuse Req
5	Illinois	20	None	
6	Pennsylvania	20	None	

7	Ohio	18	ID	
8	Georgia	16	Photo ID	
9	Michigan	16	Photo ID	
10	North Carolina	15	Photo ID	
11	New Jersey	14	**None**	
12	Virginia	13	ID	
13	Arizona	11	ID	
14	Tennessee	11	Photo ID	**Excuse Req**
15	Indiana	11	ID	**Excuse Req**
16	Massachusetts	11	**None**	
17	Washington	10	Mail	
18	Minnesota	10	**None**	
19	Missouri	10	ID	
20	Wisconsin	10	Photo ID	
21	Maryland	10	**None**	
22	Colorado	9	ID	
23	Alabama	9	Photo ID	**Excuse Req**
24	South Carolina	9	Photo ID	**Excuse Req**
25	Kentucky	8	ID	**Excuse Req**
	2020 Elector Information	**412 of 538**	**None and Mail = 179 of 270 Needed**	**Mail-In No Excuse Req = 336 of 270 Needed**
	10 Gray, 5 Light Gray, 10 White			

Gray	
Lt. Gray	
White	

2. Non-paper-based Voting Machines

Voting Machines:

- One of the most popular voting machines, the direct recording electronic (DRE) system, provides no hard copy of recorded votes. Without a paper trail, voters can't verify their vote accuracy. Validation by polling volunteers is not possible.
- The Dominion voting machine:
    - May be programmed to change votes in predetermined ratios. Dominion's technology serves 40 percent of American voters. The company also gave money to the Clinton Foundation and uses parts from China.
    - The state of Texas rejected the company's machines and problems subsequently arose with a contracted company in the Philippines with ties to George Soros.
    - Dominion Voting Systems denied rumors that the use of Sharpies invalidated people's votes in Arizona, but there were also problems with Sharpies in Pennsylvania in 2019.
- Other voting machine models provide a paper validation of the vote; however, many are older, making them more susceptible to viruses.

3. Computer Viruses

A hacker as young as eleven years old and numerous college students planted viruses on various voting machines. Proof can be found on Google. Countless voters complain that voting machines recorded their choices incorrectly. Many state voting machines are decades old and vulnerable to hackers. Whether through a virus or voting machine malfunction, the outcome is the same: incorrect votes.

Misuse of Ballots such as:

4. Mail-in

Definition: Voting in an election whereby ballots are distributed and/or returned by post to electors, in contrast to electors voting in person at a polling station or electronically via an electronic voting system.

Mail-in States: Almost all states have some version of mail-in voting. Colorado, Oregon, and Washington State have all-mail voting systems. However, they may soon be joined by California, Arizona, Montana, Hawaii, Utah, and New Jersey.

Problems: This category is wide open to voter fraud due to a lack of voter ID via mail-in ballots. There are insufficient polling workers to validate signatures (many states don't check at all), and unscrupulous voters can therefore vote as many times as they want. A small percent of these issues result in prosecuted cases of mail-in fraud because without ID, there is no proof.

5. Provisional

Definition: Process available to a person whose name does not appear on the list of registered voters, who does not present a valid voter registration certificate, or who does not present the required form of ID at the polls.

Problem: By law, states should not count these ballots unless the voter later presents the required documentation. However, some states do so anyway, and most times it goes undetected.

6. Absentee

Definition: An absentee ballot is a vote cast by someone who is unable or unwilling to attend the official polling station to which the voter is normally allocated.

Problems: There are many cases where absentee ballots are collected from their party only from voters not who would not have normally voted. Many absentee ballots magically appear after the election favoring the losing candidate. In addition, due to a lack of ID and/or not checking signatures, fraud is possible.

7. Early

Definition: Early voting is when electors can vote on a single or series of days prior to an election. Early voting can take place remotely, such as by mail, or in person, usually in designated early voting polling stations.

Problems: Same problems as the other categories above.

8. Proxy

Definition: A vote cast by one person as a representative of another.

Problem: The representative voting may vote the way they want rather than voting accurately to the person they represent. This is most prevalent if the representative receives an incomplete ballot. Google "US election proxy vote fraud" for examples.

9. Ballot Box Stuffing

Definition: A type of electoral fraud whereby a person submits multiple ballots. This can also happen when a person casts his/her vote in multiple booths instead of casting their votes in a single booth.

Problem: There are numerous reports, allegations, and prosecutions of ballot box stuffing. Many states do not verify one vote per person despite preventative technology. More votes are counted than there are registered voters in some precincts! Dead voters still "vote| each year. Google the MANY YouTube videos and articles concerning verified ballot box stuffing incidents.

10. Ballot Harvesting

Definition: A campaign tactic that exploits voters in their neighborhoods to intimidate voters and cajole them into handing over their blank ballots.

Problem: This is effective in areas where there is extreme domination of one party over another, when voters do not feel safe, and when party officials and authorities ignore it. Google for yourself—you may be shocked!

11. Voting for Inactive Voters

Definition: An inactive voter is a registrant who was sent but has not responded to a confirmation mailing sent in accordance with 42 USC 1973gg-6(d) and has not since voted.

Problem: In the many states with poor or no voter ID requirements, voters may vote on behalf of inactive voters by just knowing their name and address. They may not even need this much in the sixteen states not requiring ID at all. We all know relatives, neighbors, and friends who do not vote. Lastly, many inactive voters are removed from rolls to reduce potential votes from the opposing party. Therefore, these people cannot vote unless they reregister in time.

12. Voting in More than One State

Definition: Self-explanatory.

Problem: A 2012 study conducted by the Pew Center found that at least 2.75 million people were registered to vote in more than one state. There were few instances of votes in multiple states; however, there are numerous prosecutions for this, because it's easily detected in states with effective voter ID policies. This begs the question: How many instances are there in states without voter ID requirements?

13. Voter Impersonation

Definition: Voter impersonation (also sometimes called in-person voter fraud) is a form of electoral fraud in which a person votes under the name of another eligible voter.

Problem: In the many states with poor or no voter ID requirements, voters can vote for eligible voters by just knowing their name and address (if that is even required). If the impersonated voter, then votes, this discrepancy may go undetected with poor voting controls. For instance, the NC governor instructed voters on how to do this.

14. Unregistered Voters

Definition: Voter registration in the United States takes place at the county level and is a prerequisite to voting at federal, state, and local elections. Therefore, an unregistered voter has not met this requirement.

Problem: It is estimated that millions of unregistered voters can vote due to poor or no voter ID requirements, out-of-date voter registration rolls, and poor polling place policies.

Categories are:

- Voters who fail to register.
- Voting by felons: States like Maine and Vermont allow felons to vote. Fourteen states allow felons to vote while incarcerated. Over half of the states allow felons to vote after incarceration. Eight states allow governors to reinstate felon voting rights. One Virginia governor wrote individual letters for felons to vote until the USSC found it unconstitutional.
- Voting by refugees and undocumented immigrants: According to multiple sources, over two million voted in 2018. This is due to poor or no voter ID requirements, poor polling place policies, and people ignoring the law in support of their candidate.

Other Voting Fraud Methods:

15. Destruction and Invalidation of Legitimate Ballots

Definition: Self-explanatory.

Problem: Most US citizens over thirty years old remember the Florida "hanging and dangling chads" controversy and lawsuits. There are countless modern videos, reports, and some prosecutions of the destruction and invalidation of legitimate ballots at polling places. Google and see for yourself! This is an enormous issue, especially in areas of extreme support for one party. Both parties are guilty. The remedy is increased bipartisan oversight at polling places.

16. Organized Attacks on Polling Places

Definition: A polling place is the location where voters cast their ballots in elections. Attacks are the aggressive actions by groups with the intent of reducing votes from the opposing party.

Problem: Both parties are guilty, and there are thousands of verified events, arrests, and prosecutions involving this issue. This mostly occurs by extreme right and left groups. Remedies are on-site law enforcement, dual entries, staff awareness, parking monitors, and the admonishment of the media/politicians.

17. Vote Buying

Definition: Any reward given to a person for voting in a certain way. Vote buying is a corrupt election practice and banned in United States. A vote-buying bribe is one that has monetary value.

Problem: There are media reports, allegations, and prosecutions for vote buying in NY, CA, NV, FL, VA, PA, NC, and IL. Google for the reports. However, the more modern versions are lobbyists securing congressional votes through donations to a politician and giving rights and entitlements to illegal aliens and refugees with the intent of earning their votes.

18. Misleading and/or Confusing Information (at least 3 voter fraud methods)

Definition: Politicians and/or the media release confusing and even false information to confuse voters. Also, an election ballot may contain double negatives, wordiness, jargon, complicated words (above a 9th grade reading level), and confusing verbiage. Although this is one item in the appendix, there are many applications and methods to this category.

Problem: All too often, ballots and voter information may contain misleading or confusing voter information with an underlying intent. One of the most common methods is a double negative, where a vote for "no" is actually a "yes"! This is used most often in tax-increasing propositions.

19. Voter Manipulation of Protected Groups

Definition: Vote manipulation of the blind, mentally disabled, elderly, inebriated, and other groups incapable of making informed choices.

Problem: It is illegal, unethical, sad, and indefensible. Thankfully, this occurs *infrequently* according to media reports. Therefore, this accounts for a small number of votes compared to other voter fraud methods discussed herein.

20. Voter Suppression

Definition: A strategy to influence the outcome of an election by discouraging or preventing voters from casting a ballot. It is distinguished from political campaign attempts to change voting behavior by changing the opinions of potential voters through persuasion.

Methods: Impediments to voter registration, photo ID laws, purging of voter rolls, limitations on early and absentee voting, disinformation about voting procedures, inequality in Election Day resources, closure of DMV offices, and attempts to use the law to disqualify and/or parties.

Problem: Unfortunately, all of these occur, especially impediments to voter registration, purging of voter rolls, and disinformation about voting procedures. However, some are political accusations with little merit. Once again, all states provide free voter IDs to US citizens, negating the argument that voter IDs should not be required.

21. Politicians Moving Precinct Boundaries to Their Benefit

Definition: A precinct is a fixed number of districts, each containing one polling place, into which a city, town, etc. is divided for voting purposes.

Problem: Most issues are due to population changes. However, politicians strive to move precinct boundaries to benefit their party. This occurs yearly. Google your precinct boundaries and local media reports on their fairness.

About the Author

Dr. Rob Bryant is a USAF Vietnam-era veteran, a father of two active-duty US Marines, a PhD, and a retired VP of quality for two Fortune 150 companies. After an industrial accident left him a paraplegic, Bryant became a motivational speaker and author of three nonfiction books. He once set a Guinness World Record for rowing 3,280 miles in 117 days. He's spoken to over five hundred organizations on six continents. *Fraud President* is the first book in a series.

Learn more about Dr. Bryant by visiting:
https://robbryant.com/

www.ingramcontent.com/pod-product-compliance
Lightning Source LLC
Chambersburg PA
CBHW051104030726
47504CB00006B/1779